PENGUIN BOOKS

THE LOVE LETTERS OF VIA LULLINA

Kyra Ysabel is a Filipina author who writes heartwarming romances filled with the perfect balance of humour and heart. She is the self-published author of the *Magnolia Heights* series, an ongoing contemporary romcom collection that has resonated with readers across social media. Born and raised in the Philippines, Kyra draws inspiration from culture, connections, and the magic of everyday life.

ADVANCE PRAISE FOR
THE LOVE LETTERS OF VIA LULLINA

'Charming, sweet, and full of joy, *The Love Letters of Via Lullina* will leave its readers smiling and giddy long after the last page.'

—Hannah Bonam-Young,
New York Times bestselling author

The Love Letters of
VIA LULLINA

KYRA YSABEL

PENGUIN BOOKS
An imprint of Penguin Random House

PENGUIN BOOKS

Penguin Books is an imprint of the Penguin Random House group of companies whose addresses can be found at global.penguinrandomhouse.com

Published by Penguin Random House SEA Pte Ltd
40 Penjuru Lane, #03-12, Block 2
Singapore 609216

Penguin Random House SEA

First published in Penguin Books by Penguin Random House SEA 2026

10 9 8 7 6 5 4 3 2 1

ISBN 9789815362152

Typeset in Cormorant Garamond by MAP Systems, Bengaluru, India

www.penguin.sg

Before this book existed, there was a trip. My husband captured Florence, Rome, and everywhere in between while I wandered around falling in love with every crumbling wall, sparking Isla's story.
Scan to see what I saw and feel what I felt.

To those who believe in signs
To those who believe in choice
And to those, who like me, are learning to believe in both

(And to my husband Patrick, who brought me to Italy, so now I'm legally bound to include him)

1

Isla

Some people believe in signs.

Fortune cookies, horoscope apps, the way your left eye twitches when something bad's about to happen, all that. Me? I don't *just* believe in signs. I let them narrate my entire life. I treat them like divine instructions from the universe, and I follow them. Religiously. Blindly. Embarrassingly.

Most of my decisions are based on the alignment of the stars or something insanely cheesier. One time, I bailed on a date because my horoscope warned me about a dark-haired stranger who would waste my time. The guy was brunette and five minutes late, and I took it as a cosmic no. (Granted, I was in the Philippines where everyone is dark-haired and perpetually late, but that's beside the point.)

I'm a writer from Manila, and when my last book limped its way through a hundred pity purchases in months—half of them from relatives—I took it as another sign. A flashing neon one. Time to write something new. And when that new manuscript stalled at the meet-cute for three agonizing weeks, I took that as yet another sign. This time, it was to stop staring at my laptop and go out into the real world to hunt for inspiration. Preferably somewhere far.

After all, they say you should travel.

Immerse yourself in different cultures, talk to strangers, become someone else entirely. Go anywhere except home. Do all that and inspiration will come knocking on your door like an old friend holding a bottle of wine, begging to catch up.

Travelling also heals us, they say. It gives us a sense of calm. It gives us *perspective* (which I honestly think is just a buzzword my therapist uses when I tell her I'm tired of everything).

And when you're travelling to a place like Italy, as every book I've ever read and every movie I've ever seen say, its uneven cobblestones alone will supposedly jolt your brain back into alignment, and your problems will dissolve somewhere between your first espresso and your third gelato.

That's why Italy became my 'someday' place. The star of all my Pinterest boards. The reason why *Roman Holiday* is now my favourite movie and why Dean Martin is suspiciously high on my Spotify Wrapped. So, yeah, there's no place more magical than Italy. Even back when I hadn't been there yet, I believed that.

And now that I'm here? I stand by that sentence. I will throw that sentence into every conversation. I will mention it every chance I get. Hell, I will print it on a T-shirt and wear it in a crowded mall. That's how much I believe in it.

Unfortunately, what they forget to say about travelling, especially travelling alone, is that it also comes with the very real possibility of not experiencing the magic on day one.

In fact, the far more realistic scenario is that you will arrive three hours late, wearing a sweater that seemed like a good idea when you were in an air-conditioned airport but now feels like a portable sauna, and you'll spend your first night in your hotel room, wondering which light switch opens what.

Oh, and you'll stare at a porcelain bowl for ten minutes before googling to check if it's a sink for short people. It's a bidet, by the way. And then you'll wonder why they don't just use the telephone-wired ones back home.

And then, once the jet lag hits, you'll sleep for twelve hours and wake up confused, dehydrated, and slightly regretting not bringing anyone along while you procrastinate writing your novel.

Well, okay, technically I already have a few chapters. But that's all I have. So I remind myself of why I'm here.

Because I firmly believe that stories will always find their way to you when you need them the most.

Or at least that's the poetic way I choose to say it every time people ask me what I'm doing in Italy for a month. They don't need to know that the reason I'm here is because I'm doubting all my abilities as a writer. Between ghostwriting projects that pay the bills but drain my soul and crafting stories that no one is interested in, I've grown tired. The kind that makes you question if you were ever good at this to begin with.

Writing used to feel effortless, like it was muscle memory. But lately, every sentence feels forced, every word weighed down by doubt. My publisher noticed, my editors noticed, even my neighbour noticed. They kept saying that my writing isn't what it used to be. Of course, I'm not what I used to be either. Losing a sister does that to you.

'You need to go out and find your muse, Isla.' Harriet, my editor and best friend, said. Her voice still rings in my head, clear as the day she ambushed me with that ridiculous suggestion.

I remember sinking deeper into my chair, glaring at the screen during our Zoom call. 'There's nothing I can't research these days,' I argued, waving vaguely at the stack of books and open tabs cluttering my desk. 'I don't need to physically be somewhere to write about it. I've done it from right here before.'

She sighed in a way that told me she was two seconds away from strangling me through the screen. 'Isla, you're writing about history, the culture, the feeling of Italy—don't you think you should actually experience it?' Harriet's obnoxiously red hair bounced as she emphasized my need to *experience* Italy. 'I swear, if I see a description in there that says a Roman alley feels like *nostalgia*, I'm gonna throw your laptop across the room.'

I scoffed. 'So you want me to fly across the world for the sake of vibes?'

'It's not for the vibes. It's called being a responsible writer.'

I rolled my eyes. 'That's just a fancy way of saying you want me to spend thousands of euros to stroke my ego.'

'No, it's a fancy way of saying you need to remember why you love this.'

That shut me up.

I'm currently pushing past multiple deadlines for a fiction drama I was so sure would be easy to write. I had it all planned out. The protagonist is an art curator—brilliant, sharp, deeply in love with paintings and sculptures, but going through some difficult shit in life.

I thought if I walked the same halls as Caravaggio, stood in front of Botticelli's brushstrokes, or breathed in the scent of old parchment in historic libraries, something would click. The words would come back to me, and the story would unravel itself, effortless and clear.

So that's why I'm here. Where else am I going to get inspiration if not in the most artistic country in the world?

Joke's on me, though. Because the most artistic country in the world is also the most confusing one. Why does it feel like I've circled the same fountain over and over? And I'm almost sure I passed this gelateria earlier. And there's no way that it's a coincidence that a man with a white beard is playing an accordion on the street.

I have spent the morning trying to follow some online guide about hidden literary spots in the city. The guide mentions tiny hole-in-the-wall bookstores and cafes where famous authors allegedly wrote their masterpieces, but so far, all I have found are overpriced restaurants and maybe a million pigeons. Still, it's a stark contrast to Manila's scenery of tall buildings, thick smog, and terrible traffic.

After another run-through with the gelateria, I admit to myself that I'm lost. And not the cute, self-discovery, eat-pray-love type of lost. It's the sweaty, exhausted, phone-at-one-percent type.

With a sigh, I collapse onto a worn stone bench and stretch out my legs, wincing at the poor life choices that led me here—namely, my decision to wear ballet flats while navigating Florence's notoriously unforgiving streets. I slip one shoe off, rubbing at my aching heel, and glance around, hoping for a miracle. Or at least a street name I vaguely recognize from the tour-guide list.

And that's when I see it.

Tucked between two yellow buildings is a small, narrow alleyway. Now, Florence is *full* of small, narrow alleyways—some charming, some ominous, others looking like mafia meet-up places—but this one feels . . . different. Like I'm sure it wasn't there before. I swear on my last surviving brain cell. The air around it seems quieter, and something about it makes my skin prickle. I stand, curiosity outweighing exhaustion, and move closer, tilting my head to read the street sign.

Via Lullina.

2

Isla

Okay, weird.

I squint, making sure I read it right, because I thoroughly researched Florence—with all the determination an author can manage—before I got here, but not once did that name pop up. Of course, I don't trust my own memory, so, with a frown, I pull out my phone and attempt one last desperate check on my maps app. The signal is terrible, but sometimes, if I tilt the phone at just the right angle, I get a bar or two. Not this time. My phone screen goes black. *Dead.* Of course.

I exhale through my nose and shrug. I'm lost anyway—what's one more detour?

Glancing around the streets to confirm that I am indeed still lost, I enter Via Lullina. And the moment my feet touch the cobblestones, I sense the eeriness. In here, the city sounds are completely muffled. And it's so quiet, I have to look behind me one more time to make sure that the street I came from is still there.

The buildings lining the street are older than the ones I've seen so far. But they appear untouched as if this is the first time they've been unwrapped. Old balconies are tangled with vines, shopfronts are lined with faded awnings, windows are filled with books, antiques, and things that seem plucked from a different century.

A whisper of unease snakes up my spine. Maybe it's just an abandoned street. Or maybe—God, I hate my Filipino roots for imprinting this in my brain—it's cursed. Ugh. *No, Isla.*

Cursed or not, I should probably turn back. This is the part in every slasher film where the audience screams at the screen because the dumb main character is willingly walking towards her demise when she has the perfect opportunity to avoid it.

But then, out of the corner of my eye, I spot something. I turn to my right to see a neon 'OPEN' sign, glowing faintly in the window of a shop. And behind the counter, a woman.

Okay. This is fine. This is totally normal. Normal streets have open signs. Normal streets have people. Normal streets don't swallow travellers whole.

I take a cautious step forward.

Maybe it's not a cursed alley. Maybe it's just . . . boring. A tiny, overlooked street, forgotten by time and Google Maps. Probably home to a dusty antique store or one of those bizarre specialty shops that sell things like vintage jewellery and old porcelain dolls.

Yeah. That's all. Nothing sinister here.

I tuck my brown curls behind my ears, even though I know they'll spring back the moment I let go. My dress—a soft linen one that I thought would be perfect for wandering the streets of Florence—now clings to my skin, wrinkled and slightly damp from the heat (and, frankly, the anxiety). Still,

I straighten the hem, run my hands through the fabric, and take a few steps forward.

The shop is small, and it looks as if it's been squeezed into existence. Vines curl around the edges of its stone walls; leaves brush against the frame of a wooden door that looks older than the street itself. Above it, a faded painted sign in elegant golden letters reads 'Librería dell'Amore Perduto'.

The Bookshop of Lost Love.

It's either fate, a prank, or a very strategic marketing ploy designed to lure in sentimental fools like me. Either way, the hopeless romantic in me can't just walk away.

I *have* to go inside.

The second I push open the door, a soft chime rings through the shop from one of those old-school bells attached to the doorframe.

The woman behind the counter looks up from her book. She has silver-streaked hair and glasses perched on the tip of her nose. She gives me a slow, knowing smile.

'*Buongiorno*,' she says cheerfully.

I nod, smiling back like I totally belong here.

The shop is bigger than it looked from the outside. Like, way bigger. Shelves stretch up to the ceiling, crammed with weathered hardcovers and paperbacks. A rolling ladder leans against one of them, and there's a table in the centre.

The air smells like vanilla, old parchment, and something else I can't quite place—dried flowers, maybe? No music plays, but I swear there's a faint hum, like a whispered conversation happening just outside my hearing range.

I trail my fingers over a stack of books on a nearby table. Some titles are in Italian, some in English, and some in . . . okay, I'm not sure what language that is. I glance back at the woman behind the counter. She's still watching me, her smile amused.

'Looking for something in particular?' she asks.

I open my mouth, hesitant. 'I . . . don't know yet.'

Her smile widens. 'Ah. Those are the best kinds of stories.' She steps out from behind the counter and motions for me to follow her. 'Perhaps you can begin with this,' she says as she takes a large book from the centre-shelf and hands it to me.

I take it in my hands and examine it. It looks like an old fairy-tale book. You know those books at the beginning of old Disney films? It looks exactly like that, except less golden and bejewelled, and more . . . torn and old. Dust has built up on the cover, but the title is still clear: *The Book of Amore*. Cute.

'It's a collection of love letters from people who came here,' she repeats, softer this time. 'Stories of missed connections, of lost and found love, of letters never meant to be sent.'

I tilt my head. 'Letters never meant to be sent?'

She shrugs, a small, knowing smile playing on her lips. 'Not all love stories end neatly, *cara*. Some are left unfinished. Some, well . . . have a way of finding their endings long after they were written.'

'What does that even—' I start, but the woman turns back.

'You can have the book, Miss. I'm closing soon.' She disappears behind a curtain near the counter.

Should I follow her? Would that be weird? Probably. Besides, what would I even say? *Hi, you seem vaguely mystical. Would you like to explain why this bookshop feels like I've stepped into another dimension?*

Instead, I sigh and sink into the nearest armchair, pressing the book against my lap. The cover is soft under my fingertips, worn smooth from years of being held. I'm not sure if I heard her right but I think she said I can have this book. It doesn't matter, though. I'm not going anywhere with this heavy thing. I'll just browse a few pages, then leave.

Suddenly, something flutters to the floor. I stare at the yellowed envelope for a while, thinking if I should just leave it. Pretend I didn't see it. Just stand up and walk straight out of here because frankly, I have seen enough horror movies to know that when weird things happen, they are often followed by *weirder* things. And I'm already pushing my luck having stepped into an alley that may or may not exist.

Also, I am wildly superstitious. So superstitious that I apologize to the ground when walking past an anthill, just in case the spirits of the land are listening. I say 'tabi-tabi po' to literally everything. Which is why I believe that if I open this letter, I might suddenly become cursed or haunted.

And yet, of course, knowing me, I will not let this pass.

I wanted inspiration and a change of scenery, so it would be stupid to refuse now when it's been handed to me. I reach down and pick up the envelope, my fingers skimming over the rough paper. There's a name scrawled across the front in looping ink. As I squint to make it out, my heart sinks down to my stomach.

To: Isla Mendoza
You are the love of my life.
From: Luca Rossi

I take a few seconds to breathe. Maybe there's another Isla Mendoza out there. A much cooler, much more mysterious Isla Mendoza who frequently receives cryptic letters in charmingly suspicious bookshops.

I glance around to find the woman but she's not here any more.

The rational thing to do would be to leave this book and run as far as I can. I still have my online ticket to the Uffizi Gallery. The art. The culture. The *normal* things I came here for.

But instead of doing that, I take the book and step out of the store.

I've decided. I'm about to chase after the love of my life. A man I've never met.

In a city I barely understand.

With nothing but a book that doesn't really make any sense.

There's your story, Isla.

3

Luca

I never wanted to own a restaurant.

It wasn't my dream. It wasn't the realization of some childhood fantasy about twirling pasta in a pan like my nonna used to do. If anything, it was a last-resort decision—one made from exhaustion and the foolish idea that being my own boss would be less stressful than working for someone else.

It's not.

Right now, my kitchen looks like a war zone. The scent of burnt rosemary still lingers from when Enzo nearly set a pan on fire. The seafood delivery arrived two hours late, throwing off the entire prep schedule. And just when I thought the night was over, the last table of the evening decided they *absolutely* needed dessert, even though I'd already shut down the pastry station.

I lean against the counter, rubbing a hand down my face.

'Another fun day in paradise?' Marco smirks as he dries a glass behind the bar. My best friend has been with me since I opened the restaurant. He works the bar at night after his job as a tour guide, while I work the kitchen 24/7.

I grunt. 'If paradise includes broken ovens, last-minute orders, and a waiter quitting mid-shift because his girlfriend dumped him, then *sì, magnifico.*'

Marco chuckles. 'You could take a day off, you know.'

I snort. 'And come back to find the kitchen burned down? No, *grazie.*'

I glance around the restaurant—the dimmed pendant lights, the polished wooden tables, the wine bottles lined up behind the bar. It's nothing fancy, not the kind of place Michelin inspectors bother with, but it's mine. After years of working under high-strung chefs who treated their staff like garbage, I swore I'd never be that kind of boss. But I guess being too quiet also has its cons. Like my staff never talking to me.

Marco raises an eyebrow as I start wiping down the bar. 'You're brooding again.'

I roll my eyes. 'I don't brood.'

'You do.'

'I have a lot on my mind,' I say, dodging his smirk.

Marco leans his elbows on the counter. 'Ah. Work stress, or are you thinking about Dahlia again?'

I freeze for a second before forcing a scoff. 'I don't think about her.'

Marco hums in disbelief.

'I don't,' I insist.

'Sure, sure. That's why you look like you've aged five years since she left.'

I throw a rag at him. 'Shut up.'

Marco grins but doesn't push. He knows me well enough to drop the subject, even though we both know he's right. I rub my temples and grab a drink, a glass of red from my private stash behind the bar. Marco watches but doesn't comment. He's seen me do this every night for the past two months.

Two months since Dahlia left.

The woman who had walked into my restaurant one evening, ordered a glass of red wine, and smiled at me.

We had exactly forty-two days of what can only be called pure cinematic bliss. Midnight walks along the piazza, stolen kisses in the kitchen while I burned garlic, promises that meant everything in the moment. It was reckless and stupid but so damn good.

And then, one morning, she tilted her head and said, *You're wonderful, Luca, but I don't think I'm meant to stay in one place.*

I laughed because I thought she was joking. She wasn't.

Dahlia packed up her bags that afternoon and left for Barcelona. No dramatic goodbye, no fight to keep things going. Just a kiss on my cheek and a cab disappearing down the street.

I should be fine. It was only six weeks. Not six years. Not a lifetime.

But the thing is, I don't do halfway. I don't know how to keep my heart from jumping in with both feet, how to stop imagining futures with people who see me as nothing more than a beautiful stop on their way to something better.

So, after Dahlia, I promised never to do it again. Since I know I always go all in, I vowed to never go at all.

Marco finishes stacking the glasses and stretches. 'Well, I'm heading out. You sure you don't want to grab a drink somewhere that isn't here?'

I shake my head. 'Nah. I'll lock up.'

Marco sighs, like he's disappointed but not surprised. 'One of these days, you're going to have to leave this place and remember what fresh air feels like.'

'I get fresh air,' I argue.

Marco gives me a dry look. 'Walking out of the restaurant at midnight and immediately going home doesn't count.'

I wave him off. 'Goodnight, Marco.'

He mutters something about me being a lost cause but heads for the door, throwing me a lazy salute before leaving. When the door shuts behind him, silence settles over the restaurant.

I down my last gulp of wine. It helps me sleep better, even when thoughts of the woman I thought would be my whirlwind-turned-forever-love consume me. My nonna always tells me to not make a big deal out of it. She's always telling me to live more, to spend more time with different people. She keeps telling me that I'm not *ugly*, and that my life doesn't stop after Dahlia.

I know that. I am aware that I'm quite pleasing to look at. I get glances from women and smiles from strangers.

But I'm not like her. I don't like spending a lot of time with different people. I want to meet one woman and spend my life with her. Or at least, I *wanted* it. I don't know where another failed love puts me now. I guess it puts me here, in the barstool of the restaurant I spent my entire life building.

The bell chimes, and I turn around.

A woman barges in, her curly hair sticking to her face. She's holding a gigantic book in her arms and she looks at me with panic in her eyes.

'*Scusa, Signorina,*' I say, raising an eyebrow. 'We're closed for the day.'

She doesn't even blink. Just marches straight towards the counter like she didn't hear me, or doesn't care. She's wearing a linen dress that's seen better days, and she looks like she's been running for miles.

'Can I get you some water?' I ask.

'Are you Luca Rossi?' she ignores me and demands, breathless.

I hesitate. 'Yes?' I say slowly, suddenly very aware of how tiny and yet terrifyingly determined she looks. I stand up and face her.

Her whole face lights up. 'Hi.' She extends her hand like we're at a business meeting instead of whatever weird encounter this is. 'I'm Isla.'

I stare at her for a second before shaking her hand. 'Hello, Isla. How can I help you?'

And then, with all the confidence in the world, she says—

'I'm the love of your life.'

Of course, this is happening to *me,* of all people.

4

Isla

It wasn't easy tracking him down.

I almost gave up. Almost. But I'm nothing if not persistent. And obsessive. And borderline delusional. So here's how it played out:

First, I ran out of the bookshop like a woman possessed, and left Via Lullina to go back to the busy streets of Florence. I was breathless (partly from what I had just found out, and partly because I have the cardio stamina of a ninety-year-old grandma with asthma). So I did the responsible thing: I plopped down on the nearest bench to decompress. By nearest bench, I mean on the floor near a lamp post, because there are not many places to sit here. And by decompress, I mean gasp dramatically and wave off locals trying to offer help.

Next, I decided to be smart about it. If I wanted to find Luca Rossi, I needed my phone. Obvious solution: Charge my phone. Slightly less obvious problem: I had no idea where to do that. Florence has many wonderful things—stunning architecture, charming cafes, streets that make you feel like you've been transported into an old romance film. You know what it doesn't have? An abundance of easy-to-spot charging stations. I wandered around looking for one, but I'm not exactly known for my ability to navigate.

After a solid twenty minutes of fruitless searching, I decided to go old school. I looked for a phone directory. Yes, a literal, printed, analogue phone directory. This was met with the exact reaction you'd expect. The lady at the newsstand gave me a look that can only be described as pity mixed with concern. Like I'd just asked her if people still send messages by carrier pigeon. To her credit, she actually tried looking for one, digging through old stacks of God-knows-what before handing me a dusty, outdated directory that probably hadn't been touched since the early 2000s. Unsurprisingly, it was useless.

I realized that I had better chances of looking for Luca Rossi if I had a phone with an internet connection. So I decided to search for my hotel instead. I knew it was within walking distance because I hadn't gone very far on foot. So I tried to retrace my steps. Of course, I failed.

So I did what any self-respecting traveller would do—I gave up. Not on the whole thing, just on this part. I decided to grab something to eat and take a taxi back. A girl's gotta have priorities.

And that's when the magic happened.

I grabbed a pamphlet for tourists and checked the dining section. I imagined celebratory music in the background when I read the words 'Trattoria Rossi'. My heart soared. This was it. A place with his name. A sign from the universe. Or at the very least, a sign from the Florence tourism board. Either way, it was *something*. Thankfully, it was so close. But they were already closed. But I didn't really care. I sprinted to the restaurant.

And now I'm here, face to face with the supposed love of my life. My superstitious, romantic self thought I'd feel butterflies and fireworks when I saw him. But instead, I feel . . . nothing. I mean, yeah, sure, he's good-looking. Tall, brown hair, green eyes, scruffy but still neat—goes with the whole effortlessly attractive, broody chef thing he has going on.

But magic? Destiny? True love knocking on my heart's door?

Nope. Nothing. Not even a polite little tap.

'Scusa?' Luca exclaims.

'I'm the love of your life . . . or at least that's what it says here.' I hand him the letter. He takes it from my hand, and even as his fingers brush mine, there's nothing. Not even a slight static shock. Honestly, I've felt more electricity shaking hands with my dentist.

He holds the envelope and flips it once. 'I don't get it.' He looks at me with a pointed expression. 'This is just an envelope with our names on it.' He speaks with a thick Italian accent that I admit is really cute.

'Yes, but *look*,' I say, tapping my finger on the inscription.

He squints. 'Okay . . . and?'

'You obviously wrote to me telling me I'm the love of your life!' I stomp my foot in annoyance. 'I haven't opened it yet because I want us to open it together. It might mean something. You know? Like *fate*.'

He stares at me for a few seconds. Silence stretches and I can hear nothing in the dim light of the closed restaurant. Then, suddenly, Luca snorts. And before I can stop him, he laughs. Loud and unapologetic. 'Grazie, Isla,' he says between chuckles. 'Truly. I haven't had a laugh like that in ages.'

'I'm not joking!' I protest, indignation bubbling up. 'I stumbled upon this little street called Via Lullina, and I went into this dusty old bookshop—like straight out of a movie, I *swear*—and there was this book.' I wave the giant, slightly worn book at him. 'It's a collection of anonymous love letters. And *this*'—I hold up the envelope like a relic—'this just fell out. Addressed to me. From you!'

Luca tilts his head thoughtfully, humouring me. 'Okay,' he says slowly. 'Let me get this straight. You walked down a street that doesn't exist, into a bookstore I've never heard of, picked up a magical book of love letters, and one of them just so happens to be written by me, for you? And you think this means we're soulmates?'

I blink. 'Well, when you put it like that, you make it sound . . . insane.'

He lifts an eyebrow. 'That's because it is.'

I huff. 'First of all, there *is* a street called Via Lullina. I was there. I saw the sign. I even touched the bricks. It felt very street-like.'

'Street-like,' he repeats, shaking his head. With a sigh, he says, 'Signorina, there is no street in Florence called Via Lullina.'

'But—' I start but he holds out a finger to cut me off.

'Trust me. I live here.'

'Fine, but don't you want to at least see what's inside?' I ask.

'Will that make this night end quicker?' he says with exaggerated patience.

'Duh,' I say, rolling my eyes. 'Or it'll lead to a twist. Who knows?'

He looks at me like I'm deranged (and honestly, I don't blame him), then at the envelope, then back at me. And for a second, I think I see it—the tiniest flicker of curiosity behind the green in his eyes.

I hear a rattling sound coming from outside the restaurant. I jump, startled, because every single nerve in my body is known to overreact. Luca just narrows his eyes at me, like he's not sure if I'm being serious. I don't say anything, and I stare at him in return, angling my face to make me look scary.

Yes, intimidation.

He sighs in surrender.

'Fine,' he mutters, handing me the letter. 'Let's open the envelope from the universe.'

'Really?' I say, clutching it closer to my chest. I didn't expect him to agree. I thought it would take more convincing. 'No takebacks?'

He gives me a look. 'Open it before I change my mind and call the *polizia*.'

'Right, right,' I say, carefully tearing the flap open. The paper inside is aged, yellowed at the edges, but the handwriting is surprisingly neat. It's inked in deep blue, slanted just slightly, like the words were written in a hurry. I hold my breath as I unfold it.

Luca leans in, arms crossed but eyes focused.

I read it aloud.

Isla,

I don't know how else to say this, except I miss you. I've missed you every day since that night on the bridge near my trattoria, when we stood in silence because we knew if we spoke, everything would change.

You were wearing that ridiculous sun hat you insisted looked mysterious even though it kept flying off in the wind. I hated that hat. I still dream about it.

You said you were leaving Florence, but I didn't think you meant for good. And now you're gone, and I can't find the words to say what I should have said then.

I love you.
Luca

I slowly lower the paper. My heart thumps as I glance at him. He looks at me, still obviously weirded out.

'That is not me.' Luca says this like it's the most obvious thing in the world.

'But you're Luca Rossi.'

'There are thousands of men named Luca Rossi in Italy.'

'You are the Luca Rossi who owns a trattoria,' I say, deadpan. 'And this is your handwriting.'

'How do you know it's my handwriting?'

'It's very chef-y.' I wave my hand in the air.

'Chef-y?'

'You know. Masculine. A little aggressive. Like you wrote it with a lot of wrist.'

Before, Luca was staring at me like he thought I was deranged. Now, he's looking at me like I'm a dangerous psychiatric patient who escaped this evening.

'Look.' I sigh. 'I don't know how any of this works. I'm just a writer on vacation trying to find inspiration for my novel, and then *this* happens. I didn't come to Florence looking for you. But here you are.'

'Okay,' he says finally. 'Let's say, *hypothetically*, this letter came from me. What now? You expect me to fall madly in love with you because some dusty book says so?'

'No,' I say, lifting my chin. 'I expect you to help me figure out what's going on.'

'And why would I do that?' he asks again, slower this time. Like I'm a child. Or a malfunctioning robot.

I fold my arms. 'Because if someone out there is writing our story for us, don't you want to know what their endgame is? Don't you want to make sure they didn't write you as the villain?'

He snorts. 'Please. I'd be the brooding anti-hero at worst.'

'Oh, right,' I say, eyes wide with faux reverence. 'The tortured soul with trust issues.'

Luca sighs so deeply it sounds like his soul is trying to escape through his nose. 'Okay. Let me make this simple for you, Isla.' He says my name like it's the filthiest name in the world. 'Whatever this book is, whatever fantasy plot you think you're in, I want no part of it. I'm not playing along. I have a business to run, real problems to deal with, and no time for love letter scavenger hunts.'

'But—'

'No.' He cuts me off with a sharp shake of his head. 'No more letters. No more bookshop hallucinations. And definitely no more showing up here with your . . . wide eyes and dramatic speeches.'

I blink. 'That feels like a compliment in disguise.'

'It wasn't,' he says. 'This kitchen is closed. And so is this conversation.'

'But—'

He turns away, already heading back into the depths of the restaurant. '*Buona notte*, Signorina.'

And just like that, I'm being shooed out of a trattoria by the supposed love of my life. Who, to be fair, does not love me. Or believe me. Or particularly like me.

Yet.

5

Luca

I'm pretty sure she's a scamming tourist. I know her type well. She uses her charm and innocence to lure locals, I'm sure.

She's attractive. I'm not blind, I can see that. Big eyes, sharp mind, and that restless energy. The kind of woman who talks with her whole body, so animated and . . . noisy. I'm not interested.

I'm not.

I've seen enough to know better. And I don't care how magical her little letter sounds, or how 'chef-y' she thinks my handwriting is.

But still, I barely slept last night. Not because of her—because of that damn letter. Because it *was* my handwriting. Down to the way I cross my t's and curve my l's like little ladles. So I guess the girl isn't completely crazy. But it still makes no sense because I don't know her. And I'm sure not the type to write love letters to women I don't know.

I've only ever written one love letter in my life. It was three days after Dahlia left me. I wrote a pathetic note where I begged her to explain why she left, because I wasn't convinced that it was only because she didn't want to settle. I could've gone with her, if she asked. That's how lovestruck I was. Thinking about it now, it seems reckless. And it would have been a recipe for disaster. I would've secretly blamed her for my sadness, and she would've resented me for some other reason.

So, no. I didn't write that letter. But it's in my handwriting. Still, it's not enough reason for me to waste my time finding out. Why would I?

'Sorry, we're still closed, Signorina,' I hear Marco say. I'm in the kitchen, preparing for the day, while he sets up tables.

'Jeez, does this restaurant ever open? In Manila, food places are open twenty-four hours.'

God, I know that voice. I peek out past the kitchen door and see that it's Isla. Now wearing a pair of shorts and a white, linen top.

'Just one more hour, madam,' Marco says nicely.

'No, I'm not here to eat. I'm here for your grumpy chef.'

I groan and duck back behind the door. Maybe if I stay quiet, she'll go away. Except, she doesn't. The door hits my back just as I'm stepping away.

'Finally!' she exclaims.

Marco peeps into the kitchen, right behind her, and says, 'Scusa, I couldn't stop her.'

'Not sure anyone could.' I shrug. 'Thanks, anyway.'

He closes the door behind him, but I know he's probably still there, lingering.

'Signorina,' I begin, 'I thought I made myself clear yesterday.'

'You did. Very clear. Borderline rude, actually.' Isla huffs as she places the book on the counter.

'I don't have time for riddles.' I take the book and add, 'That's not sanitary.'

She rolls her eyes but takes the book again to open it. She very dramatically points to a page. 'There,' she says. 'That one is dated three weeks from now. It's my letter to you. Care to read it?'

'I'm pretty sure you've already read it, so spare me the suspense.'

'Nope. Read. It.' She spoke with terrifying conviction.

I sigh and turn to place myself beside her. She's tiny, but like a giant burst of energy that's impossible to ignore. I clear my throat.

'Okay, *Dearest Luca*,' I look at her and she urges me to go on. '*I'm sorry about your restaurant. I know how much hard work you put into this. We're going to find a way to open it again.*' My stomach sinks for some reason, but I don't let her notice. Instead, I turn to face her, hoping I look nonchalant as I snort. 'So?'

'So,' she leans in, her voice dropping slightly, 'if this book is even remotely real . . . then maybe it's warning you.'

'Or maybe,' I reply, 'it's just an elaborate prank by someone with too much time and access to my old handwriting samples.'

Her lips curve, not into a full smile, but something knowing. 'You didn't sleep either, huh?'

I don't answer. Which is answer enough.

'I'm not asking you to believe,' she says. 'Just . . . humour me. Indulge a tourist. Help me find out why this is happening. One week. Or two. That's all I'm asking.' She flails her hand with each sentence she says.

'And after that?' I cross my arms.

'After that, if we find nothing—if it really is just a bunch of pretty letters and coincidence—I'll leave you alone forever.'

Before I can answer, the kitchen door opens. 'Sorry, I didn't mean to eavesdrop . . . no, I actually did,' Marco says. 'But let me just get this straight.'

We look at him with eyebrows raised.

'There's a magic book,' he says.

'Yes!' Isla says.

'Allegedly,' I correct.

'And a beautiful signorina is begging you to help her uncover its secrets? Is that right?'

Isla blushes and smiles sweetly as I roll my eyes.

'And you're rejecting her?' Marco looks at me. 'You're messed up in the head, *amico mio*.'

I don't answer right away. I know what he's doing. He doesn't really care about the book, he just wants me to go out with a girl again after Dahlia. To live a little. And . . . I guess it wouldn't hurt. I get a change of scene, I finally talk to someone who isn't Marco or my nonna. If we find something about the book, then I guess it's just an added bonus.

I look at Isla again, her eyes so hopeful. This still isn't making any sense. I'm not whimsical. I'm not superstitious. I don't care about fate and destiny. But maybe I care about even the tiniest possibility that the restaurant I worked so hard for will close.

'One week,' I say finally. 'That's it. After that, you're on your own.'

Isla squeals and jumps. She claps her hands and says, 'Great! Deal. We'll start tomorrow. I have a list!'

'God help me,' I mutter.

Marco clasps me on my shoulder and grins. 'I'm proud of you.' I just shrug away from him and head back to the kitchen.

'He's more fun than that, don't worry.' I hear him say to Isla.

'I don't care. I'm fun enough for the both of us.'

'Now tell me more about that magic book,' Marco says as they step out of the kitchen. I shake my head. Marco is a bit more romantic than I am. He believes in stuff like Isla—destiny and soulmates. All that bullshit.

He was the reason Dahlia and I happened. He introduced us and convinced me that we were meant to be. I believed him until she left. Even then, he told me that it doesn't just end like that. That I should chase the next one. The next spark. The next love. Make fate happen all over again, which was ironic, since fate isn't really something you *make.*

For a while, I thought I could live like him, flee from one thrill to the next. I tried to, but I couldn't. As much as I deny it, I feel everything.

And I feel it deeply. Loud. Consuming. Very inconvenient.

Which is why, as I chop these onions with a bit more pressure than necessary, I try to convince myself that it's not about Isla. It's not about believing in magic. All I'm doing is finding out who's pranking us with that book. That's it. It's not a weird journey of falling in love with another person.

Because I'm not Marco. More importantly, I'm not my father.

He was like Marco, but worse. The kind of hopeless romantic who packed a suitcase and walked out on me and my mother to 'chase his destiny'. Said he loved us. Said he'd come back when the timing was right. I guess the timing never was.

So, no. I don't believe in fate. Or books that tell the future. Or letters that show you who you're meant to be with. That stuff is for people who can afford to lose everything for a dream.

'Hey, grouch.' I hear a voice beside me and see Isla standing in the entrance.

'Stop barging into my kitchen. It's—'

'Unsanitary, yeah, yeah, I know.' She rolls her eyes. 'Just wanna say that I'm leaving for the day. I got your number from your very lovely friend Marco, and I'm coming back for you tomorrow. *Ciao*, my love!' She winks.

She doesn't give me time to respond. I just sigh and go back to my chopping.

I guess there's no turning back now.

6

Isla

I'm committed to spending this day as a regular tourist.

Which is how I find myself baking slowly under the Tuscan sun, standing in line for a sandwich I read about at 2 a.m. during a jet-lagged TikTok spiral. Something about mortadella and pistachio cream that 'changed people's lives'. I don't know about *life-changing*, but I'm hungry enough to lick a basil leaf off the cobblestone if it's topped with cheese.

The streets of Florence stretch out before me, and I can't help but grin despite myself. The buildings are warm terracotta and golden yellows, just the way I imagined them to be. The smell of fresh pastries mingles with the warm scent of leather from the shops along Via dei Neri.

'I know that you are the most superstitious person in the world,' Harriet says from the other end of the line. Her voice is warm and familiar, even with the delay from a continent away. In the background, I can hear her fork scraping against her plate. It's dinnertime in Manila. She's probably eating tapsilog in her pyjamas. 'But a magic book? Come on, Isla, even you must think that's delusional.'

'I know, Har, I *know*.' I take a small step as the line shuffles forward. The guy in front of me smells like cologne and cigarettes, and I inch back to reclaim my personal space. 'But I told you what happened.' I keep my voice low. 'That letter. The handwriting. The street that's not on Google Maps. The chef!'

She hums sceptically through a mouthful of food. 'Maybe your brain is just making stuff up to give you the plot you're looking for. Like, your subconscious is bored and starved for inspiration, so it conjures up some magical little street as your muse.'

I let that hang in the air for a second.

Because the truth is, she's not entirely wrong. I am here to get unstuck. To get over the last book that tanked and write something bold, something true, something me. Well, nothing can be more *me* than the last book I wrote, but still.

'There's no point trying to explain,' I mumble. 'You had to be there.'

She sighs. 'You're just lonely. Don't make this a destiny thing. It's not one of your weird signs.'

'Excuse me, my signs are real.' I almost never do anything unless I find a sign from the universe. I know, a thirty-year-old shouldn't care what the universe thinks she should order for breakfast, but that's just the way I'm wired now. 'And this has to mean something. Even if it turns out to be a giant joke for some reason, it's still a sign. And I'm going to figure it out.'

'Fine, whatever. Go on your little magic scavenger hunt. Just make sure a good story comes out of it.'

'Of course, that's what I'm here for. I gotta go,' I add. 'It's almost my turn to order the sandwich that will heal my spirit.'

'Don't cry when it's just bread and cheese.'

I bite back a smile and move along, the truffle-scented air filling my nose. The woman behind the counter smiles at me. I grin back and gesture to the sandwich board. '*Una sandwich con tutto*, *per favore*,' I say, surprising even myself with my not-atrocious Italian.

The sandwich comes out, glistening in the sun, with the rich green of the pistachio cream practically glowing.

As I take my first bite, I can't help but laugh. It's not life-changing, not even close. The flavours are good, but it's just a sandwich. Still, maybe it's a sign. Maybe it means I don't need to expect too much from the things around me. Or maybe it's telling me that this whole 'magic scavenger hunt' with Luca isn't about finding answers, but about learning about myself along the way.

Or maybe I'm just trying to make sense of things, reading too much into a sandwich.

Yep. Probably.

I walk the old streets of Florence to find a bench where I can eat in peace. I scour the surroundings, but after rounding multiple corners, I conclude that Italians hate sitting. So, instead, I just walk. I don't know if it's culturally appropriate to walk in Italy while eating, and I'm grateful when I don't get any judgmental looks. One man even points to my sandwich and nods appreciatively. So maybe it's fine. Maybe walking and eating is my new thing.

Just a few metres away is the Accademia Gallery, where Michelangelo's David is housed. Which is *great*, because that's in the original list of things that I wanted to see—from before *the* letter. In my journal, it's called 'David and his glutes'. The travel blogs I've read said that one look at the masterpiece will make you question reality. I don't know if I need more things to make me question reality (and my sanity), but I find myself walking towards the museum anyway.

Even as I'm walking through the streets of this beautiful city, eating this subpar sandwich, I can't help but think of *the* book.

Yesterday, when I got home after ambushing Luca in his restaurant, I read more pages of the book. This time, I wasn't surprised when I saw that, along with the other letters from strangers, there were more from him to me, and vice versa. Unlike the one in the envelope, these letters had dates on them. And all the dates were within the timeframe I plan to be here in Italy. Which makes the book feel less coincidental, and all the more ominous and freakier.

So far, I had read three letters. The first letter is the one I had showed Luca, where I am consoling him about his restaurant getting shut down. Another is a letter from him, telling me that he can't wait to see me again so we can enjoy gelato along the Arno. Like it's something we did. Like it's our thing. And the last one is a letter from me, thanking him for taking me to the Uffizi, which was supposedly the same day we were at the Arno.

I don't know why, but it all makes me feel excited somehow. Not because the letters are romantic, necessarily. But because they feel . . . familiar. Like someone has written down the version of my life that I've always hoped for but never dared to believe I could have.

And okay, maybe that makes me a little delusional. Or overly sentimental. Or just deeply in need of a really good story to believe in. But I don't care. I want to know how it all plays out. Which is why, instead of going immediately inside the gallery, I fire a message to Luca.

Me: Ciao! Can I come back there tonight and bring the book?

He doesn't reply immediately, which is fair—he must be busy in the kitchen. So I go get my ticket to the gallery. The line moves slowly, giving me just enough time to cycle through the full range of texting anxiety: optimism, mild dread, regret, hope again, a quick internal debate about whether to follow up with a 'jk' message, and finally, surrender. Twenty minutes pass. I'm just stepping through the tall museum doors when my phone buzzes.

Luca: I'm assuming this is Isla? If yes, I'm sure you won't take no for an answer.

I smile as I enter.

The Accademia is smaller than I expected—like the studio apartment version of a museum—but it packs an intimidating amount of culture per square inch. Which is great, because I'm supposed to be here doing serious research for my novel. You know, the one with an art curator as the main character who's smart and emotionally complex.

Anyway, I'm here to find inspiration. To research. To channel my inner art enthusiast. I even brought a notebook (though it's mostly full of doodles and vague notes like 'david's butt = unfair' but still, it counts).

The first few rooms are full of religious paintings. Gold everywhere. I try to study brushstrokes and palettes like a professional, but mostly I'm just looking at the art in awe.

Then there's the Hall of Prisoners—or as I like to call it, the Marble Thirst Trap. Giant blocks of stone with half-formed men clawing their way out. They are an example of *non-finito* sculpting—the unfinished. But they look more alive than the men I've dated in the past. No offence. (Actually, offence to some of them.)

And finally, at the end of the hall, there he is. David. I take photos like everyone does, and I try to observe him the way my FMC aka female main character might: examining proportions, artistic intent, political context. But then I get distracted by the veins on his hand and forget what century I'm in. Michelangelo was way ahead of his time. The veins on David's hand might be the sixteenth century equivalent of Mr Darcy's hand flex in the 2005 adaptation.

I jot some notes in the margins of my notebook.

→ FMC hosts a lecture on the evolution of the male form in sculpture

→ she lowkey thirsts over David but makes it academic

→ possibility of MMC catching her in the act = tension??

After a few more rounds of 'research', I step out of the gallery. Surprisingly, it's already afternoon, and even more surprisingly, I have a text from Luca.

Luca: Where are you? Can we meet somewhere else?

Isla: Why? Afraid I'll spread germs in your kitchen?

Luca: Honestly, yes.

I roll my eyes but tell him that we can meet in the cafe below the hotel I'm staying in.

I spend the rest of the afternoon organizing my notes for the book I'm writing—dialogues out of context, half-finished scenes, questions on the plot. That's how it usually goes for me. I form stories from half-crafted ideas. As frustrating as it is, I let myself be comforted by the fact that this is a privilege most don't get.

I'm here with an idea of a good story, with what I want to believe is still a talent in crafting one. But I have to admit, even in the presence of The Great Italy, the words aren't coming easily. Not yet. I'm still stuck.

But maybe that's not the worst place to be.

Maybe being stuck just means the story's not ready to be told yet.

7

Luca

I spot her the second I walk into the cafe. It's not hard. The cafe is small and subtle, almost dim, with velvet seats and dark walls. While Isla is small too, nothing about her is subtle. She's waving both hands like we haven't seen each other in ages. I walk towards her table and take a seat across from her.

'Ciao!' she says enthusiastically. 'So, what do you wanna eat?' Her voice is so chirpy. It's annoying, but I admit it somehow works for her.

'I already had dinner. I'll just get a glass of wine.'

'Okay, I'm already a bit full too, so I'll get a sangria.' She shuts the menu dramatically and places it flat on the table. 'Can I get that with a little umbrella on top?' She mimics the movement.

'Umbrella? It's not a pina colada.'

'Why? Are there cocktail rules?' she asks, bewildered. 'Or worse, are there superstitions? Am I not supposed to drink a sangria with a tiny umbrella? Is it bad luck?' She looks around her to confirm.

'Relax, Signorina,' I start.

'Is it one of those very specific Italian rules that no one talks about until you get publicly shamed for breaking it? Like espresso after 4 p.m.?' She scrunches her nose like she's disgusted by the fact that it's unusual to drink coffee at night.

'No, Isla. Just uncommon.'

'Oh. Well.' She shrugs.

When the waiter arrives and we order our drinks and a shared plate of cheese and cold cuts, he looks at Isla one more time.

'Just to confirm, you want a tiny umbrella on your drink, Miss?'

'Oh my God, yes. How controversial!' She rolls her eyes. The waiter nods once and scurries away from our table.

'You scared him, poor guy,' I say as I put a block of cheese in my mouth.

'No, I didn't, come on. I'm bringing tropical joy to this dungeon.' She gestures to the surroundings, which, to be honest, do look like a dungeon. Isla ties her hair into a knot on top of her head using a single pen. Impressive.

'Alright,' she says squarely. She takes out the giant book from her tote bag and sets it on the table with a loud thud that makes the cutlery bounce.

'What are you doing?' I hiss. 'Put that back.' I push the book towards her, and she reluctantly places it back in her bag.

'Why?' she asks. 'I wanted to show it to you.'

'Yes, but it's eye-catching.'

'So?' She looks like she genuinely does not care.

'I don't like attention.'

'You don't say.' She chuckles. When I don't respond, she adds, 'Fine, do you wanna go up to my room, then?'

I am too appalled that I choke on air. I clear my throat and ask, 'Scusa? You're inviting me to your room?'

'To look at the book,' she clarifies. 'Not for whatever you think, Luca. You may be the love of my life, but I don't like you like that.'

I sigh. Her arms are flailing every time she speaks. It's supposed to be unsettling, but I suppose it's part of who she is. 'Fine, I'll have the drinks brought up.'

Isla's room is not neat and tidy. Definitely not guest-friendly. Clothes draped over the bed, a towel on the chair, skin products half-open. I have to move a sweater and what I hope is a clean sock to take a seat in the armchair.

'So, what's the plan?' I ask. 'Do we light a candle? Chant?'

Isla ignores me and sits on the foot of the bed, just beside my chair, and drops the book beside her. 'Okay, so there are three letters here in this book, right about—' she stops. Her eyebrows scrunch, in the way that stretches her entire face. She's so animated. She flips a few more pages, then back again. 'Oh my gosh.'

'What?'

'It changed.'

'What changed?'

'This! What's written in here! Remember that restaurant note I showed you earlier?' she asks. 'The one about your place getting closed?'

'Yes . . .' I reluctantly reply. It's all I've been thinking about.

'Well, it's gone. Look at this now. This is dated that same day of your restaurant's supposed closure.' She extends the book to me, so I can see. On top of the page is the date, three weeks from now.

Isla reads the letter out loud.

Dear Luca,

That kiss was wonderful. Thank you for taking me to the Uffizi, for the afternoon by the Arno, beside the lamp post, and the dinner in your restaurant. I don't think I can ever leave this place.

Isla

'So we kissed at the Arno?' I snort. 'Charming. How cliché of me. Did I also quote Dante and feed you gelato while serenading you with a mandolin? It doesn't get more Italian than that.'

She swats my arm. 'Don't you see this? The book is changing. I don't know what prompts it to change, but the letters change. The dates change.'

I exhale slowly, rubbing the back of my neck. I hate how accepting she is about this. Like she expects me to be equally whimsical. But I run a restaurant. I rely on predictability. Systems. Schedules. Health inspections.

'This makes no sense,' I grumble. 'You realize that, right? Books don't change on their own. Letters don't rearrange themselves because you stared at them too hard.'

'I'm not saying I understand it,' she says, 'but it's happening.'

I sigh. If I'm being honest, I want nothing to do with this. My life is fine. It's systematic. Safe. Normal. Coffee at seven. Market at nine. Prepping at noon. And getting lost in the chaos of the kitchen for the rest of the day. I go home. I wake up. Repeat.

But if I'm being more honest, this book is scaring me. When Isla mentioned that kiss by the Arno, my stomach dropped. No one knows that's my favourite spot in Florence. It's where my parents used to take me when I was little. We would sit on the stones and they would tell me about how they fell in love. It was a time in my life when everything was perfect. When my dad hadn't left. When my mom was still alive.

When I got older, I swore to myself that if I found someone I really cared about, really loved, I would take her there. Kiss her there. Not on the Ponte Vecchio like most tourists would, no. Down by the river. Near the lamp post. Where I used to go to with my parents.

So far, I hadn't taken anyone. Not even Dahlia.

Why does the book know? And why did I take Isla? I rub my hands over my face and accept my fate.

'Okay,' I begin. 'Maybe we can start with that street that doesn't exist.'

'But if it doesn't exist, then it isn't there any more.' She stands up and takes the pen out of her hair in one swift motion. Her wavy hair falls down her back effortlessly. Like those shampoo commercials.

I shake my head. 'Do you remember where it is?'

'Of course not, I got lost inside an H&M once.'

Of course she did.

I pause for a while, trying to concentrate, and think of how to approach this. 'Fine. Then maybe we can read through the book, find something or someone familiar, and start from there.'

Isla takes her glass of sangria and gulps it down. 'Thank you for finally locking in, Luc . . . Can I call you Luc?'

'Do I have a choice?'

She just smirks and hands me my glass. I down it in one gulp too, and she and I make eye contact.

'More?' she asks.

'A lot more.' I reply.

It's gonna be a long night.

8

Isla

If I had exerted myself to put the same amount of emotional, mental, and (let's face it) obsessive energy that I was putting into my adventure with the Book of Amore into preparing for my novel, I'd have a finished manuscript by now. But I'm still convincing myself that solving this mystery is the super-secret key to finishing my novel. It's . . . *yes*, you guessed it . . . a sign.

'Isla.' Luca's voice brings me back. 'You're staring into nothing again.' I just brush him off as he says, 'Anyway, you have a letter for me here. You're saying I hope I enjoyed the gelato you got. I have to say, the version of you in these letters is far kinder.'

'I am kind if you're not a grinch. That's just how it is,' I say.

Luca just chuckles, and I can't help but notice how the green in his eyes adjusts to the light in the room. Outside, they're so green. In here, it's like the corners are grey and the green is just reduced to tiny spots around his irises. Like water colour seeping into paper.

'You're scaring me,' he says. Apparently I've been staring at him for too long.

'Sorry,' I reply. 'It's just . . . you have really nice eyes.'

'Are you flirting with me now, Isla?' He chuckles.

'Yeah, wanted to see if there were sparks. It would've been easier if we just fell in love and did all the things in that book.'

'What makes you think it would've been easier?' Luca starts. He shuts the book, then looks at me. 'For starters, you're not staying in Italy. I can't move out of here. If anything, being in love would be very, very difficult for the both of us.'.

I let the silence stretch a moment before saying lightly, 'You're really good at killing a vibe.'

'And you're really good at ignoring red flags.'

We both smile. And for a second, I can't help but wonder what the book would write about this moment.

It's now seven in the morning, and I'm trying to untangle my hair. It somehow got stuck in my earring and my necklace at the same time. Luca, on the other hand, has unexpectedly spent the night. Nothing happened. He didn't even take off his shoes. The closest we got to any action was when he rejected the blanket I offered him in what I can only assume is masculine defiance.

We spent the rest of the night drinking wine and rummaging through the godforsaken book. We didn't find anything remarkable, but there was something. He stumbled upon a letter from a shoemaker, to his love, a sales lady at a clothing store. Her name isn't mentioned, but his name is Giodani. So, our next step is to find a romantic cobbler, which, according to Luca, should be easy enough for me to do while he works at the restaurant.

'*Dio mio*,' Luca exclaims. 'Did I sleep here? And is it *seven*?' He scrambles to his feet and looks at me. 'I need to get to the restaurant. Call me if you need any help with the cobbler.'

He peeks into the bathroom to fix his dishevelled hair, gives me a wave, and then he's out the door.

So I guess I'm on my own. I chuckle, because I contemplate telling Harriet about it, but it sounds ridiculous when I rehearse it in my head: *So the cute Italian chef slept over in my hotel, so we could unlock the magic book's secret together. But nothing happened. Clothes and shoes were kept on.*

It doesn't sound like a story she would want to hear anyway. So I just brush it off and think about how I'll find Giodani.

I take a quick shower and slip on a pair of white capris and a gingham top. I twist my damp hair into a loose bun, sling my bag over my shoulder, and step outside . . . only to be met by the aggressive Florentine sun. It's hot, but still, it's not like the Manila heat where the humidity feels like it's trying to cook you, slowly and from the inside out.

My hotel is near the train station, which, in hindsight, was a tactical error. Florence isn't a place you conquer by rail—it's a place you wander through. Hopefully not to the point that you get lost in a magic street.

A quick google search points me towards the Arno, where most of the artisan shops are clustered. I don't know exactly what I'm looking for—some sign that says 'Giodani the Lovesick Shoemaker, est. 1974' would be ideal—but I'm willing to follow the breadcrumbs.

I walk slowly, trying to savour the scenery around me. The view at every turn is like a photo on a postcard. My phone camera doesn't do it justice. It's one of those places where you just have to be there. I glance at my maps app from time to time, and slow to a stop, nearly colliding with a group of tourists taking selfies with a handheld fan between them.

It says here that I'm standing on the Ponte Vecchio. It's one of the grandest bridges in the world, so I thought it would announce itself more—you know, maybe a giant sign. Maybe a '5 min away' warning on the streets. But no. It's just . . . there. Blending into the rhythm of this beautiful city. It's lined with buildings that look like they grew from the ground itself. Their wooden shutters are perched precariously over the edge. Shops line the walkway, gold glinting behind glass like treasure.

My sandals click softly as I walk past shop after shop, each window gleaming with gold rings, delicate chains, and lockets that look like something out of a grandmother's jewellery box. I pause before one window, marvelling at a bracelet so fine, it looks like starlight spun into metal. So simple but eccentric. Quietly dazzling.

Much like my sister Ivy.

God, Ivy. My eyes sting at the mere thought of her. I usually try my hardest to keep her out of my thoughts, for as long as I can, but then there are moments like this. Moments where I find something she would've liked, something she would've picked up and called 'ridiculously perfect'.

I chuckle even as my eyes water, because even in the grief she left behind, Ivy is a force to be reckoned with. Even in her absence, she's powerful. Even in memory, Ivy is bright in the shadows.

I wipe a tear away and focus on the goal. I'll have plenty of time to visit my grief.

So I continue onto the streets to Via De' Guicciardini, where most leather goods are. The further I wander from the bridge, the quieter it gets. The crowds thin, replaced by the comforting chatter of smaller groups. The scent shifts too. Gone is the river breeze tinged with perfume and sweat. It's still hot, but somehow, it's calmer.

I pass a row of leather shops, each like the last—hand-stitched bags hanging in doorways, belts coiled like snakes on velvet-lined shelves, shoes that look like they belong to royalty. Everything looks handcrafted and deeply loved.

I pause outside one with old wooden signage that reads 'Calzolaio e Figli' in faded gold letters. The window display features rows of shoes such as Oxfords and boots, heels and slippers. There's even a little sign in the corner that says: 'Custom orders and repairs welcome'.

Could be nothing. Could be everything.

A bell chimes as I push the door open, and the smell of leather and sawdust hits me.

'Buongiorno,' a voice calls out from the back, followed by the distinct squeak of a workbench stool.

I take a step inside and offer a cautious smile to the man who appears from behind a curtain. He's old, probably in his sixties, with silver-streaked curls and kind eyes framed by glasses that sit slightly crooked on his nose. His apron is covered in chalk dust and thread, and he has the look of someone who's been in this shop since birth and wouldn't dream of being anywhere else.

'Buongiorno,' I echo, then hesitate. 'Do you happen to know a shoemaker named Giodani?'

He lifts an eyebrow. 'Giodani?' He repeats the name like it's a question, then smiles, a little wistfully. 'Ah. *Il romantico.*'

My heart does something irrational, like a skip or a swerve.

'You know him?'

He chuckles, walking towards a low shelf and pulling out a worn ledger with a leather cover and hand-inked tabs. 'Everyone in this part of Florence knows Giodani. He used to work just a few streets away before he retired. Always left little poems in the boxes with his shoes. Drove the clients wild.'

I can't help but smile at that. It's always a treat to get a personalized something in your purchases. And this city looks like the exact place to get those.

'Do you know where I can find him now?'

He closes the ledger slowly, like savouring a memory. 'Possibly. Are you up for cappuccino and pastries?'

I look at him in confusion, and he laughs as he registers this. 'No, no, Signorina, I am not being a creep.' He steps out from behind the counter and walks towards the exit. 'There's a cafe just around the corner. Bar Giuseppe. Giodani goes there sometimes. Orders a sweet pastry and reads the newspaper, like he's always waiting for someone.'

I thank him, promise to return if I strike out, and head back into the sunlight with the directions he gave me scrawled on the back of a business card. Before I continue, I dial Luca's number.

'Sì?' His response is immediate.

'I think I found him,' I say, walking slowly, like the words might shift if I say them too fast.

'Okay,' Luca replies, not missing a beat. There's a clatter, followed by a sharp voice of an angry man . . . Yep, definitely the kitchen. 'I'll go with you.'

'You sure?' I ask, weaving through a small group of school kids.

'Yes. Don't start without me.'

The line clicks and for some reason, despite the uncertainty of it all, I find myself smiling.

9

Luca

Bar Giuseppe is tucked into the curve of a quiet street, the kind of place you'd walk right past if you weren't looking for it. I used to come here sometimes, back when I had time to myself to just . . . relax and slow down. I barely get that these days.

I spot Isla before she sees me. She's sitting by the window, tracing a circle on the rim of her cup with one finger. A strand of hair is escaping from the bun she has twisted it into. The sun hits her just right, and she looks like a painting. Her skin tan and hair dark—glowing.

She glances up, catches me looking, and smiles. She has a nice smile.

I slide into the seat across from her and nod towards the counter. 'You didn't order me anything?'

'You're late,' she says, picking up her fork again. 'The pastry window has rules.'

I snort. 'Of course it does.'

'I got a tip,' she says, lowering her voice like we're in some kind of spy movie. 'Giodani comes here. Orders the same thing. Always sits by the window.'

I glance around. 'Then let's wait.' I raise my hand to call for the waiter. 'Might as well make a decent brunch out of it.'

Isla tears off a bit of croissant and pops it into her mouth. I watch the sugar icing cling to the side of her mouth. 'You've got . . .' I trail off, gesturing vaguely towards my own face. 'Sugar. Just there.'

She swipes at her cheek, completely missing it.

'Nope. Still there.'

She tries again, getting nowhere close.

'Ay, Dio,' I say before I can talk myself out of it. I reach across the table to guide her wrist to the right spot, but I pause. 'May I?'

She blinks, surprised. 'Uh. Sure.'

I take her wrist gently and move her hand towards the spot, my thumb lightly pressing against the back of her hand. It's nothing—barely a touch—but her skin is warm from the sun, and she's suddenly very still, like even she wasn't expecting to say yes.

'There,' I say quietly, releasing her hand once she gets the sugar. 'Crisis averted.'

She looks at me for a beat too long, then clears her throat and reaches for her coffee. 'Thanks,' she says. 'Uh . . . it's okay for you to leave the restaurant?'

'Yeah, Marco basically pushed me out. Said they can handle it.' I can't deny that I'm still a bit worried. Marco can get carried away by trivial things.

'I'm sure they can,' she says absentmindedly. 'Worst case scenario is you close for the day, right?'

'I suppose. But then Marissa, our waitress, won't have enough tips to get her daughter through her surgery. Enzo, the chef, will struggle with child support. And my nonna will never let me live through it.' I chuckle.

She looks at me for a while, something new glistening in her eyes. 'Who knew,' she says.

'Who knew what?'

'That the grump has a heart.'

I laugh. 'I'm not a grump, I just find it hard to believe in fate and destiny, Signorina. It's all a waste of time . . . no offence.'

The waiter places a warm plate of pudding in front of me, accompanied by a cup of espresso. The smell alone makes me happier.

'None taken,' Isla responds. 'You're close with your nonna?' she asks.

I nod as I take a sip of coffee. 'Very, she practically raised me,' I reply. 'My parents, they . . .' I trail off. 'They left me. My father moved out when I was ten. My mother died when I was nineteen. I've been with my nonna ever since.'

She looks at me with that expression again. Wide eyes and a meaningful pout. 'Don't,' I say. 'Don't look at me with pity.'

'Oh, this is not pity,' she replies. 'This is wonder. Amusement.' She takes a clean spoon and digs into the pudding.

Just as I'm about to scold her for taking my food, the door to the bar opens. An old man enters, wearing a tailored suit and leather shoes, like he's attending a black-tie event. He goes to the counter and grabs a powdered pastry, then takes a seat beside our table. He opens a newspaper and starts reading.

'That him?' I ask Isla, who's already gawking at the old man. Her gaze turns to me, and she nods vehemently.

Before I can ask about the plan, she clears her throat and turns to face the man. 'Hello,' she says cheerfully. The man peers at her over the rim of his round glasses. He doesn't speak, so Isla continues. 'Scusa, *Signor*, but are you, by any chance, Giodani?'

The man folds his newspaper and places it on his table. 'And who is asking?'

'I am Isla,' she says and then gestures to me. 'This is my . . . friend, Luca. We're here to ask you about a letter in a book . . .' Isla trails off.

The man freezes for a while. Then he looks out the window. For a few seconds, I wonder if I should nudge him, or ask Isla to talk again, but he returns his attention to us, and says, 'Amore mio.'

Isla looks at me, raises her eyebrows, and widens her eyes. I understand her and quickly turn to Giodani. 'Scusi, so you are Giodani? And you know about the book of amore?'

'Know about it? I am still living it,' he says. Isla gasps loudly and I shush her, but instead of being more subtle, she drags her chair to the next table and plops her elbows on it.

'Could you maybe tell us about your experience with it?' she says, her eyes twinkling.

Giodani sighs. 'Well, it comes and goes, that book. Always shows up when someone needs it most.'

I arch an eyebrow. 'Right. And it just *magically* knows who's in need of unsolicited love letters.'

He chuckles and points a finger at me. 'Scepticism. That's how I was too. Until I met her.'

I narrow my eyes at him, and he smiles at me. 'Her name was Margarette,' Giodani starts. 'I already knew her, and I'd been secretly harbouring an attraction towards her. Any man would, at the time. She was gorgeous by all means.' He stirs his espresso cup as he stares in the distance, smiling. 'One day, I found the book tucked in an alley stall in Venice.'

He looks at me, then Isla, then back into the void. 'Inside was a letter to me from Margarette. She knew everything about me. That I hum when I cook, that I like the rain, and . . . that I wanted to run away from my wedding.'

Isla gasps. 'You were getting married?'

Giodani nods. 'To a woman everyone approved of. Everyone but me.'

That's absurd. I don't say it out loud, but I will never understand how anyone could go as far as discussing marriage with someone they don't approve of. I'm starting to lose respect for this old man.

'When I found the letter,' Giodani continues, 'I went straight to Margarette. Of course when I confronted her, she denied it. That's when we started to spend more time together. And we fell in love so quickly. It was like . . . the book had carved a path and we just walked on blindly.'

He stops, looking at his hands. 'And then, one morning,' he adds, 'she was just gone. And she had left the book open on a page that I hadn't seen before.'

'What did it say?' Isla asks.

'*When the time is right, I'll meet you where we dreamed. Until then, live for both of us*,' Giodani says. 'Those were her exact words. And so here I am. Every single day, I'm here where we dreamed.'

'And you've been coming back ever since?' I asked, unable to process the absurdity of it all.

'Every Thursday.' He smiles faintly. 'She said she'd come back. That was twenty-three years ago.'

Isla bites her lip. 'Do you think she will?'

He doesn't answer right away. Just folds his napkin and sets it neatly beside the plate. 'The book hasn't been wrong yet,' he says. There's something fragile in his voice. 'And love doesn't end. Sometimes it just . . . takes a while to come home.'

Then, like some old movie scene, he stands, adjusts his cuffs, and takes a slow, measured breath.

'You're leaving? So soon?' Isla asks.

'I'll come back another day.' Giodani smiles, but I have a feeling he just doesn't like being in the company of people who currently have the book. 'I hope whatever you find in that book, you treat it kindly,' he adds.

'Wait!' I say. 'So . . . that's it? You can't tell us anything about this book at all?'

I look at Giodani, hoping for a sensible answer. But knowing that he spends an hour or two every week in this bar hoping to reconnect with an estranged lover, I'm not so sure.

'That book shows us who we're destined to be with. That's what I believe.'

I can't help but roll my eyes. 'Scusa, Signor,' I start. 'Let me get this straight.' I try to keep my voice even. 'You found a book. It had a letter inside, addressed to you. From a woman who swears she didn't write it . . .'

'It told me things only I knew,' he says calmly. 'Things no one else could have written.'

I exhale sharply. 'It's a parlour trick. A hoax. People see what they want to see. You were already in love with Margarette, weren't you? The book didn't do anything—you did. You left your fiancée. You chased after someone you already had feelings for. It's not destiny, it's . . . projection.'

Isla shoots me a warning glance, but I press on.

'You waited twenty-three years. For someone who may not even exist in the way you think she does. All because of a page in a book.'

Giodani considers me for a long moment, then leans slightly forward, like he's about to share a secret.

'Tell me, Luca,' he says, voice quiet but clear. 'Have you ever been in love?'

I narrow my eyes at him. 'Of course I have,' I say, picturing Dahlia's big blue eyes.

'Then you must know,' he says, 'that if there's even the slightest chance for you to be with the one you love again, the smallest hope, you will take it.' He smiles kindly, making me feel bad for calling him out. 'But if it makes you feel better, *ragazzo*, I tried to forget the book. I tried to choose logic. But logic never made me feel alive. Love did.'

He buttons his coat with deliberate slowness, and tips his hat off to us. 'You don't have to believe me,' he says. 'Most people don't. But when the book speaks to you, you'll understand.'

And just like that, he turns and walks out the door, leaving me feeling like shit.

10

Isla

'Well, I hope you're happy,' I mutter, slamming my espresso cup down. 'You made the old signor feel like a fool.'

I take a sip and make a face. Bitter drinks are only good when they're hot. I take another regretful sip, glaring at him over the rim of the chipped cup.

'It wasn't my intention,' he says with a sigh. He turns to me and takes another bite of his pudding.

'Oh no, of course not,' I say, gesturing dramatically. 'You just accidentally crushed a lovely old man's twenty-three-year-long hope with your aggressively rational worldview. Happens to the best of us.' I shrug.

He gives me a look. 'I was being honest.'

'No, you were being a dream breaker with nice eyes.'

Luca blinks. 'That was . . . a compliment?'

I roll my eyes. 'You made him feel delusional. You are officially the Grinch of romance.'

'You're only learning that now?' He raises his eyebrows. 'I told you I don't believe in all that.' He takes a few seconds before he continues, 'I wasn't trying to ruin the mood, Isla.

But someone has to ask the practical questions. You really think this book just magically knows things? That it's a portal to your soulmate?'

'Don't twist my words. I don't know what it is yet,' I admit. 'But I know how it made me feel. And I know it's not normal. You have to admit that much.'

He scrubs a hand down his face, clearly fighting the urge to argue again. 'Fine. It's weird. But weird doesn't mean mystical. I'm still not ruling out that it's a prank. Maybe it's a psychological experiment. Someone's trying to see how far people will go when they think something is fate.'

'Oh my god.' I throw my hands up. 'It's okay to believe in something without knowing how it works, Luca.'

'That's how people join cults, Isla.' He says my name in the same bitter way I said his.

'It's how people fall in love, idiot.'

We stay in silence for a moment, thankfully. An elaborately dressed woman walks past the window, pulling her dog, a beagle, on a leash. We used to have a dog like that, but he died shortly after Ivy did.

'Remind me again why I'm doing this with you?' Luca says.

'Because,' I say, distracting myself from thoughts about Ivy again, 'deep down, you love mysteries. And me.' I smirk.

'I do *not* love y—' Luca says.

'Shh,' I say. 'Don't argue. You'll hurt the book's feelings.'

He rolls his eyes but doesn't argue. Progress.

'So now what?'

I look ahead for a while. 'Now, we just check if the book changes again, then see where we can go from there.'

'Or,' Luca says, 'we can . . . not look at it for an entire day, and live our lives the way we would. Maybe it will change. Maybe our names will be forgotten.'

I consider what he's saying. It's not like we have anything else to get us going.

The slight pause in his tone makes me glance at him. 'You're just gonna . . . spend the day with me?' I ask, sceptical of what he really meant.

Luca looks at me, caught off-guard, like he hadn't realized what he was suggesting until I said it out loud. 'Isla,' he starts, 'don't flatter yourself. I just . . .' he mutters, running his hands through his hair. 'I think it's better than having to hear you babble about the book again, you know? Maybe we can just leave it for a while.'

I stare at him with obvious confusion. He shifts, clears his throat, then adds, 'Besides, I've already cleared the rest of my day.'

'Hmm . . .' I say, still not convinced. I know he's just trying to humour me. Or himself.

As tempted as I am to check the book one more time, I agree with him. 'Okay . . .' I say. 'What do you suggest we do?'

Luca shrugs. 'You're the tourist. You have a local at your disposal.' He gestures to himself. 'What do you want to do?'

I get excited and pull out my phone. 'I have a gazillion things. I wanna go to the Duomo, the Uffizi, Palazzo Pitti, and everything else that Klook suggested.'

He chuckles. 'Alright. We can go to the Duomo, then work our way back here. If time allows.'

'Perfect!' I exclaim as I stand up, already buzzing. 'Adventure awaits, Signor Sceptic.'

He grabs his sunglasses, sighing. 'Lead the way, Signorina Cult Recruit.'

'So, tell me,' Luca says as we walk back through the Ponte Vecchio. 'Why are you really here in Italy?'

'I told you,' I say, scanning the array of necklaces. 'I'm a writer. I'm suffering from a terrible writer's block. I'm here to find inspiration.'

He nods thoughtfully as he removes his sunglasses and hangs them on his shirt collar. He looks straight ahead, his green eyes illuminated by the sunlight. His hair is a mixture of all shades of brown, and it lightens under the sun. 'Okay, that's your press release,' he says. 'What's the real reason?' He stops to look at me, and for the first time since I met him, I study him sincerely. He's wearing jeans and a white button-down, his hair tousled but swaying perfectly with the wind.

'What are you talking about?' I feign innocence. 'That is the real reason. I'm writing a book set in Italy, and I'm here to, you know . . .' I wave my hand towards the Arno, 'soak up the vibes, find my muse, all that.'

'So is it heartbreak?' he asks, ignoring me. 'Quarter-life crisis? Legal problems?'

'First of all, thank you for thinking I'm only twenty-five. Second, I don't know what you want from me, I'm telling you the truth.'

'Suit yourself. I'll find out eventually,' Luca says.

We walk in comfortable silence for a few beats, the city humming around us. I want to convince myself that I'm only here for my writing. Of course, that is one of the primary reasons. I do need to learn about the country. But if I'm being completely honest, ever since my sister died two years ago, there's been a gaping hole in my heart. It eats me up, especially at night when I'm all alone.

Grief does that, I suppose. It makes you restless. It makes you feel that if you stay in one place for too long, the sadness will find you again.

So, you move. You go to new cities and take pictures of old bridges. Pretend you're only there for the cultural reset. You fill notebooks with other people's histories, hoping it'll distract you from your own. You keep running towards places that feel unfamiliar because that's the only way you'll find a version of yourself that isn't so broken.

Every time I land somewhere new, it's like putting a tiny, invisible patch over the hole inside me. Not a permanent fix, never that. But for a little while, the hole feels smaller, and everything feels a little bit more manageable.

Over time, though, the patch grows thin. And I have to find a new place, a new patch to cover up the hole.

I clutch the sling of my bag to ground me.

'Almost there,' Luca says beside me, and I nod without really hearing him.

The streets open up, and suddenly, there it is—the Duomo, massive and breathtaking, like it was plucked straight out of a fantasy realm and dropped into the middle of the world.

I stop walking without meaning to.

The sunlight catches on the red-tiled dome, the marble facade shimmering in white, green, and pink like a cake too beautiful to eat. It towers over everything else.

People swarm around it—taking photos, laughing, spinning in slow circles with their faces lifted to the sky.

'You there?' Luca's voice brings me back.

'Shut up, I was having a moment,' I joke.

'Yeah, you and every other tourist. Maybe you wanna have a moment while we're in line?'

'So bossy,' I say, rolling my eyes. 'So, what's in this glorified cupcake?'

'Glad you asked,' Luca says, leading the way. Without missing a beat, he shifts into lecture mode. 'The Duomo, officially Santa Maria del Fiore, is one of the largest churches in the world. Building begun in 1296. Designed by Arnolfo di Cambio. Finished with Brunelleschi's dome in the 15th century—which was a massive architectural feat at the time. No scaffolding, by the way. Just engineering genius.'

I blink at him. 'You're, like . . . weirdly cute when you know facts.'

'I am what they call a history nerd,' he says sheepishly. I brace myself for the awkward silence that usually follows moments like that—moments where I say something flirty without thinking. But it doesn't come. It still feels easy between us. By easy, I mean so very platonic. I've given up hoping that this book brought me to my soulmate, but I'm still determined to know what its purpose really is.

I try not to think about the book, though. In case it can read my thoughts and update its words in real time. So, instead, I observe the people around me. As a writer, I'm fond of people-watching. It's where I get little quirks, notice little mannerisms, and connect with strangers in the way I would connect with my characters.

To my left, there's a guy with a camera lens longer than my entire forearm, whispering sweet nothings to the facade of the cathedral. At one point, he even calls it his baby. Directly in front of us in the line is a couple: They honestly look like they don't care where they are as long as they're inhaling each other's faces. You go, guys.

I've decided that the character I'm writing, while an excellent art curator, is also weirdly grounded in reality (good for her, right?), so I'm scribbling away in my phone as the line moves forward slowly.

I stop short when we enter the cathedral. It's massive. Echoes of centuries hum off the stone. The ceiling soars above us like heaven itself has been cracked open. The dome—the *cupola*, as Luca lovingly corrected me earlier—is enormous. Towering. Not just tall, but somehow infinite. Every inch is covered in frescoes, carvings, and stained glass that filters in coloured light.

'I think I just walked into a painting,' I whisper.

'It's one of the largest cathedrals in the world,' Luca says beside me, voice lower now, almost reverent. 'Designed to overwhelm you. It's supposed to make you feel small. Remind you how vast faith—or art—can be.'

'Well,' I say, turning in a slow circle, 'mission accomplished. I feel like an ingrown toenail.'

Luca chuckles, but doesn't reply. He lets me take in the scenery. Despite the warmth outside, it's cold in here. Probably because of the marble. And everything is so well-preserved that I can't imagine it's been here for centuries.

I glance at him, and he's studying a patch of fresco above the altar, face tilted up, soft light catching on the angles of his cheekbones, his jaw. His lashes are annoyingly long. The kind of lashes girls would buy fake versions of.

He looks like a painting straight from the museums I've visited so far.

I blink, startled at myself. Why am I looking at him when there's centuries of art around me?

I look away before my brain can make it a whole thing. It's probably just the lighting. Or the art. Or the altitude.

Yes. Stupid altitude.

11

Luca

It's always a treat to see tourists fall in love with your country.

Italy draws people in. It's the food, the history, the art. Some places take time to get under your skin, but Italy doesn't wait. It grabs you immediately. Every day, I thank whatever force put me here. Not just in this country, but in this city. In this moment.

Isla is quiet for the first time since I met her. It's nice.

I mean, don't get me wrong—I like her ridiculous commentary. I like that she compared one of the greatest architectural masterpieces in the world to a 'glorified cupcake'. I like how most people would say 'wow' or 'it's beautiful', but Isla said it makes her feel like an ingrown toenail. But I think I like this version too. The one who whispers when she's in awe and just observes.

I wonder what the book would write about this moment. Would it describe the way the afternoon light filters through the stained glass and lands right on her shoulder? Would it mention that, for the first time, I'm not thinking about how strange all of this is?

Or maybe it's already written it. Maybe we're living a line I haven't read yet.

I shake my head.

No. No book. Not today. That was the deal.

Isla finishes taking a dozen photos, and then pulls out a little notebook from her bag. She scribbles something quickly, brows furrowed in focus.

I watch her, even though I shouldn't.

When she finally looks up, I ask, 'So what's your book about?'

She blinks like I just pulled her out of a dream, then she huffs a laugh and clears her throat. 'Right. Um. So, my main character's an art curator. She gets sent to Italy to acquire this painting for the Philippine National Museum, but this guy—some local art restorer or dealer, I haven't decided—refuses to give it up.'

I nod slowly. 'So, enemies to lovers? Marco loves reading that stuff.'

She gives me a narrow look. 'Not everything has to be a romance, you know.'

'Right,' I say. 'Of course. But is it?'

She sighs dramatically. 'Yes, fine. He's grumpy, she's determined. Sparks fly, feelings get hurt, sparks fly again.'

'Very realistic,' I say, deadpan.

She grins, and I notice for the first time that she has a tiny freckle near her jawline. It's not something you'd see right away, not unless you're looking closely. Not unless you're maybe standing too close . . .

I step back half a pace.

'Anyway,' she continues, twirling the pen between her fingers, 'it's a mess right now. I've only got fragments—

scenes that don't connect yet, bits of dialogue, questions I haven't answered. But that's how it always starts for me. The character comes first. Plot comes later.'

'Sounds familiar,' I say.

She cocks her head. 'What do you mean?'

I hesitate, then shrug. 'I just mean . . . life doesn't usually start with a clear plot either. Just people. And then . . . everything else just happens.'

'Exactly!' Isla exclaims. 'That's what I always say. Stories, especially romance in the "real" world'—she adds air quotations—'should be character-driven. They unfold through people. Their choices. Their weird little habits. Their contradictions.'

She's fully animated now, hands up in the air, and her notebook almost falling.

I watch her while she talks more about the technicalities of writing a romance, observing the way her whole face lights up when she's passionate.

I clear my throat. 'So . . . is that what your story is? A messy love story?'

'Well, I sure hope so,' she replies quietly. 'Messy means it moved. That something shifted or mattered enough to shake the ground. People think mess is a sign something's gone wrong, but I think it's proof that something is in progress.' She glances at me, almost shyly now. 'Besides, a story without mess is just a summary.' She shrugs.

I blink at her. I haven't thought of it that way. Everything in my life is measured—when I cook, everything is precise, down to the last drop. I like knowing what comes next. What step follows what.

She talks like she believes in the beauty of the mess, but I've seen the way she freezes when the plan falls apart. The way she checks for omens in spilled salt, flinches at coincidences that feel too pointed. She wants things to be spontaneous, sure—but only if they still feel like fate. Pre-approved by the stars. She wants signs. Arrows. Cosmic winks. Not open roads with no map.

She craves control just as much as I do . . . only hers wears romance like perfume, while mine comes labelled and alphabetized.

Funny how people can be so different, and still—still end up sitting next to each other like this.

'So,' Isla says. 'Any interesting facts?' She holds up a finger, then adds, 'Emphasis on interesting.'

'Okay, so you say your novel is about an artist,' I say.

'Art curator.'

'Then look up,' I instruct.

She blinks at me, then tilts her head. 'That's . . . the dome I've been gawking over for the past ten minutes.'

'The painting,' I say, calmly, 'is called *The Last Judgment*. Vasari. Sixteenth century. He designed it to cover Brunelleschi's—the architect's—original dome, which, at the time, was considered a masterpiece in its own right.'

Isla studies it a moment longer. 'It looks . . . chaotic.'

'It is,' I reply. 'It's meant to be. Heaven at the top, hell below. A whole spectrum of humanity caught between grace and punishment. The artist was trying to make it true.'

She lowers her gaze slowly, thoughtful now. 'That's kind of depressing.'

'Or just real,' I say. 'Depends on how you look at it.'

She scribbles in her little notebook again. I admire her determination. I have to give her that. Despite everything that's happened since she arrived in Italy, she still hasn't lost touch with what her purpose really was. For a second, I think about purchasing a book she's published before. Just to see how she works her ideas into pages.

I know what it feels to be so immersed in your passion. It's a thin line between being passionate and self-destructive, by the way. And I'm teetering towards the latter.

The truth is, the reason I'm doing all this is because of that haunted letter that mentioned my restaurant shutting down. If I were at any other point in my career, I'd brush it off. But this time, this is all I've got. And it's not doing well. It's not as easy to maintain a restaurant in the heart of Florence. I'm not situated in a tourist-heavy place, and the locals don't spend so much on stuff they can prepare at home.

I was nineteen when I started working in a restaurant. It was a Michelin star restaurant where chefs screamed as often as pans rattled. Every single day, I wanted to walk out. But I didn't. Because my mother passed away and I had to care for my nonna. I walked away when she started getting sick often. Not that she needed much care, she's still strong. But she always told me that it's important to have something in this world that you can call your own. Whether it's a family, a career, anything. As long as you've curated it yourself. She said humans are simple beings. We all need a little validation.

So I started the restaurant a few years after my mom died. At first, I was proud. I was happy. But lately, it's getting harder to get people to eat there. Sure, we're still busy most days, but sometimes, I feel like it's not enough.

'What's down there?' Isla asks, breaking into my thoughts. She points to the staircase situated near the entrance.

'Another museum. In the crypt.'

'Underground? That's *so* cool. Come on.' She grabs my arm and pulls me with her. She's tiny, but she's surprisingly strong. 'You can be my personal tour guide.'

I let her drag me along. Maybe because it's easier than saying no. Or maybe because, for just a moment, it feels good to be needed for something other than cooking.

Humans *are* simple creatures, I suppose.

12

Isla

When we were kids, Ivy used to tell me, 'Go where your feet take you.'

At first, I thought it was a stupid thing to say. Like, *Duh, Ivy. That's literally how feet work.* They're the ones doing the walking. Did she want me to levitate? Teleport? Ride a magic carpet into the unknown?

When I grew older and slightly more self-aware, I understood what she meant. Of course, it's not about feet. It's about instinct. About letting yourself drift towards the thing that sparks something in you, even if it makes no sense.

Ever since she died, I have had trouble doing that. I can't seem to just do something because I feel like it. But right now, standing in this weird dungeon-museum, the basement of the cathedral, and considering everything that led me to this moment, I feel like she would've been proud of me.

My feet are definitely taking me places now, Ivy. I only wish yours were walking with mine.

I blink fast because the air down here is cold and damp and my eyes are stinging (possibly from something other than the air, but we're not going there).

The thought of Ivy once again sits heavy in my chest, and I don't know what to do with the weight. So, naturally, I do what I always do when things feel too real and too heavy.

I glance at Luca, and he immediately turns to me.

'This better not be where you murder me,' I tell him. This underground museum doesn't have many tourists. Unsurprising, since it is mostly in ruins. Just crumbling stone walls, remnants of mosaic tiles, and a few dusty spotlights. 'Because if it is, just know I left my other notebooks in the hotel room, and someone will find it and make a really subpar movie about my life.'

Luca chuckles quietly. 'Relax, if I were to murder you, I wouldn't do it beneath a cathedral.'

'Thanks. Comforting.' I shrug.

We don't spend a lot of time in the crypt. All I find out is that it showcases the remains of the ancient basilica of Santa Reparata, which served as Florence's cathedral from the fifth century until its demolition. And the architect is buried there, too. I think.

'Isla,' Luca says. I look up at him and see concern in his eyes.

'What's wrong?'

'Nothing, just . . . I need to check on my nonna. She wasn't feeling well this morning, and I told her I'd bring her some medicine after five.'

'Oh.' I nod quickly, trying to sound understanding, even though a small knot forms in my chest. I didn't want the day to be over yet. I didn't want to go back to my empty hotel room with nothing but my unfinished manuscript and the ache of missing Ivy to keep me company.

So instead of letting the moment end, I blurt, 'Do you need help?'

Luca blinks, visibly surprised. 'Help?'

'Yeah,' I say, shrugging. 'I'm an excellent medicine delivery assistant. And I make great small talk with Italian grandmothers.'

A beat passes. Then, to my shock, he chuckles. 'You're serious.'

'Completely.'

He hesitates for a second more, then nods. 'Okay. But if she tries to feed you something the size of your head, that's on you.'

'I've trained for this my entire life,' I deadpan. 'Let's go.'

Like most places in Florence, Luca's home is within walkable distance. We stop by a pharmacy for the pills, and he grabs some aranciata and a fresh loaf of bread from a nearby bakery 'just in case Nonna hasn't eaten'. Then we wind through quieter streets until we reach a yellow-toned corner house with green shutters and colourful flower boxes.

The building is old, but charming in the way that only this city seems to pull off. He unlocks the door and gestures for me to enter first.

Inside, it smells like rosemary and lemon and . . . mothballs. Typical grandma stuff. Except, in the Philippines, rosemary is replaced by Efficascent oil and lemon with that floral scent that clings to the upholstery.

There's a wooden side table by the door with a little orange bowl full of keys and coins. The walls are lined with photos in mismatched frames: black-and-white portraits beside polaroids, faded prints of people smiling at birthdays, holding babies, or standing beside Christmas trees. A few pressed herbs hang from a hook in the kitchen, and a cat is curled up in a chair near the window, its tail flicking lazily as we walk past.

'This is cozy,' I whisper.

'It's old,' he replies, but not dismissively. He says it like it's something he's proud of.

He leads me down a narrow hallway and knocks once on a wooden door. 'Nonna?' he calls softly.

There's a moment of silence, then a voice—hoarse but chipper—answers in Italian.

He cracks open the door. 'It's just me. I brought your medicine.'

'And a girl,' she says before we've even stepped in. 'I heard a girl's voice. Don't lie to me.'

I blink. 'Wow, you're good.'

The door opens fully and I see her: tiny and sharp-eyed, her silver hair swept into a tidy bun beneath a floral scarf. She's sitting upright in bed, her back straight, with a pink cardigan wrapped around her shoulders and a bowl of clementines on her nightstand. There's a stack of crossword puzzles beside her and a remote control tucked into her lap like a sword.

'Well, well,' she says, appraising me. 'She's pretty.'

'Nonna,' Luca groans.

'What?' She shrugs. 'I may be old, but I'm not blind. Come in, sit down. Don't hover like a nurse.'

I smile and step into the room, letting the warmth and clutter wrap around me. There's a small crucifix on the wall, a landscape painting of Rome that looks hand-painted, and a dusty bookshelf filled with old Italian novels and what look like cookbooks from the 1950s.

Nonna pats the edge of her bed. 'Sit, cara. Tell me your name.'

'Hi, I'm Isla,' I say, settling beside her.

'Like the island?'

'Exactly.' My parents were outdoorsy when they were young. They've travelled the Philippines from its forests to its beaches. Which is why we're named Ivy and Isla.

She squints at me. 'Not Italian.'

'Filipina,' I reply.

'Ah,' she says, pleased. 'I like Filipinas. Warm. And kind.'

'And loud.' Luca scoffs, and I glare at him. He is still hovering near the door, holding the pack of medicine. 'I thought you were sick. You don't look sick at all, Nonna.'

She waves off her hand. 'I am, I am. Get me a glass of water,' she says as Luca scurries out. She then leans a bit closer to me and adds, 'Between you and me, I'm not sick. But I need to give that man something to do to make him feel useful, you know?'

'Why would he need that?'

'Ever since he gave his heart and soul to that Dahlia, and she left him, he has lost all belief in love,' she says. 'No, actually he's never been a believer of love. Then he believed for a brief moment. And now, he's more cynical than ever.'

I try to wrap my head around that. I've always thought that he was just a natural walking-rain cloud. And I admit, that was dismissive of me. Of all people, I should know that there's a story behind every person. One that usually makes them who they are.

Luca re-emerges with a glass of water and the medicine. He places it on his nonna's bedside table.

'So,' Nonna says, 'what is the story between you two?'

'There's no story,' Luca says. His nonna eyes him, until he says, 'She just needs help. That's all.'

Nonna doesn't let it go. She turns to me and says, 'And you, Isla? What's your version of the story?'

'There's just this book I want to study.'

'And my grandson is whom you chose to study with?' She's not convinced.

'Well,' I say reluctantly. 'It's hard to explain. It's just . . . I'm a very superstitious person, and there's this book that's been making me more superstitious by the hour. I just wanna put an explanation to it. It's weird, and confusing . . .' I trail off.

'Amore,' she mutters. Her eyes widen slightly, like she's had a revelation, but she returns to nonchalance shortly.

'You know?' Luca asks, brows furrowed.

His nonna chuckles. '*Know?* Dio mio, it's all your mother ever talked about.' She immediately stops, like she just said something she wasn't supposed to.

Luca frowns. 'What?'

I feel like I should slide off the bed and tiptoe out of the room backwards. I am not family. I am a random girl who has an obsession with horoscopes. I am not supposed to be here for a decades-old family drama reveal.

Nonna sighs and straightens her shoulders. 'It's the reason your father left,' she says plainly. 'That *book.* Or maybe not that exact one, but something like it. Same message. Same promise. He decided—*decided,* mind you—that he was meant for a love more poetic than the one he had.

'He told your mother that love was a calling,' she says, rolling her eyes so hard, it made me worry for her optic nerves. 'That it would find him somewhere else. Some mystical city. Some *destined woman.* I told him, "Philip, you are not a character in a telenovela." But he didn't listen.'

Luca closes his eyes and rubs his temples, like he's resigned himself to the idea. He sighs deeply, and says, 'Well, that explains it.'

'I don't know what the book is,' Nonna continues, 'or what it contains, or how you two are now tied to it. And I'm not going to ask you to tell me. But if there's one person who might give you an explanation . . .' Her eyes drift to Luca, and she raises her eyebrows.

'I don't want to see him. It's been decades,' Luca says.

Her voice goes soft again. Gentle, but not unsure. 'He's in Rome.'

It's quiet. For a long moment, no one speaks. And we just let it settle in the air. At first, I thought this book was just a little sign from the universe, something to spark inspiration for my writing, to help me face what I've been running from since Ivy died.

But now? It's showing Luca the things he's been hiding from, too.

Maybe we're meant to be together at this point in our lives after all.

13

Luca

I think about my father from time to time, but not enough to want to see him.

To be honest, the more I find out about this book, the more I want to throw it in the fire and watch it burn. Pretend it never existed and continue living my magic book-free, Isla-free life.

But some part of me can't just let it go. For once in my life, something is nudging me forward, telling me that I don't have to face the future blind. Sure, it's not really the future. I can ignore it. I can fight it. But I can't lie: There's a weird comfort in thinking that I've been led to a breadcrumb trail. Even if I never asked for it.

That's the only reason I let Isla drag me to her hotel room again. We had promised not to look at the book at all today, to see if the pages changed with our silence. But after everything Nonna had said, silence suddenly felt like the wrong move.

Earlier, after Nonna's confession, I had expected her to throw questions at me like a machine gun. I had expected her to pry into my childhood, my father, my mother, everything in between. But Isla was surprisingly (maybe intentionally) quiet on our way here. I'm not sure if it was because she respects my privacy or if she was thinking of a strategy to get me on a train to Rome.

I take a seat on the armchair—the same one from yesterday. Or two nights ago. It's hard to tell the time any more. The chair's a lot tidier now, and the room more inviting. No clothes half-strung on surfaces, no make-up bottles half-open, no shoes missing their pair.

I ring up Marco to get some restaurant updates (slow lunch, slightly busy dinner, all as per usual). While we are talking, Isla decides to take a quick shower. Apparently, she's used to taking two showers a day because of the humidity in the Philippines. I've never been there, so I wouldn't know. Well, I haven't been around much at all, if I'm being honest. The last vacation I took, if it even counts, was my ski trip to Switzerland with Marco two years ago. But even that was just a train ride away.

A few minutes after I end the call, Isla steps out of the bathroom, drying her hair with a towel. She's wearing a matching pair of shorts and a top that are printed with palm leaves and flowers. The moment she steps out, the room starts smelling of coconut and berries.

'Okay, you ready?' she asks.

'Not really,' I admit.

'Same.' She takes the book from under her bed, and the sight of it makes me feel queasy. This book, or one like it, is the reason my mother was left to parent me alone.

When I was young, I saw my father through the rose-coloured lenses of bedtime stories and old photos. He loved my mother. Fiercely and openly. I was the front-row witness to that love, the centre of their world. But then he left. Disappeared into some other story. And if that kind of love could unravel, could be replaced by some . . . ancient book with impossible promises—do I really want to understand why?

Do I really want to track him down and ask what was in these pages that made him choose something else over us?

No.

Yes.

I don't know.

The thought coils inside me like a knot I can't undo.

Isla takes the book, and gestures for me to join her at the desk. She opens it and flips to the last few pages that are filled, where our letters are. She hovers a bit over one, then her eyes scan the page quickly as I lean over her shoulder. The smell of coconut and berries is stronger now, and I can't help but take a few more whiffs as I try to get a better view. Her head is inches from my cheek, and I suddenly realize how close we are. Before I can adjust my position, she squeals.

'Oh my god!' she says.

'What?' I move, so I'm fully beside her now, our arms touching.

'This one is new.' She points to the last letter—one addressed to her, from me. '*Rome changed everything*,' she starts. With this, she looks at me, our faces inches apart. She quickly turns her head back to the book just as I notice the mole on her eyelid. '*I didn't know it then. Not when we boarded the train, or when you spilled coffee on my luggage at the Roma Termini. Not even when I saw you argue with my father about the meaning of love.*'

Isla lets out a chuckle. 'Sounds like me,' she says. I nod as she continues.

'*But somewhere in between, I fell. Harder than I thought possible. I keep thinking: What if we hadn't gone? I would've missed the version of you that existed only there. And I would've missed the version of me that only exists when I'm with you.*' Isla stops briefly, but she continues. '*I love you. Please don't leave.*'

For a moment, there's silence. She doesn't move, and neither do I. I don't know what it is about this particular letter. It's much like the previous ones—from the future, and romantic. But this time, it somehow makes all of this seem . . . real.

I know, I know. It's been real since the moment Isla stepped into my trattoria. But back then, it was real in a way that I could easily explain: There's a hopeless romantic woman who believes in fate and true love, who thinks I'm her soulmate. Isla was an idea. Just a mere possibility. I never thought it would go beyond that.

But now, now it feels different. Now, it's not just something I'm trying to make sense of or dismiss. It's not some magic I can debunk with logic or scepticism.

Somehow, I believe it. I believe that there's a version of me in this moment, in this city, in this book, that I wouldn't even recognize. And it would all be because of Isla. Because she came into my life.

'Well?' she asks. She closes the book now, her eyes darting up to mine. 'I'm not saying come with me to Rome,' she begins. 'I'm saying that I really want to go. And I would. Even if you're not coming. But it would be much better if you came.'

'Why?' I ask.

'Because I can't speak Italian.'

I chuckle and shake my head.

I've spent much of my life closing doors. The only times I ever put myself out there were when I opened the trattoria and then met Dahlia. Even then, I didn't know it could be this way. I didn't know love could make a familiar place feel new, could change the way you see the world, make everything else fade into the background.

And so now I'm standing here, torn between the old life I know and this new one that scares me more than anything. The truth is, Isla might be right. She's been right about so much already. And maybe it's time I start listening.

'*Andiamo a Roma.*'

She stares at me in disbelief. 'So your response to me saying I can't speak Italian is . . . Italian?' She shakes her head dramatically, adding in a few tsk tsk tsks. 'I'm just gonna assume that means we're going?'

I can't help the laugh that escapes. She's so animated. The pyjamas certainly don't help tone her down. But I don't think she needs to be toned down. It fits her.

Her eyebrows are still raised, and this time, she crosses her arms and aggressively taps her foot in mock impatience.

'Correct, Signorina.'

She claps her hands. 'Just so you know, I've already booked the train tickets. We're leaving in two days.'

Of course we are.

14

Isla

Today, I'm supposed to write. I look at my little notebook of ideas and try to make sense of the nonsensical things I put in there. I wince at every turn of the page because my mind, ladies and gentlemen, is a glittery trash heap of half-formed thoughts, cryptic phrases, and doodles of anthropomorphic coffee cups for reasons even I cannot explain.

Still, I try to wrestle the nonsense into order. I start compiling everything into a shiny new document. Like a digital Marie Kondo, I'm dragging weird notes into categories and colour-coding them. Miraculously, a story starts to peek through the clutter.

Okay, so here's where we are: Julie, my extremely energetic but secretly soft main character, is in Florence for an art show. She's got tunnel vision for this one painting—apparently Filipino-owned. I have no idea what the painting is or who the artist might be. I trust Future Me to sort that out.

The scene I've been stuck in for weeks is the one where she meets with the director to acquire the painting for the

National Museum of the Philippines. But our deliciously feisty male lead stops her before she can even ask.

Miraculously, after an hour of scribbling, I move past that scene. Not only that, I also manage to outline the rest of the story. Calling it an outline is a bit of a stretch, though. It's really just a page full of arrows and random words. In fact, that outline's as good as my grocery list. A big, long list of wishful thinking. The one where I put items like carrots and lettuce only to end up with a bag full of ingredients for a dump cake I didn't plan to make. I don't know how some writers stick to their outlines. I can never do that. I'm fully convinced my outlines are there simply to give me a false sense of direction. A guide to look at when things feel out of hand, as I then proceed to duck into an alley that doesn't exist on it.

Much like life, I suppose. Ugh. I know, right? Here I go again. Relating every single thing to 'life'. But everything contributes to the way we live our lives. Life is like a giant puzzle sometimes, where you might be referring to a complete picture reference, but when you're actually doing it, half the pieces are missing, and the ones you do have don't exactly snap together neatly. They just sort of . . . hover there awkwardly until you find one that fits or give up and shove them in a drawer for later.

Or maybe it isn't a puzzle. Maybe life's a mosaic made from broken coffee mugs, crumpled receipts, and all those stray socks that vanished in the laundry. Individually, those pieces are ugly, useless, and kind of sad. But shove them all together and somehow, it's art. A hot mess of beautiful chaos.

Life is a combination of everything we do, every thought we have, every person we meet.

So yes, this book is a reflection of life. My life to be exact. And maybe that's why I'm having such a hard time writing it. Because I'm not just figuring out Julie's story, I'm figuring out mine. Drawing the map while walking the journey (and I think we've established that I'm not so good with maps).

Anyway, I was able to write at least a few thousand words today. And that warrants a celebration. And because I have this irrational superstition that if I don't say the win out loud it'll disappear, I reach for my phone and dial Harriet's number.

I fumble with my pen until she answers on the third ring, voice groggy. 'I hope you know how time zones work, jerk.' I quickly check the clock to see that it's 9 p.m. here, which means it's . . . Yikes. 3 a.m. in Manila.

'Sorry, Har!' I say, trying to speak softly as if that would be any better. 'But I just want to tell you that I'm feeling really good about the story!'

There's a brief silence. 'This is exactly what people say when they get called into meetings that could've been an email,' Harriet says. 'This could've been a text, Isla. And I would've responded with enthusiasm. In the morning.'

I laugh. Harriet has always been snarky. But that's her love language. Really. The greater the insult, the greater the love. So instead of getting offended, I say, 'Since you're already awake, you could respond with enthusiasm now.'

She dramatically clears her throat and says, 'Wow, sweetie, I'm so proud of you. Tell me about it in the morning, I beg you, darling!' And then she hangs up.

I receive a text a few seconds later saying, *Really. Tell me about it in the morning. Love u. Zzzzz.*

I chuckle. But it doesn't feel enough. I still feel that need for validation and expression. So, I scroll through my phone as I look for someone who's in the same time zone. And since there's only one person who fits the description . . .

I stare at Luca's number.

We're . . . friendly-ish? He agreed to go to Rome with me. That counts for something. I don't know what level of friendship we're at, but I do know that he tends to answer quickly and already knows my superstitious side.

I call before I can talk myself out of it.

He picks up immediately.

'Sì?'

'Oh. Hey! Hi! Um . . .' Great start, Isla. Really confident. 'Sorry if this is weird. I just—I wrote today. Like, properly wrote. And I'm kind of freaking out about it, and I know this is probably not what you expected, but I have this thing. This compulsion? Ritual? I don't know what to call it. But I have to say it out loud to someone or it feels like it didn't happen.'

There's silence. Oh no.

'And not to make it weirder, but it's kind of like reverse-jinxing. I have to talk about my wins or they vanish. Which I know is not how jinxes work, but for some reason the whole "keep it to yourself" thing just makes my accomplishments shrivel up like—'

'Isla,' he says gently.

'Yeah?'

'Do you want to come to the restaurant?'

I blink. 'What?'

'I'll make you a celebratory carbonara,' he says, casually, like it's no big deal. 'And I might also need a hand with some prep.'

'Oh,' I say. I don't know what I was expecting. Maybe a quick 'congrats, Signorina'. Or a snarky comment. But definitely not an invitation to dine. I'll take it, though. 'I'd love to!'

'I can come get you. It's late, and—' he starts.

'No, no.' I jump off my bed and rush to the bathroom. 'I don't mind walking alone. It's sort of therapeutic for me,' I say as I stare at my puffy face in the mirror. 'And also I don't want to bother you, you're already cooking.'

'It's not a bother, really, it's—' he starts.

'No, it's fine! I really enjoy walking alone.'

'Fine. Just watch out for pickpockets. Be mindful. You can get pretty caught up in your head. Once, you walked straight into a street sign.'

'That street sign jumped out at me,' I lie.

'You were narrating to yourself. Loudly.' I hear him chuckle a bit before the sound of cutlery clashing interrupts.

'It was dialogue practice!'

'Okay,' he says. 'Just be careful.'

'Yeah, yeah.' I roll my eyes, but I feel a smile tugging on my lips.

When I hang up, I'm still staring at my reflection in the mirror. I'm already dressed for bed. Already in my floral pyjamas and tied-up hair. I could've just settled for phone call validation, but I agreed to go to his restaurant at 9 p.m. What is wrong with me?

I mean, he did mention a celebratory carbonara. And no woman in her right mind would say no to a carbonara by an Italian chef.

As I think of more ways to convince myself that I'm doing the right thing, I change into comfortable clothes—a tank top and my trusty jeans. I grab a sweater because the air at night is a bit chillier than the morning. I slip into the sweater, put on some lipstick, and step out of the hotel.

15

Luca

I don't usually ask for help in the kitchen. Not from Marco. Not from the staff. And definitely not from someone I barely know. But I'm leaving for a few days, and the kitchen needs to be set up before I go—prep sheets finalized, stock checked, deliveries confirmed, and stations organized, so no one burns the place down while I'm gone.

Marco would've helped. Normally, he would. But tonight he's out with that girl he's been talking about for months. I told him to go. Told him I could handle things.

That was a lie.

My next option would've been Enzo. Or someone from the team. But I've already asked enough of them. Leaving them to run the kitchen while I disappear to Rome with a stranger isn't exactly fair. I can't bring myself to ask for anything more.

Which leaves Isla.

After all, she's the one who roped me into this trip. I was about to call her when she called me, talking about the progress she had made with her novel. Good to know something's actually happening with that, since it it's the reason she came to Italy in the first place.

I know that it takes around twenty minutes from her hotel to my restaurant, so I wait for her outside. I don't know why. Genuine concern for a friend, maybe. If I can already call her that. Also, as beautiful as Italian streets are, they're also scary. Especially for tourists.

A few minutes later, I see Isla speed-walking towards me. As soon as she sees me, she smiles and waves.

'I'm ready for that carbonara now,' she says as a greeting.

'No "Hi, Luca" or anything?' I open the door as we step inside the empty restaurant.

'Hi, Luca,' she says, removing her sweater. 'I'm ready for my carbonara now.'

I chuckle. 'I'm about to make it.' She widens her gaze, so I continue, 'Don't worry. It only takes minutes. Do you want to come?'

She walks towards me and then past, into the kitchen. 'Are you sure you want me in there?'

'I'll take my chances.' I toss her an apron and she attempts to catch it, but it falls down to the floor. Isla picks it up, but then hits her head against the table, and grunts in pain.

'Chances aren't looking good, to be honest,' I say. She glares at me. I chuckle. She ties the apron around her waist. Without accident.

'So, what do you need help with?'

I gather the ingredients for her—eggs, pecorino, guanciale, and pepper.

'I just need to make sure the restaurant is ready for the next few days that I'm gone. Just some minor preparations. Will you put these noodles in the pan?' I hand Isla some noodles I hand-rolled earlier. She obeys, dropping them in the boiling water.

'So you thought I'm the best person to ask for help in the kitchen?' she says sceptically.

'Yes. The same way you thought I'm the best person to rant to about your writing achievement. Which is good, by the way, congratulations.' I grate some of the cheese and set it aside.

'Ah. Last resort too?' She covers her mouth. 'I didn't mean that in a negative way, just that there are a million other people I would've called instead of you.'

'Yes, that's not negative at all.' Isla rolls her eyes and tosses an eggshell at me. 'Okay, no playing in the kitchen, Isla.'

She chuckles. 'You know, in the Philippines, carbonara is made with cream and ham. And mushrooms.' She eyes me like she's lit a fuse. 'Are you triggered? Offended?'

I shrug. 'Why would I be?'

'Because . . . cream. And ham. In carbonara.' She looks around like the hidden Italian ancestors might strike her down.

I grab the pepper and keep my voice casual. 'If it works for Filipinos, then it works. Call it carbonara.'

She blinks. 'Wait, what?'

'Look, people use what's available. Cream's easier to find than pecorino. Ham's cheaper than guanciale. If it feeds people and makes them happy, why argue over a name?'

'I don't know what to do with this information,' she says, hands in the air. 'I was ready for a whole lecture. Italians on social media have no control.'

I laugh. 'I never understood the way people treat recipes like museum exhibits. Food evolves. People adapt. That's the whole point.'

'You're a good one, Chef.' Isla grabs the grater and helps with the pecorino, still processing. 'So . . . you're also not offended by Filipino spaghetti? You know, with the sweet sauce and the hotdogs?'

I raise a brow as I beat the eggs. 'Do I look offended?'

She leans forward like she's whispering a state secret. 'It has sugar. In the sauce.'

I shrug. 'And? Childhood tastes like weird choices.'

She laughs, a real, belly laugh, and the sound warms the kitchen. 'Wow. You're like . . . really chill.'

'Thanks, I try.'

She snorts and picks up the bowl of grated pecorino. 'Here,' she says, handing it over. Our fingers brush. Just lightly. The kind of touch that shouldn't mean anything.

But this time, it does.

It's not the first time we've touched accidentally, but this one zings. Like static electricity. Or a voltage I wasn't prepared for. I almost convince myself it's just the cold in the kitchen, but then I see her pull back, too fast. Like the bowl suddenly burned her.

When I glance up, she's already looking at me, and for a second neither of us says a word. Her cheeks are flushed. Rosy. But she's still holding my gaze. Almost defiantly.

Then she blinks, breaks eye contact, and stares down at the countertop like it's the most fascinating thing she's ever seen. 'Anyway,' she mutters, voice a little lower, a little unsteady. 'The book's gonna have a field day with that moment.'

I freeze. Just slightly. Did she just . . . acknowledge it? 'You felt that too?'

'Yeah,' Isla says, rubbing her hands together. 'But that's nothing, right? I mean, it's not like the book can magically make us feel things.'

I shrug, and before I can stop myself, I say, 'Maybe it has nothing to do with the book.'

Her eyes widen, and I instantly regret what I said. So I retract, 'What I mean is that it's nothing. Just cold in the kitchen or whatever.'

She nods approvingly. 'You're right.'

To avoid any lingering awkwardness, I continue to cook the carbonara. Isla sits there scrolling through her phone. She pretends not to sneak glances at me, and I pretend not to notice.

After a few minutes, I place the bowl in front of her and hand her a fork. '*Buon appetito*,' I say.

Isla sets her phone down and excitedly twirls the pasta. 'Oh this smells amazing. It smells like . . . dreams.'

I chuckle as she starts to eat. Once she begins chewing, she makes these weird little moans. 'Oh, wow,' she says as she twirls another bite onto her fork. 'I'd marry you for this carbonara alone.'

I raise an eyebrow. 'Careful. Say that too loud, and tomorrow we'll open the book and find a letter describing our wedding in graphic detail.'

She chuckles. 'Definitely.' After another bite, she asks, 'Are you not going to eat?'

'I didn't plan to,' I say. 'But watching you eat is weirdly making me hungry.'

'Right? I've been told I'm too animated with my movements. So much so that it's influential.' She offers me her fork. 'Go on, then.'

'Good that you know you're animated. Your hands move every time you talk.' I mimic her hand movements, and she swats me with the fork.

I take it from her hands, and take my serving of carbonara. I have to admit, it's really good. I'm getting the hang of this.

We spend the next few minutes finishing the carbonara and talking about her book. She tells me about how she has structure now, but she says she doesn't trust it enough to actually follow it. I, for one, find her book amusing so far. I'm not usually a romance reader (to be honest, I barely have time to read these days), but it sounds like something I'd start reading out of boredom, then accidentally lose an entire night to.

As I head to the sink to wash the bowl, she drawls, 'Sooooo, what do you need help with? I'm ready, Chef. Command me.' When I glance back at her, she has her hands on her hips like she's waiting for instructions.

'You can start with cutting these strawberries into small pieces. Doesn't matter how, I'm gonna make it into jam anyway.'

She proceeds to follow orders, and hums to herself while she does. I don't know what it is about Isla but her presence is making the kitchen seem less stressful.

And if I'm being honest, it's not just the kitchen.

16

Isla

I check out of my hotel, the one I was supposed to call home for an entire month. But, as it turns out, life had other plans. I tell myself that it's just a short trip to Rome—a few days at most. But I know myself well enough to know that there's every chance I won't return to this room. Or Florence at all.

The man behind the counter is middle-aged, his hair swept neatly to the side and his blazer perfectly pressed. There's something about Italian men and how effortlessly elegant they are, like they walk straight out of a cologne ad and into real life. Refined. Timeless.

'Signorina, will you still return?' he asks, eyes scanning the computer screen. 'You booked until the 26th, sì? I can refund you for the unused days, but I just want to confirm—are you coming back?'

I hesitate. 'I hope so,' I say softly. 'But I don't know when I'll be back yet.'

'Very well,' he nods, as though he's heard this before. There's no pressure in his tone. With swift, practised hands, he arranges the refund and prints out a receipt, sliding it towards me with a smile.

'Grazie for staying with us. Spread your sunshine to Roma, *bella donna*.'

His words make me blush, and I duck my head slightly. 'Thank you, Signor. I'll try.'

I wheel my suitcases—one giant one and another smaller carry-on—towards the doors, the familiar click of the wheels over the marble floor suddenly feeling final. When I step outside, I pause. Florence is warm this morning, and the air smells faintly of espresso and stone warmed by the sun. I take one last glance around, letting my eyes sweep over the street I've stayed in for days. And just as I turn to the left, I see him.

Luca.

He's walking towards me, and for a second, the world slows down. (Okay, dramatic, but he just looks so different.) He's dressed for travel, and somehow, it makes him look even more attractive than usual. His hair is brushed back, revealing more of his face, the sunlight catching on the rich shades of brown. He's wearing a crisp white collared shirt, tucked into subtly plaid navy trousers. There's a leather-strapped watch on his wrist, sunglasses in his hand, and that unmistakable expression of his—somewhere between sceptical and resigned, like he still isn't sure if this whole thing is completely stupid.

But he showed up.

And that counts for something.

Maybe everything.

'Hey,' I say as he stops in front of me. I can't help but notice how strikingly different we are. He looks regal and refined, every bit European. I look like a vacation-themed sticker pack with my lemon-printed mini dress. Which I love, by the way.

'Ciao,' he replies, lips twitching into a half-smile. 'Ready to go mess up the universe?'

I grin. 'You mean fulfil its grand romantic design?'

He rolls his eyes. 'Same thing.' As if to hide incoming eye rolls, he puts on his sunglasses, pushing them up the bridge of his nose. A strand of hair falls over his forehead, but he ignores it, instead reaching for his suitcase. It's a sleek, matte black carry-on that looks comically small next to my overstuffed, yellow monstrosity.

But just as he's about to take his first step forward, he pauses. His eyes flick to me, then to my luggage. There's the faintest furrow between his brows before, without saying a word, he shifts his stance.

In one swift, practised move, he lifts his own suitcase and places it squarely on top of mine, balancing them. Then he reaches for my smaller suitcase—the one I always forget has a wheel that sticks—and takes it in his free hand.

I blink. 'I can take that one,' I say embarrassingly, already reaching for the handle.

He just shakes his head, barely glancing at me. 'No trouble, Isla.'

'It has a sticky wheel.'

'I have a really strong hand.'

And just like that, he starts walking, dragging my luggage set-up with the calm determination of someone who's made peace with his life choices.

'So,' I begin, sliding into my seat with a soft thud, 'Rome's just an hour away?'

The train hums softly beneath us, with wide windows and warm sunlight spilling through them. I claim the window seat without a fight. Luca didn't even let me lift a finger with the luggage. One second I was reaching for a handle, and the next, everything was stored neatly overhead like magic. Or more accurately, like a very efficient Italian man who refuses help.

'Yes,' he says, settling into the seat across from me. The train has those little tables in between the seats that face each other, which admittedly excites me enough to make sure I use them properly. So I plop my purse down with a satisfying thud, then start unpacking the modest mountain of snacks I've just bought at the station: two croissants, a couple of chocolate bars, some biscotti, a can of Pringles, and coffee.

Luca raises an eyebrow. 'Which is why all those snacks are unnecessary.' He gestures towards my stack disapprovingly.

I take a dramatic sip of my still-too-hot latte and look him straight in the eye. 'It doesn't hurt to be prepared, Luca.'

He leans back, folding his arms. 'Prepared for what? Famine?'

I shrug and unwrap a croissant. 'Yep, hunger. Mood swings. The sudden need to bribe someone. You never know.'

He just shakes his head lazily and reaches for a croissant.

'Thought it was unnecessary.'

Luca shrugs, and says, 'Eh, I got hungry from hauling all that luggage.' Once again, I remind him that I offered to help. To which he replies that it would only slow us down. I don't have a response to that.

The scenery outside has transformed into rolling hills dotted with cypress trees—their tall, lean silhouettes cutting against the pale blue sky. Rows of vineyards flash by like green braids woven into the land, and every now and then, we pass through sleepy towns with terracotta roofs and laundry swaying from balconies. It's the kind of postcard-perfect view that makes you forget you're in transit, and for a moment, I just breathe it in.

It's easy to reflect in the silence. I still can't believe I'm in this beautiful country. Every view feels like it's something I just conjured from my imagination. Something I wish I could immortalize.

So I try. I take photos. I scribble a few sentences about how the light flickers through the olive trees or how the train hums beneath our feet or how I wish we had speed-rails back home (and briefly daydream about how quick the daily commute would be if we did).

And like always, the silence, the scenery, the overall feel of this moment make me think about my novel. I picture myself as the main character I'm writing, trying to write what would go on in her head. Maybe she would think that art isn't just in the museums. Art is in every corner of Italy. Art is in the way the leaves sway or the mountains roll. It's in the way the terracotta rooftops look like they hold magic. Even the way the laundry sways in the balconies. Everything about this place is so unbelievably artistic.

'Are you ready to see your father again?' I ask, without turning from the window.

There's a pause. Long enough that I begin to wonder if I said it too softly for him to hear.

'I don't know,' he says finally, voice low and even. 'As ready as I could be, I guess.' It's like he's not entirely sure whether his words are true.

I glance at him then, catching the edge of his profile in the golden light—stoic and unreadable. And for a brief moment, I wish I could write him, too. Figure out what's going on beneath all that quiet. All that control.

But for now, I just nod.

And quietly slide the chocolate bar a little closer to him on the table. Just in case.

We spend the rest of the ride in silence, and I even drift off for a few minutes. When we reach Rome, I hurriedly stow away the leftover snacks in my tote bag as Luca effortlessly takes the luggage out. I alight the train in slow steps, bracing myself for what greets me in this new city.

'This is the train station, Isla, no scenery here,' Luca says, snapping me back, as a child rushes past me and his mother calls out to him. I look around, and, sure enough, it looks like a shopping mall. Fluorescent writing, shops lined up, people walking. I chuckle softly to myself.

I wasn't being dramatic. (Okay, maybe a little.) I just really love romanticizing things. I learned that from Ivy. Or rather, I learned that *because* of her.

Ivy was always the one with the plan. She used to think that life is short, so she lived like she always had somewhere to be—always three steps ahead, always in motion. For a long time, I thought she liked it that way. That it thrilled her, the rush of it all. But now I think maybe she just didn't want to stop. Because when you slow down, you start to feel everything. The weight of things. The ache. The questions you can't answer.

And maybe she didn't want to *feel* life.

But I do.

I used to think I didn't. After Ivy died, I felt like a balloon with the air punched out—flat and quiet and drifting. For a while, therapy helped me float again. Writing helped me breathe. It didn't make the grief disappear, but it gave it somewhere to go.

And now, I romanticize everything.

How a city might shift my heartbeat. The awkwardness of small talk. Bathtubs. Pasta. Eating cake. Laughing until your sides hurt. The silence after someone tells you something real.

Because life *is* short.

But that doesn't mean rushing through it.

Because rushing only steals the moments worth feeling.

17

Isla

'Coffee? Again?' Luca asks me as we arrive at Rome's central terminal. We're taking a regional train set to leave in twenty minutes, and I'm taking a sip of my afternoon latte.

'You know,' I say, 'for a country known for its espressos, you sure seem to have an issue with me and my coffee-drinking obsession?'

'Isla, that is your third cup for the day.' He looks at me in disbelief.

'Exactly. I'm still one cup away from my daily intake.'

I don't know what it is about the Philippines, but everyone loves their coffee. And when I say we love coffee, I don't mean we're passionate about the way the espresso smells or whatever, we literally inhale the damn thing. Multiple times a day. Even when the sun is scorching, I guarantee there are people sipping hot coffee. Outdoors.

'That's crazy,' he says and just rolls his eyes. I don't blame him. In Italy, coffee has rules. Protocols. A kind of sacred choreography. No cappuccino after eleven. No takeaway cups. Sweeteners are discouraged. Frappuccinos don't exist, but somehow, an espresso shot with ice cream does.

I continue to sip my unapproved afternoon latte, and a man beside me side-eyes me like I've committed a crime. I ignore him. And Luca. And the nation of Italy.

The digital schedule board flickers above us, shuffling like a deck of cards. Then—there it is. Our train. Flashing like an alarm bell.

'Oh no.'

In a blur of panic, I grab Luca's arm for support and accidentally bump the flimsy cafe table. My latte tips, tilts, and spills, slow-motion style, directly onto Luca's luggage. The foam clings to the zipper.

I freeze.

Luca glances down at his bag, lets out the quietest sigh imaginable, and pulls out a tissue in very impressive nonchalance.

'Can't say I'm surprised, really,' he says, dabbing his luggage with clinical precision. 'This tracks.'

He's talking about how the book predicted exactly that I'd spill coffee at the Roma Termini railway station. I don't know why, but before this, I assumed the book was just messing with us and making up possible future events and hoping we'll play along. But now, standing here, looking at Luca's bag, I can't pretend this was something I planned. If anything, I was doing the opposite. I was deliberately trying to avoid following the book.

But somehow, here we are now.

'I'm so sorry,' I say, reaching for my own napkins, now way too late to be helpful. 'But our train leaves in—what, two minutes?'

He doesn't even flinch. Just keeps blotting. Calm. Unbothered.

'No, Isla,' he says, still patting down the soaked corner. 'That's the time it arrives.'

I whirl around, and, true enough, our train is arriving at the station.

The address Nonna gave us is situated somewhere around Trastevere. A new wave of excitement courses through me. Rome wasn't on my itinerary. I know, I know—what kind of person would go to Italy and not visit Rome, right? But I really wanted to focus on the art and the museums. Florence was always on the top of lists for that. And I always thought of Florence as a painting, and Rome, a movie.

I suppose, even without the book, I would've gone to Rome anyway. I don't know how or what cosmic sign would have urged me to, but I know I would have.

Luca leads us to a boutique hotel in the area. It's dinnertime by now, and I can't help but ask him, 'How's your restaurant while you're gone?'

'Marco and my sous chef Enzo can handle it.' He looks ahead, probably doubting whatever it is he said. But before I can provide a sliver of comfort, a man arrives at the check-in counter.

Luca speaks with him in Italian while I look around. The hotel is nice. Quaint. It's not homey like my hotel in Florence. Rome is a bit more . . . tourist friendly. Florence looks like it's been preserved in the 1800s, while Rome looks like a modern world with bits of historical architecture squeezed in.

The hotel looks every bit of a boutique hotel. White walls, abstract paintings, indoor plants, and elevators. For a moment, it doesn't even feel like Italy. It looks like the lobby of my condo back home.

'Isla?' Luca's voice brings me back.

'Hm?'

'There's only one room left.' Luca looks at me, waiting for me to answer him. 'Should we check others?'

I think about that. Do I want to walk around just to find another hotel which probably doesn't have enough spare rooms? No.

'I don't mind,' I say. Suddenly aware of what I might have insinuated, I add, 'Do you?'

Because if he minds, then I'll mind. That's just the way the world works. My brows knit, and I see his lips twitch up to a slight smile. 'I don't,' he says. 'But your face is making it hard for me to believe we're in agreement.'

'Oh,' I say, putting on what I hope is a neutral expression. 'It's fine, really.'

He nods, then takes the keycard and hands me the spare. He proceeds to take all our luggage, and I'm once again left with my personal tote bag.

It's nice . . . to be helped like this. I'm so used to carrying most things that I had almost forgotten what it felt like to have someone there for me.

I think somewhere along the way, I rewired my brain to believe that love always came with strings attached and heartache. That having a boyfriend meant bracing myself for the inevitable unravelling. After enough toxic relationships, you start to confuse survival mode with independence.

I dated people who made me feel like needing help was a character flaw and asking for support was something to be ashamed of.

'Where did you learn to be such a gentleman?' I ask.

'I don't know what kind of men you've met, Isla,' he says, still effortlessly carrying three suitcases, 'but carrying a lady's heavy baggage is the bare minimum.'

I open my mouth to respond, but nothing comes out. Because the sad, honest truth is . . . I have met some terrible men in this life. Like, actual goblins. My most recent ex (if you could call five years ago recent, which I do, because that was the last time I let myself try) basically squatted in my condo, used my electricity and water, ate food I bought with my own money . . . and then had the audacity to cheat on me. With a girl he claimed was 'just a friend from work'.

After that, I didn't just stop dating. I shut the whole door to my heart and bolted it shut.

Also, if I'm being honest, being superstitious made me fear love in a way. Like, if I dated someone, it would never be just casual. I could never just 'see where it goes'. I would always think that the person in front of me was strategically handpicked by the universe.

And now, that's how I see Luca.

We step into the room, and the universe—that chaotic little minx—decides to dial things up.

My eyes immediately land on the queen-sized bed in the centre.

One bed. Just one. No sofa. No rollaway. Not even a rug big enough to dramatically sleep on like a martyr.

I blink.

'Oh' is all I manage to say. I glance at Luca as he sets the luggage down and scans the room. He's still alarmingly nonchalant.

'Is it going to be a problem?' he asks as he looks at me.

Is it a problem? Oh, only if you count *sharing a bed with the man a possibly magical book has named as my soulmate* a problem. Or if you count the fact that I haven't stopped blushing around him since he showed up looking refined this morning. Or if you consider that I once told Harriet that I'd rather sleep on broken glass than share a bed with a guy I wasn't dating. (Okay, that may have been a little dramatic, but I was twenty and hormonal.)

And now here I am, standing in a hotel room in Rome—*Rome!*—with Luca . . . and we're going to share a bed?

No, wait. Maybe we're not. Maybe I can sleep on the floor. I've done worse. I once took a nap on a pile of laundry that included a belt buckle. I can suffer. I'm a martyr. Filipino blood runs deep in my veins. I'll make a blanket nest on the floor and pretend it's part of some rustic European experience.

But then again . . . what if I'm the only one seeing the romantic implication? What if he's looking at this bed like it's a bed and I'm looking at it like it's a divine sign from the heavens?

I feel the heat rush to my cheeks, because that's just how my own overthinking betrays me.

'Isla?' he confirms.

I stare at him. My mouth opens. Closes. Opens again. I'm a goldfish. A goldfish caught in a weird scenario.

'Nope!' I say, with a voice that sounds like I inhaled helium.

'*Perfetto*,' he says, and proceeds to go to the bathroom.

Yes, Luca, nothing is more perfect than my existential dread.

I try to brush it off. This shouldn't be so bad. To regain control of my life, I remove my wedge sandals and place them neatly near the door. I slowly take my small luggage to the other corner of the room, which I mentally claim as mine. Maybe the view from the window will help distract me from everything. I walk over there, pushing the curtains aside, and sure enough, it does.

The rooftops stretch out like soft, warm waves. Light pools between the chimneys and the alleys, making the scene look like a beautiful painting. Far off in the distance, I catch sight of the Colosseum, standing tall and ancient. There was a time in my life when the only way I could see the Colosseum was by watching the Lizzie McGuire movie. She wasn't lying when she said this is what dreams are made of.

The sun is still up, but it's starting to dip lower in the sky, its golden light like a blanket that completes the beauty of Rome.

Sunsets are one of my favourite things in the world. As a night owl, they feel like a slow sigh from the universe, as if it's finally time for the world to be quiet and my thoughts to be heard. There's a calmness in sunsets that cannot be quantified, and maybe that's why I love them so much.

Ivy was the opposite, though. She was a sunrise girl, through and through. She used to say they were proof that you get another chance. For me, though, sunrises feel . . . expectant. Full of promise—and pressure. They demand motion. Action. A list of things to get done, hopes to rise to, lives to live fully. And those kinds of beginnings scare the hell out of me.

I think people are either sunrises or sunsets. Beginnings or endings. Ivy was a sunrise—always rushing to make something of the day even before it started. I'm a sunset. I like to linger, savour, and stretch the last light into something beautiful, even if it's brief.

I look at the bathroom door behind me, and wonder for a moment what Luca is. But I've got nothing. Maybe he's midday. Noon. Or that part at twilight when you don't know if the light is coming or going.

Or, you know, maybe he's just too nonchalant to care about what colour the sky is.

18

Luca

'Dio mio, just get out there,' Marco groans from the other line. 'Is it your first time with a woman?'

'Marco, you don't understand.' I shift my phone to my other ear. 'She's a woman, yes, a beautiful one. But we're not . . . together. We're not even almost together. We're strangers sharing a bed.'

There's a long pause, followed by a low chuckle. 'Sounds like the beginning of a very good story.'

'To you, maybe,' I say, pacing the bathroom one more time. 'I'm not like you.'

'And that is your problem, amico mio.' I hear him shift. 'I've got to go, I'm busy trying to keep your restaurant running.'

I've officially been in the bathroom way longer than anyone would need to be. I've washed my hands three times. Brushed my teeth again, even though I haven't eaten since lunch. I considered shaving but realized I didn't bring my razor. So now I'm just . . . hiding. Because I'm not used to this proximity.

I splash some water on my face for the final time, and pluck up the courage to step out of the bathroom.

Isla is on one side of the bed, staring out the window. She's still wearing her absurdly bright lemon dress that no woman over twenty-five should be able to pull off, but she does.

'Took you long enough,' she says, looking at me. 'Did you get lost in there?'

I chuckle. 'I got distracted by Marco's messages.' Lie.

'Do you want to go check out the address today? It's still a bit early.' Isla stands up, finger-combs her hair, and raises her eyebrows. 'Or, we could do it tomorrow, and just get something to eat.'

'You're still hungry after all that train snack?'

'Key word: snack. Not meal. I need my carbs.'

There's a part of me that wants to get it over with, but an even bigger part wants to preserve the peace I've created for myself for years. It takes a lot of strength to step up when a father leaves. It would've been easier if he was taken from us by death or some sort of phenomenon. But for him to decide to leave, just because he wanted to . . . that was hard for ten-year-old me. I kept asking why, and when the answers didn't come, I filled in the blanks myself. Maybe we were too much for him. Maybe I wasn't enough to keep him around. Maybe he didn't really love us.

That was something no child could move on from. But I did. And I want to hold on to that victory a little bit longer.

'Let's go get something to eat then.'

Isla smiles widely, and tucks a strand of hair behind her ear. As she walks closer to me, I notice she has changed her earrings. There are now two giant flowers dangling from her ears.

'You changed your earrings,' I say before I can stop myself.

'Very good observation. I felt like flowers suited my mood more.' She goes out of the room, and I follow close behind. I just stare at her, narrowing my eyes because I know she doesn't just do things.

'Fine!' she exclaims. 'I had a dream, when I fell asleep on the train, that someone gave me white flowers. My lola—my grandma—used to say that means change is coming and you have to welcome it or risk bad luck. So, flower earrings.'

I chuckle. 'Knew it.'

'Don't feel too good about yourself. I know why you chose to eat instead of going straight to your dad,' she says over her shoulder as we step into the elevator.

'And why is that?' I ask, curious.

She leans against the mirrored wall, arms crossed, her tone suddenly softer, almost too casual. 'Because deep down, you don't think he deserves your effort. Or attention. So you're holding back. Making him wait.'

She's not wrong.

Maybe I *am* making him wait. Not because I want to punish him exactly. But because after all these years, after the healing and the work and the life I built without him, I'm not sure he deserves to be part of it now. Maybe I'm afraid that seeing him again will unravel all the knots I've spent years tying tight.

Or worse, maybe I'm afraid it won't affect me at all.

That the person who once broke me doesn't hold any power any more. That he's just a man who left, and I'm just someone who got over it.

What does that make me? Stronger? Colder?

The elevator dings. Isla walks out first, not turning around, so I follow. She doesn't wait for a response. Thank God, because admitting it out loud feels wrong.

We exit the hotel as the sunlight dips, making the streets look golden. I'm used to the beauty of Italy. Florence is more artistic and historical, if you ask me. But Rome has something else. It has . . . freedom. I don't know how to explain that, exactly. Freedom is not a place. Freedom, for me, is the absence of something. The absence of expectations. Pressure. Pretensions. And Rome just feels like that. Like I don't have to be someone whenever I'm here.

Isla puts on her sunglasses even though the sun is almost gone. The sky is streaked in burnt oranges and blush pinks, and in this light, her dark hair carries a warm undertone—almost auburn, like wine catching fire. The wind picks up the ends of it, lifting strands across her cheek.

'Why are you so quiet?'

'I'm always quiet.'

'Yes, but usually you're quiet because you're busy. Or you're concentrating on a thought or something.'

'So you've observed me? That's sweet, Isla,' I say as she rolls her eyes. 'What makes you think I'm not thinking right now?'

She stops walking and looks at me inquisitively. 'What are you thinking about?' she asks. I shake my head and continue walking. She keeps up with me and continues, 'Do you think my earrings are actually cute?' As she flips her hair, the two oversized, flower-shaped pieces swing like pendulums.

I can't help the laugh that escapes me. 'Yes, Isla, I am deep in thought about how adorable you are,' I say, and then quickly backtrack. 'Your earrings, I mean.'

She pretends not to notice the slip, or maybe she genuinely doesn't care.

We turn down a narrow side street, swarming with locals and tourists alike. At the far end of the street, a hand-painted sign that reads 'Trattoria Mariano' sways gently in the breeze, illuminated by a warm glow from inside.

'Are you sad?' she asks softly. 'Angry? I can never tell with you.'

'Stop trying to analyse me.'

'I'm not analysing. I'm asking,' she presses.

'I don't know, really,' I say, which is the truth.

She hums thoughtfully. 'You know,' she begins, 'someone used to tell me that sadness is like a currency. Not because it buys you anything, but when you carry it around for so long, it starts to weigh you down. Then if you spend it—in words, in tears, whatever—you make space for something else.'

I glance at her, surprised by the insight.

'And I think it's the same for all emotions,' she continues. 'Even anger. Even guilt. Maybe if we let ourselves spend a little of it, we wouldn't be so full all the time.'

Isla is an enigma. Sometimes she says things that are so absurd. Like how we're star-crossed lovers made by a magic book. But then she says something like this, and I understand why she's a writer. It's not just her imagination. It's her precision. Her timing. The way she names things I haven't found words for yet.

When we reach the trattoria's front steps, I pause before going in.

'Was that your way of telling me to talk more?' I ask.

She gives me a small smile—mischievous but not unkind. 'No,' she says. 'It was my way of saying stop being a party pooper.'

I chuckle, the tension loosening in my chest. We enter the restaurant, the door closing softly behind us. The trattoria smells of garlic, fresh basil, and slow-simmered tomato sauce—something that has become a new normal with the restaurant, but it still feels good. The low murmur of conversation mingles with soft Italian music, and flickering candles on each table cast warm halos of light.

I pull a chair for Isla and once again see the surprise in her eyes when I do. 'Again,' I say, 'you must have met some pretty terrible men.'

'You have no idea,' she says, rolling her eyes.

The waiter hands us the menu, and Isla does a quick scan before looking at me. 'Surprise me, Chef.'

As I read through the menu, I think about my restaurant back home. I'm sure it's doing well tonight, as it is most nights. But even full houses can't always fix what's broken beneath the surface. The rising rent. The staff turnover. The repairs, maintenance, everything.

I glance up at Isla. She's on her phone. Or maybe writing a note to herself. Her brow is furrowed, nose slightly scrunched. Lip caught between her teeth in a way that I'm starting to recognize.

'You always make that face when you're deep in thought,' I say.

She looks up, surprised. 'What face?'

I mimic her—furrowed brow, exaggerated concentration. 'That one. You had the same expression at the Duomo. I'd bet good money you're thinking through a plot twist for your novel.'

She narrows her eyes at me. 'Wow. And here I thought you were aloof.'

I shrug and raise a hand for the waitress. 'I notice things.'

Isla leans forward, propping her elbows on the table and fluttering her lashes dramatically. 'So you've been observing me. That's sweet, Luca.'

I guess I have.

19

Isla

'I can cook better than that,' Luca says as we step out of the restaurant. We had a hearty meal of cacio e pepe and steak. Italian food is good. It really is, but I'm starting to get a wee bit tired of it. I miss some comforting sinigang and rice.

'I'm sure you can,' I reply. 'But that wasn't so bad.'

Luca shrugs, and we head down a narrow alley towards the hotel.

And there it is again—the reminder of our room. Our shared room. And the one singular bed waiting inside. I've been dreading it all evening. Not because of Luca, exactly, but because of everything it suggests, and everything I'm not sure I want to think about.

I pivot hard. 'Do you want some gelato? My treat!' I say a little too brightly.

He glances at me. 'Sure,' he says, and shrugs again.

We pass three, five, ten gelaterias. He doesn't stop for any of them.

'Okay, I'm sorry,' I say, eyeing yet another brightly lit shop with a rainbow of flavours. 'Did we not just pass fifty-seven gelato places?'

He glances at me, unimpressed by the hyperbole. 'None of them look good.'

I blink. 'How can you tell? You haven't even looked inside most of them.'

Luca slows, finally stopping in front of one without a flashy display. The counter is understated, the signage barely visible. 'Because the good ones keep the gelato in metal tins. With lids.'

I squint at the counter. Sure enough—metal tins. Minimalist. I follow him inside.

The man behind the counter greets us cheerfully. I smile and scan the assortment of flavours, which isn't a lot. Just pistachio, hazelnut, and dark chocolate. I get a scoop of pistachio while Luca gets chocolate.

We return to the hotel, because we've apparently done everything we could to delay it, and now all places in Rome are either closed, far, or ridiculous to squeeze into last-minute.

Now, how do I approach this? Do I sleep with my back turned like a cold-hearted mannequin? Or do I face him and risk eye contact mid-dream? Do I wear the oversized shirt I packed, or will that read as inviting? Will he be shirtless? Oh God. What if he's shirtless?

I shake my head like I can physically knock the thoughts out.

'Are you okay?' Luca asks as I step out of the bathroom (wearing my oversized shirt *with* pyjamas).

'I'm fine!' I squeal. He's sitting on the foot of the bed, holding a change of clothes.

He stands up quickly to walk towards the bathroom, and I move to make way for him, but he moves in the same direction, so now we're aggressively swaying left and right. He puts both hands on my arms to steady me, and then he walks around me while chuckling to himself.

Great. That's not awkward at all.

I walk towards the mirrors to brush my hair, and dial a quick call to Harriet.

After about five rings, she answers. 'Isla, I swear to *God*. Do you hate clocks for some reason?!'

'I'm sorry, I'm sorry, but there's only one bed,' I say in panic.

'You have to help me here, girl, I have been awake for exactly five seconds,' Harriet says, but I feel her shuffling in her bed. 'Is something wrong?' Her voice turns serious.

'No,' I answer. 'I mean yes. No. I don't know. Just . . . there's a bed.'

'Are beds a foreign concept to you? Have you been dropped on Earth five minutes ago?'

'Ugh! Here's the deal. I am in Rome with Luca and we're sharing a room with a singular queen bed, with no sofas or recliners or any other option for sleeping. Unless you count the carpet. Which, if you think about it, is soft—' I trail off.

'Okay . . . are you afraid of sleeping with someone? Is this your first time? Don't bullshit me. I know it's not.'

'Harriet!' I whisper. 'We're not here to do *that*. We are here on a very platonic mission to decode that magic book.'

'Oh, shit.'

I'm about to launch into a full-blown monologue about boundary pillows when the bathroom door opens.

I whip around instinctively. Luca steps out, his hair damp. He has a grey shirt slung over one shoulder. He's wearing striped pyjamas, and his chest . . . is very much bare.

Harriet is still on the phone.

'Um,' I whisper.

'He's shirtless, isn't he?' she says from the other line. I can almost hear the teasing smile in her voice. 'Oh, I love this.'

I let out a strangled sound that might have been a laugh or a tiny gasp for air. 'I gotta go.'

I hang up on her mid-cackle.

'Everything okay?' Luca asks as he takes his grey shirt and shakes it. 'Sorry. I will sleep with a shirt on. This one just fell in the shower and is a little bit damp. Give me a few minutes.'

'Okay, but how are you like this?' I gesture to his form.

'Like what?'

'You look like David. The sculpture,' I say before I can stop myself. He's silent for a while before he laughs. But it's not a real laugh. It's that dry, disbelieving kind of laugh. Like a scoff.

'You think I look like David?' He tilts his head, eyes squinting slightly as he walks past me. 'You do realize David is, like, five feet tall and anatomically underwhelming.' He walks towards me, and the faint scent of his soap—something clean and woodsy—lingers in the air as he moves. He drapes the damp shirt over the back of a chair.

'I meant vibe, okay? Not . . . proportions,' I mumble, already regretting every life choice that has led me to this hotel room.

He glances at me, not unkindly. 'Okay, Isla,' he says gently. I walk towards the bed slowly, as he adds, 'Look, I don't want this to be weird.'

'I agree,' I say. 'We should put up a pillow wall.'

He stares at me, deadpan. 'I didn't mean that kind of weird.'

There's a pause.

He sits on the bed and puts his feet up. 'Let's not make this awkward. Let's just . . . talk.' His voice softens like he's offering a way out. Or maybe a way in.

I perch cautiously on my side—not my side, just the side, though the possessive language in my head is not helping. The mattress dips beneath me, and I feel the give of it, the quiet rustle of sheets. The whole room smells faintly like hotel linen.

'Talk?' I echo.

'Yeah. Tell me something about yourself,' he says, gaze now fixed on the wall in front of him.

'What is this? Fifty questions before bedtime?' I try to joke, but it comes out too tight.

'I don't mean anything serious,' he says, ignoring the deflection. 'Just . . . anything. I at least want to feel like we're friends, you know?'

'You think we're friends?' I ask, glancing sideways at him.

He meets my eyes. 'Well,' he says, lips twitching into something almost like a smile, 'I wouldn't cook carbonara for a stranger. For free.'

That makes me laugh—a small, surprised sound. It slips out before I can stop it.

'Okay,' I say, voice softer now. 'But let's not make it boring.'

'What do you have in mind?'

I get up, crossing the room to where his half-unzipped suitcase lies. I put my hands on my hips. 'Each of us picks something from the other's luggage. Then the person has to tell the story behind it.'

Luca raises an eyebrow. 'How do you come up with this stuff?'

'I'm a writer. I live on writing prompts.'

He laughs, then checks on his grey shirt before walking to the bathroom to get a new towel to drape over his shoulders. 'Choose, then.'

I dig around, fingers brushing over a rolled-up sock, a crumpled receipt, a half-used packet of mints, and then—something more interesting. I tug out a pair of beat-up wired headphones.

'Seriously?' I hold them up by the wire, letting them dangle like a limp squid. 'These still work?'

He approaches me and cranes his neck to look. 'Barely. One side cuts out if you move your head too fast.'

'So naturally, you packed them.'

'Of course. They're reliable.'

I snort. 'In what world is "cuts out if you move your head" reliable?'

He grins, taking the headphones from my hands. 'It's more about comfort. I used to wear them every night when I lived in Naples. Couldn't sleep in silence. Music helped. Or made me think I was sleeping.'

I take them back to finger the fraying padding on one ear. 'What did you listen to?'

'Jazz. Rain. Piano. Once, an audiobook on Roman history that put me out cold every time.'

'That's adorable.'

'It's sad.'

'No,' I say, sitting back on my heels. 'It's very you.'

He blinks, caught off guard. 'What does that mean?'

'You don't throw things away just because they stop working perfectly. There's something . . . kind about that.'

He just shrugs, and makes his way towards the bed and sits on the corner.

For a second, we're just sitting there, him on the bed, me on the floor, and the air between us feeling like a pause in time.

'Just frugal. You're really good at making things sound better than they are,' he says, not quite teasing.

'And you're really good at pretending they don't matter when they do,' I reply, softer than I intend.

A second passes. Then another.

I break the quiet, holding the headphones up. 'Alright, your turn. My suitcase is a landmine of strange. Choose wisely.'

Luca stands and walks over to my luggage, his fingers hovering over a mess of toiletries, books, and fabric. Then he pauses, brow furrowing as he pulls something out slowly. A small duck-themed timer.

He stares at it. Then at me. 'Do I want to know?'

I sit up straighter, already grinning. 'Ah. That's Quackson.'

He blinks. 'You named your timer.'

'Duh,' I say.

'So what's the story behind Quackson?'

'I have the attention span of a fruit fly. I regularly get distracted by things around me. When I'm writing, especially when I'm writing,' I roll my eyes, 'I become hyper aware of my surroundings.' I scoot over and take Quackson from his hand, and fumble with it. 'This was a gift from my sister. She said I should schedule fifteen-minute writing sprints. No distractions, no overthinking, just words on the page. She gave me this so I could . . . you know, put my ducks in a row.'

Luca laughs, and his eyes crinkle a little. 'Your sister is smart. You should thank her again.'

I chuckle back, even when it hurts. 'She *was* smart,' I say quietly. 'Really smart.'

He sits on the floor beside me, his expression softening. I know the moment the past tense lands.

He shifts like he's suddenly unsure what to do with his hands. 'I'm sorry. I didn't realize—'

'It's okay,' I interrupt, even though it isn't. Not really. It hasn't been okay for a long time. But I've learned to carry the grief like a second skin—tight in places, invisible in others, always there.

Still, I don't want to end the night on that note, so I clear my throat and force a smile that feels like it barely makes it past my cheeks. 'Anyway. Should we do another round?'

Luca gently plucks Quackson from my hands and places it back inside my suitcase, then zips it closed. He pulls me up.

'It's not fine, Isla,' he says softly, not looking at me. 'And you don't have to pretend it is.'

He tucks the suitcase by the edge of the bed with careful precision. When he finally turns to face me, there's no pity in his expression, no patronizing softness—just understanding.

'I'm not going to tell you how to grieve,' he continues. 'I wouldn't even know where to start. But just . . . know it's okay if it still hurts. It doesn't make you weak. It just means you loved her enough to miss her.'

My throat tightens without warning. I walk to the head of the bed, just to avoid looking at him again. I blink quickly, hoping to keep the tears from spilling over, but of course they rise anyway. Stupid traitors. Always showing up when I least want them. Whether it's sadness or joy or some infuriating mix of both, they never miss an opportunity to betray me.

I wipe under my eye and let out a breath that shakes at the end. 'Great. Cool. Now I'm crying in Rome. Very on-brand.'

Luca chuckles gently. 'It's a good city to cry in. Dramatic. Cinematic.'

I grab a pillow and throw it at him.

He catches it easily and tosses it back onto the bed. 'Let's just sleep,' he says as he crawls into the left side of the bed. I mirror his movements by moving to the other side.

I place the pillow wall between us. 'Don't get ideas, okay?'

Luca lies down and says, 'Tell that to the book.' He winks at me and then turns to the other side.

It isn't so bad after all.

20

Luca

I can't sleep. It's physically impossible. Not with a woman lying next to me, just one pillow wall away. My brain refuses to power down. I keep thinking about all the ways I might accidentally embarrass myself in the morning—drooling, talking in my sleep, dreaming about something I definitely shouldn't be dreaming about. So instead, I drift in and out—mini comas that last five minutes, maybe ten, at a time.

Isla, on the other hand, is thriving. Or at least, she's asleep, which already makes her superior to me. She's hugging the pillow wall, her face far too close for comfort. Her mouth is slightly open, and she's making these soft, gurgling sounds.

If she's comfortable enough to sleep like that, then I guess I should feel honoured. It means she doesn't see me as a threat. Or a *man*. Just a cohabitant of this singular-bed arrangement. Which is . . . fine. Probably for the best.

Still, I lie here and stare at the ceiling, trying not to think about how she smells like something warm and sweet. Like sugar and something citrus-y and completely distracting.

God, I need sleep.

After a few more mini power naps, it's officially morning. Isla moves beside me and stretches her arms.

'Good morning,' she says with a smile. And then, like a switch flipped, her eyes widen. 'Sorry, was I loud? Did I bother you?'

'You were loud, yes,' I say. 'Bother me? Not so much,' I lie.

'Oh good. You slept well?' She stands up and immediately places the pillow back on the head of the bed. She walks towards the bathroom, but stops midway to raise her eyebrows at me, waiting for my answer.

'Um, yes, quite well,' I say as I nod, hoping I sound convincing.

Apparently satisfied, she disappears into the bathroom.

Alone now, I start making the bed with automatic, practised movements, then move to the window. The street outside is waking up, scooters buzzing faintly in the distance, sunlight cutting sharp across cobblestones. Today's the day we go to that address. The one that belongs to my father. The one I've been pretending not to dread.

I wish I could delay it. Just a few more hours of make-believe, that this is just a weird vacation with a woman who builds pillow walls and names her timer Quackson. But no. Time's up.

Best to rip the Band-Aid off, I guess.

Or, knowing our luck, it'll rip itself off and reveal something worse underneath.

We don't say much over breakfast. She's probably giving me the space she thinks I need, but really, I could use loud Isla today. But I guess it's also a good thing I get to reflect before I go there.

After breakfast, we head out, walking for several minutes, following the map. The neighbourhood is situated in the hidden parts of Rome. In here, the city doesn't look too special.

We pass more houses until I find myself face to face with an apartment that's about five stories tall, its walls painted a soft blue. It's nothing special. It looks exactly like the ones beside it. But I glance at the house in front of me, then back to the paper Nonna gave. The numbers are correct. The street is correct. This is it.

'Are you ready? We can turn back if you're not,' Isla says beside me.

'We came all this way,' I say.

'That's not an answer, Luca. You need to tell me if you're okay with this. We can make a detour to the Trevi Fountain and wish for some good juju,' she tilts her head and smiles. The wind sweeps her hair towards her eyes, and she tucks the strands behind her ear.

'It's fine. I'm fine,' I say, smiling back. 'We can go to the Trevi Fountain later and wish for whatever I might need after this.'

'That's the spirit!' she exclaims as she rings the doorbell before I can second-guess myself.

The intercom crackles, and suddenly, a man's voice speaks. 'Ciao,' he says. It makes me shiver slightly, but I try to ground myself. It's just his voice. *You can do this.*

Isla jumps into cheerful mode. 'Um, hi, Signor! I'm here to talk about a book. But not in a weird way! My friend has something to—well, we have something to—look, may we come up?'

There's silence, and for a moment, I wonder if we've wasted our time. Maybe that isn't my father. Or maybe that is my father and he still doesn't want to see us.

Just as I'm about to accept defeat, I hear a buzz. Then the gates open.

The stairwell smells faintly of old marble and furniture polish. The walls are painted a dull cream with olive-green trim, and the tiles under our feet are cracked and mismatched. As we climb, each step creaks slightly beneath our shoes, and I try to match Isla's pace, but my feet feel heavier with every floor.

She goes ahead of me—light and steady—and I follow, feeling the tension coil tighter with each landing.

I try to rehearse what I'll say.

Hi. I think you might be my father.

Hello. It's been twenty-three years—how have you been?

Nothing sounds right. Nothing sounds like me.

The staircase ends in a short hallway. There's a dusty umbrella stand by the wall and a faded rug leading to a wooden door. The paint is peeling at the edges. The number is written in brass above the knocker.

I stop in front of it and take a breath. My palms feel damp, so I swipe them on my trousers. The collar of my shirt suddenly feels too tight.

And then the door opens.

And there he is.

I don't know what I expected to feel when I came face to face with my estranged father. I ran through every possibility.

Maybe I'd feel a flicker of the childhood we shared—those early, hazy memories before he left. Maybe I'd feel anger. Maybe peace. I even tried to prepare myself for happiness, in case something cracked open in me.

But I didn't expect to feel . . . grief.

Not fresh, but resurfaced. Grief that you think you've buried until a breeze carries it back. This isn't the grief of losing someone, like how I felt with my mother. If I'm being honest, that was an easier grief to navigate. I lost someone I loved because she got sick. It was hard to move on from, but at least it made sense. It was something I understood.

But this one . . . this grief is weird. Murky. I guess I've been subconsciously holding space for him, unintentionally justifying his absence in my head. Part of me wished that when he opened that door, there would be a visible sign of distress. Illness, disability, anything that would have explained why he didn't come back.

But he looks annoyingly ordinary.

And somehow, that's what hurts the most. That he was always capable of showing up, and simply chose not to. There's no illness, no great tragedy to explain the silence. Just choice.

The father I held on to all these years—the one I imagined, justified, protected—is gone. Or maybe he never existed at all. And so the grief isn't for the man in front of me. It's for the one I made up just to survive the one who left.

And now, I have to let him go, too.

'Luca . . .' my father says. His expression shifts from nonchalance to surprise. He didn't expect to see me. 'You're here.'

'Sì,' I say. 'I'm not here for you. My friend here has something she has to confirm.' I gesture to Isla, who looks like she's witnessing a murder taking place. I widen my eyes at her to bring her back to the moment, and she shakes her head.

'Right!' She looks at my father. 'Ciao! May we enter?'

He doesn't respond, but he moves out of the way to invite us inside. His apartment looks okay, but also lifeless. It doesn't look like someone else besides him lives here. No photos on the shelves, no flower pots, no decoration, nothing. Just a soulless couch and a television. From a distance, I can see the equally soulless kitchen.

'We're here about a magic book.' Isla goes straight to the point. That's good. The sooner, the better. Let's get this over with.

My father stops short. 'You can't possibly mean—'

'The very same one!' Isla says, getting the book out of her bag and placing it on the table in front of the couch.

The silence that follows is dense. Not just awkward—but loaded. Like the moment before a storm breaks.

And all I can do is stand there, watching a stranger in my father's skin, and a woman who's more familiar to me than my own blood ever will be, in a room without memories, waiting to see what (or who) cracks first.

21

Isla

Mr Philip Rossi is a very unpleasant man. He hasn't acknowledged me once. He didn't even smile, or even grunt, and I think I deserve at least an uninterested grunt.

But this isn't about me. So I compose myself, and say, 'Have you seen this before?'

'Before I answer that, may I know who you are and how you found my son?' I feel Luca flinch at the mention of 'son'. I have to admit, my dad and I don't have a perfect relationship, but I can't imagine him abandoning me for twenty-three years and then just saying my name when I track him down. If this happened to me, the man had better be on his knees begging for my (and my mom's) forgiveness.

'Well, I'm Isla. I'm a writer from Manila, on vacation here in Italy.' I take a deep breath before I say, 'I stumbled upon this book and saw a letter from him'—I gesture to Luca—'to me. I tracked him down, and he agreed to help me figure this out.'

'You can't,' Philip says.

'Excuse me?' Luca interjects.

'I'm afraid you can't figure it out. I tried,' he says. He gestures for us to sit on the couch, and we oblige.

'This book is cursed.' He calmly sits down across from us, and looks at us with his eyebrows furrowed, as if he's deep in thought or remembering something unpleasant.

'Can you at least tell us your experience with it?' Luca says. He's way calmer than I would be in this situation. There's a giant elephant in the room and no one is addressing it.

His father sighs deeply, and starts. 'I found that book during one of my walks. Every time Eleanor—your mother—'

'I know my mother's name,' Luca interrupts.

'Sorry,' Philip replies. 'Every time Eleanor and I had a misunderstanding, I would go on a walk to clear my mind. And during one of those walks, I forget what we fought about, I was walking along the Arno and saw a street I haven't seen before. Long story short, I found this book. Similar to your experience, Signorina, I found a letter addressed to me.' He looks at me, this time with softer eyes.

'However, unlike you, I knew who the sender was. Fatima. She was a woman I loved before Eleanor. And if I'm being honest, the woman I almost married.'

I blink. 'The letter was from her?'

He nods. 'She'd written it years earlier, but somehow . . . it knew things. Things she could never have known back then. It spoke of regrets. Of chances not taken. Of a version of life I could've lived with her.' He finally looks at me, and this time, his eyes aren't cold. Just tired. 'That's the thing with this book. It shows you something possible. Maybe even beautiful. But it never tells you what it costs.'

I glance at Luca, whose jaw tightens imperceptibly.

'I tracked her down, and we fell into rhythm for a while. I was happy. Ready to introduce her to you, Luc,' he says. 'But then she left. She found another man to call a husband.' His voice shakes, and he sets his gaze down.

'That's why . . . why I left my family. You, Luca. And your mother. I left because I didn't think I could love you enough. Not in the way you deserved. Not with that other life haunting me. I thought . . . maybe if I followed the thread the book gave me, I could become someone better.'

A single tear escapes him, trailing down a cheek that looks weathered by too many choices.

I feel something snap inside me, something all too familiar.

'Well, that's incredibly unfair, don't you think, Signor?' My voice is tighter than I want it to be, but I don't bother reeling it in.

'Scusa?' Philip asks, taken aback.

'I'm sorry, but what made you think that leaving is better than staying? Who gave you the right to decide for the people you're leaving behind?'

'I suppose . . .'

'It's always like that,' I say. 'People who leave spin it into some tragic noble act. Like sacrificing love somehow makes them heroes. But most of the time? It's just cowardice.'

He flinches.

Good.

'Because leaving is easy,' I continue. 'It's easier than staying. Easier than sitting across from the people you claim to love and saying to them, "This isn't the life I imagined." Easier than trying. Than compromising. Than being honest.'

I take a breath, just to keep my voice from shaking.

'And I'm so tired of watching people sugarcoat it. Romanticize their exit like they're doing something brave. News flash—they're not. Real courage? Real love? That's choosing to stay when it's hard. Choosing to have the hard conversations. The uncomfortable truths. The messy, painful middle.'

Philip says nothing. The silence stretches, so thick it feels like the walls are holding their breath.

'And if Luca never tells you this, I will: You *should have* stayed. Not because you were perfect. But because he deserved the chance to love you anyway.'

I exhale, and sit back, fully expecting Philip to throw me out of his house. He doesn't, though. And suddenly I find myself grounded back in reality and realizing the effect of the tantrum I have just thrown. I look at Luca apologetically and say, 'I'm sorry, I—'

'Shh,' he says, patting my knee. 'You're right.'

Philip exhales like he's been holding the breath in his lungs for twenty-three years. He leans forward, elbows on knees, eyes fixed on a spot just beyond the book I had laid on the table.

'You sound like her,' he says finally. 'Eleanor. She never let me off the hook either.'

'I'll take that as a compliment,' I mutter.

Philip doesn't smile, but something in his shoulders softens. He runs a hand through his thinning hair, and for a moment, he looks exactly like someone who's not proud of the life he ended up with.

'I thought I was choosing peace,' he says, voice rough. 'I thought walking away was the only thing I had left to give. My mind kept circling this idea that I would only hurt them more by staying. That if I removed myself, maybe they could . . . I don't know. Heal better. Grow without me.'

'Look,' Luca says. 'We're not here to talk about us. We're here to find out about the book.'

I clear my throat, fully aware that he's asking me to pivot. I try to speak, but then Philip nods, leans back and says, 'I'll tell you everything I know about the book. And I'll help you if I can.'

'Thanks,' I say. 'So . . . what happened?'

Philip watches as I open the book, his eyes landing on the pages like they might bite. 'It's not like other books,' he says. 'You've probably figured that out.'

'Yeah,' I say, flipping to the page with the first letter. 'It doesn't follow any sense of order. One day it shows me something new, the next it's blank. Sometimes, the letters change.'

Philip nods. 'That's what it did to me, too. But it never repeated anything. Never let me go back.'

'What did it show you?' Luca asks. He's sitting up straighter now, eyes narrowed.

Philip doesn't answer right away. His gaze drifts to the window like he needs the sky to give him permission.

'Like I said, it started with a letter,' he says eventually. 'From Fatima. Or . . . someone pretending to be her. It mentioned a memory—something no one else could've known. It felt so real.'

'And?' I ask, though I already know how this story ends.

'I followed it. Every clue. Every hidden street and metaphor. I kept hoping it would take me somewhere that made it all worth it. But it only ever pulled me away—from Eleanor. From Luca. From everything I'd already built.'

Luca's jaw tightens. 'So you were warned.'

Philip doesn't argue. 'I was.'

We sit there for a while, letting that truth settle. The book sits open between us like an artefact, humming with secrets.

'I have a theory,' Philip says, 'that the book doesn't just show you what you want. It shows you what you're most afraid of wanting.'

My spine stiffens.

'I think,' he continues, 'that's why it's dangerous. Because sometimes, you're not ready to know.'

'And that's what you've always wanted?' I ask.

'Not Fatima, but what she represented. The possibility of being someone else.'

'You said you tracked her down, and you lived together for a while. Did she also see letters from you?' I say.

'Yes. The books were filled with our letters to each other. We followed it. Every single time we did, we grew closer to each other. So, naturally, we thought the book brought us together. However, when its letters turned from love to goodbyes, we didn't want to follow it. We tried to resist it. But it has a way of haunting you.'

Luca frowns. 'But it's still just a book. Paper. Ink. You could tear it up, burn it, throw it in the river.'

Philip lets out a slow breath, eyes drifting to the window. 'I tried. I threw it in the Arno. I watched it sink. I felt free for about a week.'

'What happened?'

'It came back.' His voice is flat. 'Showed up in my mailbox like a package. No return address. Same book, same markings. Same page folded down where it left off. Like it never left.'

I shiver.

Luca crosses his arms—always sceptical. 'So, someone must be delivering it. A person. A system. Something.'

'Maybe. Maybe not.' Philip shrugs. 'But that's the thing. It knows how to stay relevant. If you ignore it, it waits. If you fight it, it adapts. You can move to a new city, start a new life, never mention it again—and years later, a letter will appear in your coat pocket. In your own handwriting.'

There's a long silence. The book lies open, but the air around it feels closed, heavy, thick.

'I think,' Philip says finally, 'it attaches to longing. That's what anchors it to you. Wanting something badly enough gives it a way back in. It doesn't need magic. It just needs you to want.'

'And Fatima?' I ask. 'What made her leave?'

Philip's jaw tightens. He doesn't answer right away.

'She loved me,' he says, voice distant. 'For a long time, she did. We even convinced ourselves that maybe the book wanted us together. That our letters, the ones that kept appearing, were signs. Prophecies. Love notes from some kinder timeline.'

'And then?' Luca presses.

'And then the letters changed,' Philip says quietly. 'They stopped being full of longing. They started sounding like warnings. Like goodbyes.'

He exhales slowly, like the memory still scrapes his lungs.

'She said it felt like the book was preparing us to let go. Like it knew something we didn't. At first, we resisted. We stopped reading. We locked it in a drawer. But the letters kept appearing—on receipts, in journals, scrawled on the backs of postcards. Always in our handwriting. Always . . . inevitable.'

A silence settles between us.

'So she left,' he finishes. 'She said loving me while trying not to read the book felt like living in a house with the lights off. You can feel the walls closing in, even if you can't see them.'

He looks up at me then, and for the first time, he doesn't look guarded. He just looks tired.

'I don't know where she is now. One day she left, and the book stopped sending letters. As if it got what it wanted. Or gave up. Or moved on.'

A chill creeps up my arms.

'So . . . we can't win?' I ask. 'The book always decides how it ends?'

'I want to think that's not the case . . . but that's what happened to me.' Philip sits back, resigned. 'I guess once I figured out it's the life I wanted, the book took it from me.'

I glance at Luca. He's staring at the book now, like it might blink back at him. I feel for him, I really do. Here's the thing he spent his whole life surviving. And now he finds out that his father abandoned him because he wanted to. Because he found a different life he wanted for himself. And that's the worst kind of abandonment. (Not that there are good kinds, but you get it.)

Philip clears his throat. 'I lost my family in the process.'

I open my mouth, then close it again. Then I say it, gentle but honest: 'With respect, Signor, you didn't lose them. You left.'

Philip flinches like the truth has teeth. He turns to Luca. 'I'm sorry. Truly. I hope you've found someone who sees you. Who loves you.'

Then to me: 'Isla, please take care of him.'

I stiffen. Before I can think of a polite way to respond, Luca finally speaks.

'She doesn't have to take care of me.' Luca stands, and I follow. He doesn't say it in a mean way. It just sounds . . . honest. 'Thank you for your time.' He takes the book in his hand. 'You were helpful, and we now know more about the book. So, for that, thank you.'

'Luca, really, I'm deeply—'

'I don't need your apology. I've lived twenty-three years without it. But I forgive you. I hope we can find peace in the lives we've chosen to live.'

He doesn't give his father time to respond before he takes my hand. 'If you're all good, we can leave now,' he says in a tone that's much, *much* softer than the one he used on his father.

I can't bring myself to answer so I just nod. And then Luca doesn't let go of my hand until we're out of his father's apartment. He doesn't say a word, and neither do I.

But I squeeze his hand ever so slightly, just so he knows that I'm here.

22

Isla

Once we're out of the apartment and back on the streets of Rome, Luca continues to hold my hand, though his grip isn't as tight any more. 'Well,' he says after a beat, 'that went well. Could've gone worse. Could've ended with a knife in my chest.' He lets out a dry chuckle and lets go of my hand, but his eyes still carry the weight of something unresolved.

'I'm sorry,' I say, quieter than I intend. 'I shouldn't have dragged you into this. If I hadn't made such a big deal about that stupid book, you wouldn't have had to relive . . . all of that.'

He halts, then takes my hand again—like it's the most natural thing in the world. 'I'm grateful,' he says. I don't know if we've officially entered hand-holding territory, but I don't care. His hands are calloused in places, but soft in some. They're warm and steady. Dammit, I like them.

'If it weren't for you, I think some part of me would've kept waiting for that man to turn into a father.'

My chest tightens.

'He kinda sucks,' I say, because I don't know what else to do with all this ache.

Luca huffs a laugh. 'Yeah,' he says, looking down at our joined hands. 'Kinda.'

We walk again, unsure where we're going, and he continues. 'But, you know, in a way it's comforting. Peaceful, even. That some people really aren't meant to be who we hoped they'd be, no matter how hard we try to twist it in our heads.'

I nod too eagerly.

'And,' I add, 'more often than not, deep down, we already have a feeling. But we justify it all because it's easier that way. And then we get this confirmation that we've been right all along, and it sucks. But also, it's, like, not surprising.'

He agrees. We're still holding hands, still walking aimlessly. 'At least I can stop myself from secretly expecting him to show up. And I can live my life finally free of all that. Because he's just a guy who left.'

I look at him, expecting to see hurt in his eyes, or sadness. But he's right . . . He looks oddly at peace with himself. 'And you're a guy who turned out alright despite all of that.'

'You think I turned out alright?' he says as he looks at me.

'I mean, you're a giant sceptic,' I say, laughing. 'But you're kind. You try even when it's hard, and that's rare.'

'You know what else is rare?' he says, his voice a little softer now. 'Strangers who crash into your life with a magic book and somehow turn out to be the only thing that makes sense.'

Oh.

I feel my cheeks getting warm, and he notices, because he swiftly lets go of my hand. I open my mouth, then close it.

What can I possibly say to that? Should I laugh? Smile? Quote Jane Austen? Well, Jane did say, 'A lady's imagination is very rapid; it jumps from admiration to love, from love to matrimony, in a moment'.

Not that I'm thinking about matrimony.

Or love. Ugh.

I can shrug it off and treat it as a joke or a light-hearted comment (which it probably is), or I can peel off a layer and tell him that he's the only thing making sense to me too. That my life is all over the place, but being here right now somehow makes it easier . . .

But that feels too big. Too much. Too soon.

Oh my God. What if this is the book? What if it's manipulating my feelings? Then does that mean we're also doomed to—

'Do you wanna go to the Trevi?' Luca's voice pulls me back to the moment.

'Yes,' I say, way too fast. 'Yes. Please. Desperately. Give me all the clichés.'

He smiles like he knew I'd say that. But he doesn't reach for my hand this time. He just walks beside me, quiet and steady, giving me space to reassemble all my mental furniture.

The streets of Rome are still pulsing with life even with the scorching sun high in the sky. I match Luca's pace, a little slower now, like we've both decided it's okay not to be in a rush.

Every few blocks, I sneak a glance at him. His jaw's relaxed, brow smooth, hands tucked in his pockets like he's keeping them from doing something reckless—like reaching for mine again.

We don't talk. We just let Rome talk for us: mopeds buzzing by like angry bees, the smell of espresso and hot chestnuts, the uneven cobblestones tapping under our shoes like a heartbeat, a mandolin somewhere in the background that's so faint I might be imagining it.

It's oddly romantic. Which is unfortunate, because I am trying very hard not to romanticize anything right now.

Finally, we turn a corner and there it is—Fontana di Trevi—lit up and luminous, the sound of rushing water growing louder as we move closer. People are scattered around the fountain's edge, taking photos, tossing coins, making wishes they probably won't remember in the morning.

I slow down. 'You ever made a wish here before?'

'Once,' Luca says. 'I was twelve. My mom and I took a trip here, and I wished for us to be back in Florence when I woke up, because Rome is too beautiful to be in when you feel like shit.'

'Well, that's painfully dramatic.'

'Italians are born dramatic. And romantic. And passionate. I just lost my ability over the years,' he says with a chuckle.

'So did your wish work?' I ask with a smile.

He looks at me like I'm the stupidest person in the world. 'Of course not,' he says. 'I just woke up with a crick in my neck and got pigeon poop on my shoes on the same day.'

I snort. 'Well,' I say, pulling a coin from my pocket and holding it out to him, 'maybe your technique was off.'

He takes the coin, but gives me a sceptical look. 'Are you about to tell me to re-believe in magic?'

'I'm about to tell you to play along,' I say, stepping towards the edge. 'Just for today.'

Luca considers this, then steps up beside me. 'What do I wish for?'

'You're not supposed to say it out loud.' I roll my eyes at him, and turn my back to the fountain.

'What if I don't know what to wish for?'

'Then fake it. That's what most people are doing anyway.'

We look around, and everyone is turning their backs, throwing in coins with their eyes closed. I close my eyes too, inhale the scent of Rome—stone and water and some old woman's perfume—and make my wish.

I don't wish for answers, or even love. I wish for clarity. Just to be prepared for whatever happens next. For things to make sense. For my novel to make sense. For the magic book to make sense. For everything in my heart to make sense.

When I open my eyes, Luca's already thrown his coin. He glances at me like he knows I've been watching him.

'Well?' I ask. 'Feel the shift in the universe?'

He pretends to think. 'Neck still hurts. No pigeon poop, though. So we're off to a better start.'

I chuckle. He offers to take a photo of me, and I hand him my phone. When in Rome, right?

A lady approaches us and says, 'Do you want me to take a photo of you two? If you'd take a photo of me and my boyfriend.' She smiles shyly.

I hesitate, caught off guard. Not by her offer, but by her assumption. You two. As in, together. As in, couple. As in, romantic. I almost correct her—almost explain that we're not like that. That we've only recently graduated from book-related bickering to semi-occasional hand-holding. That I'm still not entirely sure what we are.

But I don't. Instead, I just nod, take my phone from Luca, and hand it over.

Luca steps beside me, close enough that our arms brush. 'You do know,' he whispers, leaning just slightly towards me, 'that she might be a pickpocket and you just handed her your phone like a gift?'

'Ever the sceptic,' I mutter, rolling my eyes, though I do tighten my grip on my bag just in case.

We turn towards the fountain and smile as the woman lifts the phone. Her boyfriend calls out something behind her in rapid Italian—something about lighting, maybe, or framing—and the whole thing feels oddly . . . normal.

Like I belong here. Like we belong here.

And for the length of a shutter click, and as Luca puts a hand on my back, I let myself believe it.

There's an *unbelievable* crowd on the way to the Colosseum. Not that I expected it to be a haven of peace on a warm summer day, but the influx of tourists is overwhelming. I know I don't have the right to complain since I am, in fact, a tourist contributing to this crowd. Luca sighs beside me, and takes a handkerchief from his back pocket. He wipes his forehead with it, and puts it back.

'Are you sure you wanna go in there?' Luca asks.

'Does going to Rome even count if I don't go the Colosseum?' I chuckle.

'It's underwhelming inside. Trust me. The outside is much more beautiful.' We walk along the street leading up to the Colosseum. I'm starting to get used to the cobblestones, but I am still somehow wearing my flattest flats.

'Then let me marvel at the outside.'

There are bikes and cars lining the street. Italian cars are not what I expected, either. I thought it would be all shiny Ferraris and stylish scooters. Instead, it's dented Fiats and boxy little vehicles that look like they've survived five popes and at least one minor explosion. Honestly, Manila has better-looking cars. But the streets of Rome are not made for modern driving—they're made for walking dramatically and basking in the city.

Before walking to the Colosseum, we had lunch at one of the sandwich places around here, so now the sun is almost down, and the city is bathed in golden honey.

We walk for a few more minutes until I get a glimpse of the *thing*.

It's gigantic, as expected, and I can only see the arches from here. Or are those holes? Windows? Historical eyelets? Whatever.

From a distance, the Colosseum looks every bit as magical as one would expect. It rises like it's built from power. Really, truly amazing. It looks like a weathered crown of stone carved out of time, just sitting in the middle of modern life like it never noticed the centuries passing. From here, the arches line up like teeth in a giant, ancient jaw—cracked and imperfect, but still standing.

As we get closer, I can see the wear and tear on every stone. Pockmarks. Erosion. Fractures. Like scars the earth itself tried to leave behind. Dramatic, I know, but that's what it feels like.

However, it's also . . . well, as Luca said, underwhelming.

Reality starts to creep in, and the crowd is massive—an overwhelming mix of backpacks, tour guides waving flags, and the hum of a hundred different languages trying to out-volume each other. The closer we get, the less I can actually see it.

Don't get me wrong. It's still magical up close. I can see the little details that add to the history of this place. The porous walls, the wearing of the structure.

'Well, you're right. It gets more underwhelming the closer we get,' I say.

Luca chuckles, and says, 'Even more so inside.'

'Still impressive. Just not in-line-for-two-hours impressive.'

Luca chuckles, hands in his pockets. 'Fair.'

I glance back one last time. The Colosseum still looks dreamlike. I imagine gladiators walking where the scooters are now. Roman emperors where the camera crews stand. And I realize that it's not underwhelming because it's unremarkable. It's underwhelming because no monument, no matter how ancient or grand, can compete with the weight of our own expectations.

Maybe some things are meant to be admired from a distance.

I turn back to Luca. 'How about you give me the Italian exclusive?'

'The what?'

'Take me somewhere that isn't in the guidebooks. Something not made for tourists. Something that matters to you.'

He tilts his head at me, his expression thoughtful. Then he nods towards a quiet alleyway that winds away from the crowd.

'You sure?'

'I'm sure.'

'There's this place I used to go to back when I took a semester here. It's a hill that overlooks the city and—'

'Perfect. I love it already,' I say, before he can even finish.

Luca lifts a brow. 'It's a few kilometres away, and it'll take an hour to walk. Maybe more with your poor choice of footwear,' he adds, glancing pointedly at my flats. 'There's a bike rental nearby. If you're up for it . . .'

'I'm up for it,' I say decidedly.

That was a lie. My feet are going to revolt.

23

Isla

The bike rental shop is exactly the kind of place you'd expect to be run by a man named Gino who accepts only cash and has absolutely no online presence. The bikes are all crammed together under a faded green awning. Mine is bubblegum pink with a bell that lets out a dainty *ting*! Luca's is a rugged, mud-streaked thing that looks like it's been to war and back.

The man behind the counter hands us helmets, and before I can do it myself, Luca reaches over and gently places mine on my head. He straps it on like it's second nature, and proceeds to give soft taps on the top of my helmet like he's sending me off to battle.

Before we know it, we're pedalling through Rome just as the sun starts its descent. I don't usually have time for this kind of thing back in Manila. I live in a condo in Makati—a city that's *technically* walkable, if you're willing to dodge jeepneys, rain puddles, and risk a heat stroke. But even then, I'm usually too wrapped up in deadlines. Always rushing to finish a manuscript, edit someone else's book, write an essay, show up for a friend, respond to a message, check something off a never-ending to-do list.

But here, in a city that's far from home, I can pedal through narrow Roman streets and feel the wind on my cheeks, free from it all—even if just for a little while. Sure, I still have a novel to finish. I still have a magic book to decode. I still have that weird flutter in my stomach whenever Luca looks at me like he knows something I don't. But right now, all of it feels lighter. Manageable. Like background music.

Luca slows down and turns towards a steeper road, one that coils upward with worn stones and cream-covered walls. 'Almost there,' he calls back, and I follow him, legs burning but heart full.

At the top, the world opens up. We alight from our bikes and push them towards the location. Luca walks beside me, but I don't notice immediately because my eyes are fixed on the big statue in the middle of the roundabout. It's one of a man riding a horse, cast in bronze, perched atop a stone sculpture.

'That's the Garibaldi statue. He was a soldier,' Luca says, obviously noticing my half-agape mouth. Behind the statue is an entirely different kind of magic.

'Welcome to Gianicolo,' he says.

Gianicolo is not crowded, like most places. No camera-toting tourists. Just a few locals murmuring on benches, a dog curled at someone's feet, and a violinist in the distance playing something mournful and sweet.

Rome in daylight is beautiful like a summer postcard. In the afternoon, it's magical. Whimsical. With the golden glow of the sun illuminating everything. But at night? At night,

Rome is like an exhale. I don't know how to explain it but there's something about the silence, the silhouettes, and the lights that make it feel relaxed.

We park our bikes near a low, time-worn stone wall. It curves gently along the edge, and it looks like a place where you could sit for hours. I hop up and dangle my legs over the side, Rome sprawling beneath us like a living storybook.

'Wait here,' Luca says, and I see him walking towards the stalls surrounding the area. He comes back minutes later with a cup of tea and some nuts for snacking. He hops up onto the stone wall, beside me, and we stare at the night sky and the ancient buildings sprawling around us.

'So, what makes this place special?' I ask.

He shifts beside me, as if weighing whether or not to tell the truth.

'I came here a lot during my semester in Rome,' he says finally. 'When everything felt like too much. School. Expectations. Loneliness. I'd sneak off here after classes. Sit right where we are now.'

He pauses, eyes scanning the view like it's speaking to him in a language only he understands.

'I was trying to figure out who I was, I guess,' he continues. 'Away from home. Away from my mama, from Nonna. There's something about this place—it's high above everything, but not in a distant way . . .'

I glance at him, the gentle curve of his mouth, the way his eyes reflect the city lights. There's something disarming about this version of him.

'You don't seem like someone who gets overwhelmed,' I say.

He chuckles. 'That's because I'm good at pretending, Signorina.'

The breeze shifts again. A car horn echoes faintly from below, swallowed quickly by the night. The violinist's song winds to a close, and for a moment, everything goes still.

I smile. He hasn't called me Signorina in days. I kinda missed it. I know I've only known him for five—six days? But I already know he's someone I won't forget. And no, it's not just going to be one of those travel experiences where you put a picture of someone in your journal and they stay there forever. Just as a memory. Luca will be something more, like a thought that will always slip into my mind in the strangest moments. Maybe I'll remember the feel of his hand when I'm holding someone else's someday. Or maybe I'll remember this skyline, this moment, when I look out of my condo's balcony. Maybe I'll remember him in my morning coffee. Every time I twirl pasta on a fork.

And it's not lost on me that this is exactly what the book said. That we would somehow grow closer when we were here in Rome. And it's also not lost on me that I only have three weeks left in Italy. And that Luca only promised to help me for one. And that's almost ending.

So, forgive me, Universe, if I ignore every impulse I have to shut this feeling down. Forgive me, if I want to turn this moment into a secret I can put into my pocket and take everywhere I go.

'Is it my turn to ask now?' Luca looks at me with a soft nudge.

'Oh is that what we're doing? Twenty questions?' I chuckle.

'We're getting to know each other. So, two, twenty, a hundred questions. However much it takes.'

I look up at him, and for a moment, our eyes hold each other's. I smile softly, and he returns it. Before the moment gets more intense, I say, 'Shoot. Ask away!'

'Are you always superstitious?' he asks. 'Do you always believe in fate and those ridiculous signs?'

I glare at him. I was dreading being asked this question. The answer will not be easy. It will not be light. Or cute. It's painful and heavy. But I have to face it one way or another.

'Isla?' Luca asks. 'Sorry, is it too personal?'

'Yes, but no, it's fine . . . it's just . . . it's a long story.' I contemplate deflecting, but part of me wants to talk about it anyway. 'It's because of my sister Ivy.'

Luca doesn't talk. He just lets me gather the courage to speak. 'I already told you she died two years ago.' He nods solemnly. 'Ivy was the uptight one. The type who always had a plan—and a plan B, a plan C—a spreadsheet, a calendar reminder for everything. She even had an alarm for when she should drink water.' I roll my eyes.

'I was the spontaneous one. The wild card. I show up without a plan, winging everything, the same way I wing the plots of my novel. And she used to say she envied that about me.'

A sad smile forms, small and shaky.

'So, one day, she decided to be spontaneous for once. She booked a solo trip. To Coron, a beautiful island in the Philippines.' I glance at him to see him looking at me intently, cautiously, like he's expecting me to break but he's ready to comfort anyway.

I continue, 'She, uh, she drowned. It was when she was hiking in this secret beach she supposedly found online. She slipped. They said the tide was too strong. That she hit her head when she fell.' My voice breaks for a second, but I keep it together. 'By the time they found her . . . it was too late.'

A long pause.

'She'd sent me a picture earlier that day. Of the cliff. She joked that it looked too scary, and that she missed her desk. And I told her . . .' I trail off. 'I told her not to chicken out. I also told her to be careful, but not in the way that matters.'

I wipe under my eye with my sleeve, though the tear never really falls.

'I didn't ask enough questions. And I ignored all the other signs. Little things that didn't sit right. The weird texts of panic before she hiked. The silence. The gut feeling that something was off. I told myself I was overthinking it. That Ivy was just being spontaneous. *Just being like me.*' I laugh once, small and bitter.

'Some part of me still believes that if I had paid attention—if I had listened to the signs—I could've done something. Stopped it. Saved her.' The breeze tugs gently at my hair. Somewhere behind us, the violinist has begun playing again.

'So, now I check horoscopes. I avoid ladders. I panic when a candle flickers too suddenly. It's stupid, I know. But when the universe whispers, I try to listen now.'

Luca's hand finds mine on the stone wall. He doesn't say I'm being silly. He doesn't tell me it wasn't my fault. He just squeezes my hand once—firm and sure—like an anchor, not letting go.

'I'm sorry you had to go through that. The grief must have been tough,' he says.

'Well . . . grief sucks, sure,' I say softly, my eyes distant and my voice lined with something even I can't identify. It sounds almost like fatigue. 'It guts you. Ruins you to the point of no return. But what really breaks you isn't the grief itself. It's the way people look at it—at you. Even your own parents. They don't see your grief as something sacred or shattering. They see it as a warning. Or a mirror, even. And when they look into your pain, all they really want is reassurance that it's not theirs. That it won't be. That your tragedy is a fluke, a footnote, a mistake they'd never make.'

I pause, feeling the emotion washing through me. But I continue talking, swallowing hard. 'When someone dies of an illness, they ask questions not to understand and sympathize, but to distance themselves. "Did she eat too much sugar?" "Was she unhealthy?" "Was it genetic?" Not out of sympathy. But to convince themselves they're safe. That if they do everything right, it won't touch them.

'And if it's an accident, they ask why, like it's a puzzle with a single solvable answer. "Maybe she wasn't crossing the right lane." "Maybe she was distracted." Because if they can find something to blame, then they can believe that they're immune.'

I turn to Luca, my eyes watering, but I don't care any more.

'And then the worst part is they turn your heartbreak into a parable. A story with a moral. A lesson in what not to do. They say things like, "That wouldn't happen to me. I'm careful. I pay attention." As if caution is a shield against loss. As if love and death and disaster are things you can outsmart. As if grief is a punishment, and they're the righteous ones.'

Luca doesn't say anything at first. He's just watching me, quiet and still. I think he wants to help, but what could he even say?

'I'm sure they mean well,' he murmurs.

A tear escapes down my cheek, and I don't wipe it away. 'Of course, they mean well. They always mean well. And that's what makes it so hard to be angry. They say all the right things: "I'm here for you", "You're so strong", and "Time heals". Like it means something. But it doesn't. They're just standing there, watching from the outside, pretending that by giving you a few words, you'll be fine. They show up for the funeral, not the aftermath. They hold your hand when your voice breaks. But they don't come for the after. They don't sit with you in the quiet. They don't stay when the silence is too loud and your grief starts to rot into loneliness. They don't see that the hardest part isn't the moment you lose someone. It's *every single day after* that they're still gone and the world keeps expecting you to function like you're not slowly unravelling.'

I exhale shakily. My voice is barely there now. 'The truth is . . . people only look at your grief long enough to feel grateful it's not their own.' I meet his eyes. 'And then they look away.'

The silence that follows is thick. Real. He doesn't try to fill it with clichés. He just stays there while I break down like I've exploded from all the things I've bottled up.

'I would,' he whispers.

I look up at him, confused. 'You would what?'

He gives the softest smile. 'I'd sit with you in the quiet.'

24

Luca

I wonder if I've said too little. Or too much. Or if I've misread the moment entirely. But she doesn't let go of my hand. Not even when her shoulders tremble again. Not even when she leans forward a little, hands on her knees, like her body has finally surrendered to the weight of everything.

Dio mio, she's been carrying so much.

And I didn't know. I had no idea.

I've spent the last week pretending I could figure her out. Isla with her sarcastic comebacks and her oversized tote bag full of scribbled notes and random clutter. Isla who walks too fast, and fills silences with jokes when things get too heavy.

But this is the real her. Or at least one of the versions she doesn't usually let people see.

And she's letting me see it. I feel . . . honoured? That sounds like the wrong word. Too formal and too sterile for something this fragile. What I really feel is this strange ache, like I want to go back in time and find her a year ago and make sure she never had to feel that alone.

I don't say that. I wouldn't know how. Instead, I remove my hand from hers to place it on her back, and rub it gently.

The breeze brushes past us again, a little cooler now. The dome of St Peter's gleams faintly in the distance, but my focus is on her. I don't know what to say. What could I say?

'Sorry,' I blurt out. 'Sorry you had to relive that. I didn't mean to push you.'

She shakes her head. 'You didn't. I had to talk about that. It's nice to finally let it out.'

'Can I just say something, though?' I ask softly. Isla looks at me with her big brown eyes, and raises her eyebrows.

'I'm not gonna tell you what to feel,' I continue. 'I'm sure people comforted you by saying that it isn't your fault.'

Her eyes narrow, as if she was expecting me to do the same. 'That's true, by the way,' I say. 'It isn't your fault. But what I'm trying to tell you is that guilt is part of grief.' I look in the distance, remembering my own experiences. 'There will always be a part of you that feels that it's your fault. Because, as you said, finding someone to blame is the default. And when we can't find someone else, we blame ourselves.'

She sighs, but continues to listen. So I continue, 'You miss someone so much that your brain tries to turn it into something you can solve. It spirals into what-ifs and could-have-beens. And none of it changes what happened. But it makes you feel like you're at least doing something. Even if that something is punishing yourself.'

Her lips part slightly, like she's about to respond. But she doesn't.

'I think Ivy wanted to be like you because she saw how alive you were,' I say. 'Because you said yes to things. Because you lived without fear. And that scared her, maybe. But it also inspired her. You gave her permission to try.'

I pause, more hesitant now. 'So maybe, yes, you encouraged her to be brave. But that's not what hurt her. What hurt her was the world being unpredictable. Cruel. Random. It wasn't you. It was the ocean.'

Isla's eyes are shimmering now. Her knuckles are white against the edge of the stone.

'And yeah,' I add, gently, 'it's kind of ironic that now you're the one second-guessing everything . . .' I trail off before I say something that triggers her. I'm not expecting her to change the way she handles grief. If she thinks this is the way, then I'll stand in support.

'I keep trying to convince myself,' Isla says after a while, 'that Ivy wouldn't want me to live this way. But I can't shake off the feeling that if I miss even one sign, another tragedy could happen.'

She lets out the faintest breath, shaky but silent. Her fingers are gripping the edge of the stone wall tighter now.

'You lost her, Isla,' I say, more quietly this time. 'But you don't have to lose yourself, too.'

She looks up at me, her eyes watering, and she smiles. The most genuine smile I've ever seen from her. She quickly wipes the tears and goes back to looking at the skyline. She leans slightly on me, her head resting lazily on my shoulder. It startles me, but I don't move.

Then she says, almost too quietly, 'It sounds stupid when you say it out loud, doesn't it? That I started believing in signs and fate and . . . cosmic warnings. All because I couldn't find a way to justify my grief.'

'No,' I say. 'It sounds like someone who's trying to make sense of things. And you don't have to justify grief.'

I can't help but notice how different we are. I was raised to believe that life is what it is. Random. Cruel. Beautiful at times, but painful nonetheless.

She fidgets with her fingers, while my hand rests behind her on the stone wall. 'Is that why you read the book and obsessed about it in the first place?'

Isla chuckles. 'Yeah,' she says. 'I think I was trying to bargain with the universe. Like, if I could just follow the signs, if I could just listen this time . . . then I wouldn't lose anything else.'

A part of me envies her. Not the pain, not the loss—but the belief that somewhere, somehow, there's an order to it all. That someone's at the wheel. I've never had that luxury. The luxury to just . . . believe.

'Do you ever get tired of waiting for signs?'

She blinks, caught off-guard. 'What do you mean?'

'I mean . . . don't you ever want to choose something without needing a divine green light first? To just let yourself want something. Or someone.'

She goes quiet again.

'I do,' she finally says. 'But it's scary. Wanting things out loud makes them real. And then it makes losing them real, too.'

I nod. 'Yeah. But it also makes having them real.'

Our eyes meet, and for a second, I swear we're saying more than either of us is ready to admit.

Then she smiles faintly. 'Okay, fine. That was poetic of you.'

She nudges me with her shoulder, and I laugh under my breath. I don't remember the last time someone made me feel like this—like the world wasn't such a closed system after all.

Then she turns to me, her gaze suddenly sharp and curious. 'Can I ask you something now?'

'Go ahead.'

'Did you turn into a sceptic after your father left?' she asks.

'Yes and no,' I say. 'I think I was always the kind of kid who needed things to make sense. Who liked cause and effect. Proof. Logic. But after he left . . .' I trail off for a second, trying to find the edges of the memory without falling too far in. 'After he left, it was like everything cracked open. All the things I used to believe about family, about permanence, about what people owe each other—they didn't hold up any more.'

She doesn't interrupt. Just listens. So I keep going.

'He said he had a different destiny,' I say, the words tasting bitter even now. 'That he wasn't meant to stay. As if leaving your family behind is some noble calling, and pain becomes profound when you sugarcoat it. I think that's when I stopped believing in all the things people romanticize. Destiny. Meant to be. Signs,' I continue. 'Because that's what he used as an excuse. And I guess . . . I didn't want to believe the universe would let someone do that and still call it love.'

Isla's face softens. 'So you don't just hate signs. You're scared of what people use them for.'

I nod. 'Yeah. People use fate like it's a hall pass for bad decisions. "It wasn't meant to be." "The universe had other plans." But sometimes the truth is simpler. Sometimes people just leave. Sometimes they choose to. And that choice hurts more than any cosmic reason ever could.'

She's quiet, and I think maybe I've said too much. But then she says softly, 'I get that. I really do.'

There's something about the way we understood each other tonight. About the way our presence made our problems less problematic. How we're somehow less lonely. And somehow, I want to lean in. In fact, I don't even realize I'm leaning closer until I feel the warmth of her shoulder against mine. My hand is still behind her, perched on the stone.

She doesn't pull away. If anything, she tilts her head slightly towards me, just enough to let me know she feels it too—that pull. That impossible gravity.

Her breath catches, just slightly. I hear it more than I see it.

She turns to me then, her gaze soft and searching. Her eyes flicker down to my lips for the briefest second, and it does something to me. When her eyes land back on mine, I'm tempted to do it.

But none of us are moving. And then, after a few more seconds, Isla whispers, 'I don't know what we're doing.'

'Me neither,' I reply, in the same voice that's barely audible.

'But it feels like something.'

'It does.'

A shout suddenly echoes from behind us. Laughter. Real, human noise, cracking through the stillness.

We both flinch slightly, blinking as the spell breaks.

Isla chuckles, and turns her head. I follow, and witness a group of people behind us, walking and talking and laughing with drinks in their hands.

'I blame the universe for that,' I mutter, half under my breath.

She laughs again, softer this time, and reaches out to pat my leg. The touch is light, but it lingers.

Maybe the kiss wasn't meant to happen tonight. Maybe the universe really does have timing. Or maybe it's just reminding us that some things are worth waiting for. Or maybe . . . probably . . . it's not gonna happen at all.

25

Isla

We're going back to Florence tomorrow. So there's only one more night of this shared bed experience. I'm not as nervous as I was last night, though.

Whatever happened earlier shifted something between us. That moment with his father, our vulnerability at Gianicolo, that almost kiss. Dammit. That moment.

How did that even happen? What does it mean? That group of friends, that stopped our kiss, that had to be a cosmic nudge. Surely, the universe is warning me. That getting too close to Luca might make me fall for him, and falling for him is not an option.

Not when we're written in a cursed book. Not when we're continents away. Not when he's an eternal sceptic with trauma and I'm a superstitious goblin with unresolved guilt. Not when the only thing we have in common is . . . being sad. Jeez, that's not romantic. That's a support group.

Still, I didn't expect to open up to him the way I did today. I don't usually talk about Ivy—not in full detail, not the messy truth. Whenever I try, I unravel. I tried it once with Harriet, and when she said, 'It's not your fault,' it felt like she was handing me an exit ticket from the conversation. Like absolution meant I should stop feeling the way I do.

But Luca didn't say that. He didn't try to comfort me. Or fix things. He listened and he validated my emotions. In a way, I know it's because we're equal parts broken. And I can't decide yet if that's beautiful or tragic.

I change into my donut-printed pyjamas, and take one last look. I catch a glimpse of myself in the mirror, and there it is: that annoying, traitorous blush. I try to smush it away with my palms, but it just makes me look more flustered, so I give up and settle for splashing my cheeks with water.

I hate to admit it, but I felt safe with Luca today. And I guess that's exactly why I should be more careful. Because it doesn't take much for safety to start feeling like home. And I can't afford that. Not here. Not now.

I step out of the bathroom, expecting to find Luca on the bed. He's nowhere to be found, so I just stay on my side, and take my laptop out. I try to squeeze in a few words for my novel, and surprisingly, the words are just . . . flowing. Something about ripping my heart bare put my brain in reset and I somehow know the right things to say.

Sometimes, I worry about inserting my own struggles into the characters I write. That my books might come across as trauma-dumping. But then I remember that we all put little pieces of ourselves into the things we make. Some people knit scarves with wonky edges because they can't seem to hold stuff together. Some people bake rainbow cookies because they couldn't have one as kids and now they're reclaiming joy. I write emotionally volatile people who fall in love in inconvenient places while dealing with unresolved baggage . . . because writing it is easier than living it.

And maybe that's the point. Creating isn't always about being clever or polished or profound. In the end, it's just about survival. About telling the truth sideways, so someone else out there can find their reflection in it too.

I look at the chapter I have written about Julie facing with a decision. Torn between the safe path she trained for and the uncertain life she actually wants. She's scared. She's confused. But she's choosing to try anyway.

I smile a little. Ivy would've liked this one. She would've called Julie reckless in that fond, sisterly way of hers—then cheered when she made the jump.

Just as I'm rereading the last paragraph, I hear the door creak open. I look up and see Luca holding a paper bag and two cans of peach iced tea (which have immediately become my favourite drink here).

'What's that?' I ask, already closing my laptop because my stomach rumbles at the mere *reminder* of food.

'Pizza al portafoglio,' he says, reaching into the bag and pulling out something wrapped in waxy paper. A corner of warm pizza dough peeks out.

I scoot towards the edge of the bed, reaching for it like a kid being handed her first candy. 'Pizza a what?'

He chuckles as he hands it to me. 'Wallet pizza. It's basically a folded pizza. Roman street food.'

I peel back the paper to reveal—yes, a pizza, folded in quarters. 'This is the coolest thing I've ever seen. I will never eat pizza the same way again. I'm a changed woman.' I take a bite, and let out a dramatic groan that probably sounds like it belongs in a distinct genre of romance novels.

Luca's watching me with an amused look, one brow raised. 'Should I give you some privacy?'

'What?' I ask, mid-chew.

'You moaned. At the pizza,' he says as he unpacks his food and sits beside me on the edge of the bed.

'I don't choose how my body reacts to divine flavour, Luca.'

He laughs. Loudly. 'I'm just offended. You didn't moan at my carbonara.'

I choke on my pizza. That carbonara was divine, if I'm being honest. But at the time, I was too careful to make any wrong impressions. But I don't admit that. Instead, I say, 'Then use it as inspiration. Do better, Chef.' I wag a finger at him. 'But fair warning—this pizza has raised the bar. It's you versus street food now.'

'Oh no,' he deadpans. 'Not the unbeatable folded pizza.'

'*Pizza al portafoglio*,' I correct with exaggerated flair. 'Please respect the local culture.'

He laughs again, and slightly nudges me. He pops open my iced tea and hands it to me like it's second nature. I pretend not to feel giddy about it, but as I take it and our fingers brush, I don't mistake the jolt making its way up to my brain.

'Do you wanna watch something?' I reach for the remote before my brain makes this a whole thing.

'Sure. But you're picking,' he says.

I flip to Netflix, and type in *Roman Holiday*. As I press play, I stand up to brush the crumbs off my pyjamas. I look at Luca and smile. 'It's the perfect movie. We're in Rome. And I'm Princess Ann.' I curtsy.

'Quite sure Princess Ann doesn't eat wallet pizza in her pyjamas.'

I gape at him. 'Then you obviously haven't seen the movie.'

He smiles sheepishly. 'You're right. I haven't.'

We both settle back on the foot of the bed, shoulder to shoulder, legs half-tangled, eating our wallet pizzas and watching Audrey Hepburn smile and wave.

'You know,' I whisper, 'Audrey's character runs away from her royal duties, gets a haircut, eats gelato, and falls in love in one day. *One.*'

'Thank you for spoiling the entire movie for me,' he says, but he doesn't stop watching.

'You'll still love it. Also, it's from 1953. The statute of limitations for spoilers has passed.' I look at him, and narrow my eyes. 'But I'm just saying. How can she do all that in one day?'

I take another bite of my pizza. Luca takes a sip of iced tea, looks at me, then says, 'Unsurprising. A lot can happen in one day.'

Our eyes meet. It's soft. Steady. Maybe a second too long.

And suddenly I get it.

All my life I thought this movie was too good to be true. Nobody falls in love in a day. But then I reflect on my own day: I confronted someone's estranged father, made a wish at the Trevi, judged the Colosseum, unpacked emotional burden at Gianicolo, ate folded pizza in bed, all while my heart shifted, tilted, leaned in towards this man beside me, whom I almost kissed.

All of that in one day.

Maybe it's Rome. Something about the city or the air, or the feeling of being away from everything familiar. This city makes impossible things possible.

I sigh. As the movie plays and we scoot over to the head of the bed, pillow wall nowhere in sight, I place my cheek softly on Luca's shoulder. He doesn't move. Doesn't even flinch. In fact, he breathes in sync with me.

By all means, Rome, I quote Princess Ann in my head, *I will cherish my visit here in memory as long as I live.*

And if I happen to fall a little more tomorrow, well . . .

That's tomorrow's problem.

26

Luca

'*Bentornato*, amico mio,' Marco's voice greets me as I enter the restaurant. I was in Rome for only three days, with the restaurant left in Marco's care. He updated me regularly, and nothing out of the ordinary happened in the restaurant.

For a moment, I think that they can survive without me after all. That maybe I don't have to stay here forever. Because if I'm being honest with myself, those three days in Rome made me think about all the possibilities of my future, ones that I never dared to think up before.

Those three days shifted the ground beneath my feet. Suddenly, that letter made sense. The one of me telling Isla not to leave because everything that happened in Rome made me love her.

Of course, I don't love her. Not yet, anyway.

'Hello?' Marco says as I walk past him, lost in thought.

'Sorry,' I say. 'Grazie, I'm just . . . not in the headspace,' I say.

Marco chuckles as he turns on the lights to get ready for the day. 'Did you get mugged or fall in love?'

I look at him in confusion.

He just shrugs and says, 'It's Rome. It's usually one or the other.'

I sigh. 'A bit of both?' I take a seat at the bar stool.

Enzo, my sous chef, enters the restaurant, and greets me. I raise a hand to say hi, and then watch as he proceeds past me, to prep the kitchen. I'm usually the one to do that, but I guess he's been doing it in my absence. I don't stop him, though. I can't function properly anyway.

'That sounds like a story for after hours,' Marco says, tossing me the apron. 'Was it Isla?'

At the mention of her name, I feel a tug in my chest. I nod at Marco, and tell him I'll indulge him later. He waves goodbye to me, resuming his job as a tour guide in various places in Florence, promising he'll return later.

I weave my way to the kitchen, relying on muscle memory to function. I can't stop myself from thinking about her. Especially that night at Gianicolo. Everything she said, everything *I* said, everything that happened and almost happened.

On the train ride back here, we were normal. We joked around, we ate snacks, we even fell asleep for fifteen minutes. But the moment we landed in Florence, it felt heavy. Or maybe it was just me. Since I live here, I feel like I have to return to a normal life, a normal routine, and just accept that Isla is nothing but a travel companion. Someone passing through.

And part of me doesn't want her to be.

I took her to her hotel last night. The same one that she stayed in before. She still has around three weeks to spend in Italy. I don't why I'm already in a state of panic that she's leaving.

It's Dahlia all over again.

I swore I'd never get this close again. Never let anyone in far enough to ruin me twice. And now I'm standing on the edge of the same cliff, looking at Isla and wondering how I got here so fast. Wondering if I'll fall again. Or worse—if I already have.

And I can't afford that. Not with her. Not with someone who lives a continent away. Not with someone who believes in signs and fate and serendipity, when I've spent my whole life trying to prove that none of it matters. That people leave because they choose to, not because the universe plotted it.

The night winds down quietly. The restaurant isn't busy—just a slow trickle of regulars and a few tourists who somehow found us. I'm wiping the counter when Enzo approaches, his brows drawn in that way that means he's been thinking about this for hours before deciding to say it.

'*Capo*,' he says. He only calls me that as a joke, since we're friends more than we're co-workers.

I look at him with raised eyebrows. 'Sì?'

'I will be straight to the point. The restaurant is not doing well,' he says with an expression of someone who genuinely cares.

'I know,' I say, scrubbing at a spot that probably doesn't exist. 'I've seen the numbers.'

'Yeah, but it's more than numbers,' Enzo presses. 'It's the energy, Luca. We've lost momentum. Fewer regulars, fewer bookings. Even that American couple who used to come every Friday night? Haven't seen them in three weeks.'

I sigh, placing the cloth on the counter. 'What do you want me to say? I've been gone three days, not three months.'

He doesn't flinch. 'And in those three days, I saw something. You left, and somehow . . . it all ran smoother. Because people stepped up. Not because they wanted to replace you—but because they had to.'

'That's good, isn't it?'

'Yes and no,' he replies. 'It means we can float. But it also means you're drifting. You're here, Luca. But lately, you're not here.'

I swallow hard.

He continues, 'Which is why I wanted to bring something up. I have a friend. Business guy. From the Philippines.'

At that, my head lifts. 'The Philippines?'

Enzo nods. 'Yeah. He's been wanting to open an Italian place in Manila. He wants someone with heart. Someone who knows the food and the story behind it.'

'And you thought of me.'

He nods vehemently. 'I told him I'd rather introduce him to someone I trust than watch him hand his dream to some flashy influencer chef with a truffle oil addiction.'

I smile faintly, but I already feel my chest tightening.

'I don't know, Enzo,' I say. 'Manila? That's a big leap.'

He leans on the other side of the counter, lowering his voice. 'Is it, though? You've been somewhere else lately. Since before Rome.'

I stiffen at the mention. 'You think this is about a girl.'

'I think this is about possibility,' he corrects gently. 'And maybe a girl. But mostly, I think you've been waiting for something to shake you out of this sleepwalk you've been in for a while now. Maybe this is it.'

He's not wrong. I have been feeling stuck at this restaurant lately. I shake my head slowly. 'It would be stupid. To follow someone halfway across the world.'

'Depends,' Enzo says. 'Are you following her, or are you following the part of yourself that finally woke up?'

That makes me pause.

Because I don't know. I don't know if it's her or the way I feel when I am with her. Alive, honest, understood.

Enzo taps the counter once, then stands straight. 'You don't have to decide now. But maybe don't dismiss the idea just because it sounds reckless. Some of the best things in life start off that way.' He gives me a pat on the back. 'See you tomorrow, Capo.'

I sigh as he leaves, leaving me to lock up.

I hear the bell ring, so I peek out of the kitchen only to see Marco return, as promised. He waves at me, then proceeds to the bar to pour us a drink for us. I sigh.

I guess we're doing this.

'Tell me all about it,' he says, handing me a glass of wine.

I honestly don't know where to start, but I try anyway. 'Well,' I down a gulp of wine. 'We went to Rome, and we spent the first day eating at a restaurant and getting gelato.'

'Sounds like a good date, congrats,' Marco says, raising his glass.

I shake my head, and continue, 'It wasn't a date. But that's not even the point.'

I tell him about Gianicolo. About the way she opened up. About the almost kiss. About how silence with her didn't feel empty. About how I've been thinking about her constantly since.

When I finish, Marco lets out a long, low whistle.

'You are so screwed,' he says, smiling into his wine glass.

'Thanks,' I mutter, but I'm smiling too.

'No, I mean it,' he says. 'This is like Dahlia, but also not.'

I raise my eyebrows, unsure of what he means. 'Please, expound,' I say.

'You were like this with Dahlia.' He waves his hand. 'You were so in love with her that you were willing to go cross-country with her.'

I remember that. I was already dead set on going with her. I was leaving the restaurant to Marco and Enzo. Leaving Nonna to be with her friends at the nursing home, even when she still lived with me. She insisted that she wanted to be there. In fact she's there even now, every day, hanging out with fellow nonnas.

'Now, I feel like you're inching towards that love again. But this time, you're more guarded. Which is a good thing.'

'I'm not inching towards—'

'Please, Luc.' He rolls his eyes. 'You're eating pizza in bed. And she defended you from your father.'

'That's more about the situation than our actual feelings. Besides, we're only here because of a book, remember?' I tap my forehead to emphasize that he is not using his brain.

'You keep making your excuses, but know that this one's different. Even the creepy magic book says so.'

I don't tell him that the book is supposedly cursed. But right now, I haven't really thought about it. All I thought about is Isla, and . . .

'Ciao!' She pops up out of nowhere.

Marco gives me a teasing grin and then Isla a friendly hug. 'Ah, Signorina!' he says. 'Long time, no see. I've heard great things about your travels.'

Isla chuckles, 'Thanks, Marco. You're very kind. Or just a people pleaser. You should meet my best friend.'

'Is she every bit the sunshine you are?'

'The opposite actually. The kind that'll put you in your place.' She winks. 'But she's got a heart somewhere, I'm sure.'

'Can't wait to meet her.' With that, Marco disappears into the kitchen, probably to whip up a last-minute meal.

'Hello,' I say to Isla as she takes my wine glass and takes a gulp.

She takes a seat beside me, and then says, 'So, it's been seven days.' She tucks a curly hair strand behind her ear and continues. 'You promised to help me for a week, and it's been a week. And you did help me. And so I'm thankful.'

She gives me a small paper bag the size of my palm. I take it and open it. It's a small pendant in the shape of an Italian horn. I laugh.

'Don't laugh!' Isla says. 'That is the *cornicello*.'

'I know what the cornicello is. I'm Italian, remember?'

'Yes, but you hate luck and all the good things in life,' she says. 'So that'll protect you from the evil eye. The—'

'*Malocchio*, yes, Isla, I am well-aware. Still Italian.'

'Anyhoo,' she says, rolling her eyes with a chuckle. 'That's my way of saying thank you for helping me. And also, look.' She puts her wrist in front of my face, and she has a charm bracelet, now adorned with a cornicello pendant, one that looks like mine. 'We're matchy! So wear that! Or I'll hex you!'

I can't believe I would even consider wearing a good luck charm, let alone *matching* with a woman who lives an ocean away. But I consider it.

'So, we haven't really been able to find out what the book actually is. Giodani says it's a book that shows us who we're destined to be with. Your father says it's cursed.' She shrugs. 'I'm going to keep digging. Try to figure out what it actually means. Since it's been more than a week, I won't pester you any more. No more emotional blackmail.'

Then she stands, brushing invisible crumbs from her skirt, and shoots me a crooked smile. 'But . . . if you want to join me? You know where to find me.'

After a few steps, she's near the door, her hand around the handle. I'm still not responding, because I don't know what to say. Isla gives me one last look, and says, 'Or not. Whatever. Totally your call.'

She disappears out the door with the tiniest jingle of her bracelet.

I look down at the charm in my hand.

She says it's for luck.

And I think it's already working.

27

Isla

I'm staring at the book. I haven't opened it since Rome.

Not when we got back. Not when I checked into the hotel. Not during the cozy, productive days I spent holed up writing and eating pretzel sticks in bed. Not even after I gave Luca the cornicello and threatened him with a fake hex.

But if I really want to know more—about this book, about us, about anything—I have to, at the very least . . . peek.

Ugh.

Back when this all started, I was obsessed. I wanted answers. Why the book existed. Why it chose me. What it meant. I was practically begging the universe to give me a cheat sheet. Some instruction to follow back to the life I was supposed to live.

But now, there's also Luca. And the scary part is . . . he matters now. Not just as a character in this story the universe may or may not be writing. But as a real person. Who says things that disarm me. Who listens like I'm not a burden. Who makes me laugh, and remembers my favourite iced tea, and somehow makes me feel less alone in the weirdest corners of my grief.

Which means whatever I read next in this book—whatever letter, prophecy, clue, or curse—it won't just be intriguing any more. It'll be terrifying.

Because if it says something bad, it'll feel like a doomed love story. And if it says something good, then it might be worse. Because then I'll have to wonder if I'd believe it.

There's no point delaying it any further. I take another step towards the book, and take it in my hands. I flip through the anonymous love letters, eager to go to the last pages. And there, I see a letter directed to me, from Luca, dated three weeks from now. The day I return to Manila.

Dear Isla,

I promised myself I wouldn't fall for another woman this way. In the way that I would willingly throw away everything for her. That I would be willing to uproot myself for her.

But I guess, in the end, I'm not as nonchalant as I thought. I love with all my heart, and all my heart wants to be with you. I don't know what's written in the stars or what this book really is. But I know this: I love you.

In the way that makes me want to stay up and cook for you when you've had a bad day. In the way that makes me want to learn every version of your laugh. In the way that makes me want to be near you.

So I'm meeting with that investor in Manila. I'm building something new. A restaurant, yes. But more than that—a life. With you, if you'll have me.

I'll love you in every city.

L

I check the next page. There's nothing else. Nothing new, except this one. What a heavy, loaded letter. There really is nothing else in here. I can't believe it. It's like the book is giving me space to spiral.

And spiral I do.

Because what do you even *do* with something like that? I close the book gently, like it might explode if I snap it shut too hard.

If there's anything I've learned in the week I've spent here, it's that the book, as crazy, as magical, as nonsensical as it is, sometimes can be true. Some letters were prophecies. Like the ones about me arguing with his father, or how I'll spill the coffee in Rome. Little moments like that were written before they happened.

But there were also letters that didn't happen. Scenes that changed. Feelings that flickered and disappeared. Sometimes they vanish altogether—like the book is revising itself. Editing our story in real time.

Which raises the million-euro question: Is it changing based on the way we feel, or is it manipulating our feelings? Because I, for one, am very easily persuaded. You give me a magical premise and a poetic metaphor, and I will follow it off a cliff.

I shake my head.

I ignore the letter. I ignore the book. I ignore every thought I'm having because of it. I still put it in my bag, though, because I want to make a plan on how I'll navigate it.

I walk out of my hotel to bask in the Florence air.

As beautiful as Rome is, I think I prefer Florence. It's less . . . expectant.

Rome feels like the kind of place you must experience as soon as you step foot in it. So many attractions, and each one vying for your attention. It's a cinematic masterpiece. Whereas Florence is more like a handwritten letter. It's slower, softer, and more personal in a way. Like a beautiful thing you get to experience just by walking along its streets. You don't go around looking for attractions, you just, somehow, discover them. If that makes sense.

I cross the street from my hotel and walk into a cafe I've passed a few times. Situated on the narrow cobblestone lane, it has flowers curling around the windows and a little hand-painted sign that reads 'Caffè Patrizia'. I walk past the two tables placed outside and walk in.

It smells like orange zest and espresso. It is small, with just two more tables, like on the outside. The barista wears a bandana with little lemons on it and hums something that might be an old lullaby. She's accompanied by an elderly woman wearing the same bandana.

I order a scone and a cappuccino, then settle at the table by the window. Just a few minutes later, I'm halfway into my first bite—crumbs already clinging to the corner of my mouth—when a woman approaches me.

She has long, sun-bleached blonde hair, piercing blue eyes, and a flowy summer dress fit for a magazine cover. She looks like she belongs in Capri, or maybe in a *Vogue* spread called 'Effortless Italian Summer'.

'Isla?' she asks, carefully.

I blink. 'Yes?'

She smiles nervously. 'Sorry, I heard you say your name at the counter, and I'm just—taking a wild chance here.' Even her accent is beautiful.

'Okay . . .' I say slowly, gesturing to the empty seat across from me. 'Want to sit?'

She does. And then, clearly, calmly says, 'I'm Dahlia.'

And just like that, Florence feels like Rome. Like a cinematic masterpiece with an unexpected plot twist.

I want to laugh. Or cry. Or spill my cappuccino in rebellion.

Because *of course.* Of course, just as I'm thinking I'm in luck, and that I might actually have a chance with Luca, the woman of his dreams shows up, in a dress that's probably worth more than my rent.

Fate, you funny little bastard. You didn't have to go this hard.

I blink at her. Smile, somehow. I'm trying to be composed, but my brain is doing five rounds of cartwheels while painfully screaming. I can't decide if I want to crawl under the table or order another scone or ten.

Now, to be fair—because I am a feminist and a grown woman and generally not an evil witch—I won't judge Dahlia for breaking Luca's heart. I don't know her side. All I've heard is what Nonna told me: that she left, and that it shattered him.

But I also know people aren't just villains or victims. Sometimes we're both.

I gather the courage in the deepest pits of my brain, and say, 'Dahlia . . . as in, Luca's Dahlia?' It tastes bitter on my tongue.

Why are you being bitter, Isla?

'No, like, the Dahlia who left him,' she says sheepishly. 'What are the chances that I'd find you here?'

You won't believe. 'You know about me?' I ask.

'This is gonna sound weird . . .' she trails off.

'Girl, try me,' I say with a chuckle.

She laughs a little too, and I can feel her loosen up a bit. 'Well,' she starts, 'I live in Spain, but I have family here, so I normally come here for a vacation. Last year, I met him in his restaurant, and we had a little more than a month of just . . . love.' She sighs. 'I never believed in whirlwind romances until that time in my life.'

She pauses for a while, as if remembering their relationship. I hate how I'm feeling some really ugly emotions right now. Like, evil-witch level of emotions. I have absolutely no right to feel jealous of this *gorgeous* woman.

'One day, when he was busy at the restaurant and I was taking a walk,' Dahlia continues, 'I found a street . . . and a book.'

Oh.

No.

'What book?' I ask breathlessly.

She looks at me carefully. 'A strange one. With love letters from strangers. I thought it was fiction until I found one with Luca's name on it. Writing love letters. Except it wasn't me he was writing to . . . it was you. I know how crazy this sounds, but—'

'Not crazy,' I say, pulling out the book from my tote.

Dahlia's eyes grow wide. 'You found it too.' She's silent for a while, just staring at the book, awestruck. 'Is that how you found him?'

I nod slowly. 'I'm here on vacation, and, like you, I found Via Lullina. Strange street. Even stranger book. I found his and my name, and I tracked him down. He's been helping me find out about it,' I say.

'So you're not . . . together?'

I don't know how to respond. The scone feels like sawdust in my mouth now. 'No,' I say, looking down at the book. 'Anyway, is this book the reason you left?' I can't blame her if it is. I wouldn't want to mess with fate like that.

'I didn't know who you were,' she says while nodding. 'But I was gutted. He was obviously meant for someone else, so I . . . I left.'

Silence balloons between us.

Not because I don't believe her. I absolutely do. But because I don't know what I'm supposed to feel. Gratitude? Guilt? Bewilderment?

'You left him because of the book?' I ask, careful not to sound accusatory.

'I left him because . . . it felt right to,' she says. 'I thought I was doing the noble thing. The selfless thing. But now, I'm not so sure.'

I look at her—really look. She doesn't seem like a rival. If anything, she seems like someone who's also been haunted by this cursed fairytale of a book. She looks tired. Not from travel, but from carrying this secret around for a year.

'Is that why you're here now?' I ask in a voice lighter than a whisper.

'To find closure,' she replies. 'To see Luca. To tell him the truth. I thought maybe . . . if I explained everything, I could finally let it go.'

I nod slowly. I get it. More than I want to admit.

And deep inside, a tiny part of me—the petty, insecure, very human part—whispers: *What if he still loves her? What if she tells him everything and he chooses her, after all this?*

I take a breath. 'You should talk to him. He deserves to know the truth. Just . . . be gentle.'

She nods, then smiles at me. 'Thank you, Isla. Really.'

Before she can stand up, and before I can leave with my cappuccino and my dignity, the door to this little cafe opens to test my ability to breathe.

'There you are,' Luca says, walking towards me, hair a little tousled like he's been running around the block. 'You weren't in your hotel, I—'

He stops short.

Because Dahlia turns around. And the world tilts on its axis. Luca freezes and his eyes flick from her to me and back again.

Three people.

One cafe.

Too much history.

And absolutely nowhere to hide.

28

Luca

There are moments you expect to be difficult. Like telling your father you don't need his apology after twenty-three years. Or opening a restaurant after a global pandemic. Or letting someone in after a year of keeping your heart in a goddamn vault.

And then there are moments that sucker punch you.

Dahlia turning around to face me in a cafe in Florence is one of those moments.

My feet are rooted to the floor and the air has thinned, somehow, like someone vacuum-sealed the entire room and I can't breathe. I look at her—the long summer dress, the hair tucked behind her ear—all of it the same. And then I look at Isla, sitting across from her, holding her coffee. Her face is unreadable.

'What . . .' My voice comes out hoarse. I clear my throat. 'What are you doing here?'

'I—' Dahlia starts, but she's interrupted by Isla's sudden movement.

'Sorry, this feels like an intimate thing,' she says, picking up her coffee and the book. What's the book doing here? Her eyes lock with mine, and she smiles. 'I'll leave you guys to talk.'

'No, you don't have to go,' I say too soon.

'Really, it's no biggie!' she says in that usual chirpy tone she has, but her eyes are betraying her. Nothing about those big brown eyes is chirpy today. She walks past Dahlia and tells her, very politely, 'It's nice to meet you, Dahlia!'

When she reaches me, her eyes drift to the amulet on my neck. The cornicello she gave me, and her lips quirk up softly.

'You really don't have to leave. This'll be quick, I just—' I stammer. I almost reach out for her, but then I hold back.

'Let's just meet later if you're still up for it.' She says it with such finality that I don't counter her. I just nod.

And then I watch her leave, in her pink linen shorts and a matching top, as her skin glows and her hair sways in the breeze outside. She crosses the street back to her hotel, and I want to follow her. But I don't, because there's a ghost from my past I have to deal with.

I turn to Dahlia. She's still stunning, I have to admit. The golden hair, blue eyes. They could still captivate a human being. But they don't have the same chokehold they had on me last year.

I walk towards her and sit in Isla's recently vacated chair, which is still warm. It smells faintly of citrus, like her perfume.

'You wear amulets now?' Dahlia jokes, nodding to the red horn around my neck. 'Didn't take you for the superstitious type.'

She's trying. I can tell. To make it light. Familiar. But it only makes things feel heavier.

I wave her off with a smile. 'It's a gift,' I say.

When Isla came into the restaurant last night to give me this, I didn't want to wear it. I laughed and rolled my eyes. But this morning, I woke up thinking about her laugh. About how her accent sounds when she attempts to speak Italian. And so I put this on. Not because I believe in luck, but because, somehow, I believe in her.

I'm not even sure what I feel—if it's love yet. But I know I want more time. I want to keep discovering her. And whatever that book is, whatever fate thinks it's doing, I'm not letting it take the choice away from me this time. That's why I tracked her down today, to tell her I'll still help her until she's convinced that the book should be completely ignored.

'You look better,' Dahlia says, fidgeting with the napkin in front of her.

I sigh. 'Why are you really here, Dahlia?' I ask. 'And how did you meet her?'

'I owe you the truth,' she says as she looks up at me.

I don't respond, giving her time to continue. After a few seconds of silence and waiting, she does. 'I left because of the book.' She looks out towards Isla's hotel.

I look at her in bewilderment. She knows about the book. When I don't respond, she goes on to tell me about how she found it. Like Isla, she stumbled upon a street that doesn't exist. Unlike Isla, though, she didn't tell me.

'I'm sorry I didn't tell you. I should've.'

I nod slowly. 'Sì,' I say. 'You should've.'

I think about the times I wondered why. The times I blamed myself. Like I had for my father. It may have been just a fling to someone else, but for me, it was another reminder that I'm not good enough to stay for. That maybe I really am the problem.

Over the past months, I tried to rebuild myself. Busied myself in the kitchen, established routines, ignored any possibility of someone entering my life. Shut the door before they could even enter.

And then Isla came along. And I could have rejected her, but I didn't. I couldn't. I couldn't be another person who turns someone away when they need something—anything. Even if I didn't understand what she needed yet.

'I came here for closure,' Dahlia says. 'But I admit that seeing you now is making me regret everything. I should've told you. I should've trusted you. But instead I . . . I panicked. I thought the universe was handing me the truth on a platter. That maybe I was just a detour. That you were destined for someone else.' She sighs.

I don't know what to tell her. Part of me goes back to the moments we shared. I look at her face, her eyes, and everything replays. Every moment she spun around in the kitchen while I cooked. Every moment she asked me to do something I would never do if it weren't for her. And then I think about what could be. If I give her another chance. I expect to see it in my head. The future we can have together.

But she's not there any more.

'Do you love her?' Dahlia asks quietly.

This time, I answer. 'I don't know,' I say.

'But she's your soulmate,' she says with a dry chuckle.

'Honestly, Dahlia, I think it's you. No one has ever swept me up like that before. No one's ever swept me off my feet the way you did. Being with you felt like wind and fire and every wild thing I've ever wanted.'

She blinks, startled, like she didn't expect that.

'But that's the thing about soulmates,' I continue. 'I don't believe in them.'

'No?'

'No.' I shake my head. 'I don't even believe in the book. I believe in showing up. In putting in the work. In choosing someone not because of some damn universe, but because you want it. Love is . . . it's . . .' My throat tightens. 'It's something you build, day by day. Decision by decision.' I shrug. 'It's not magic. No matter what you—or Isla—believe, it's not fate.'

Dahlia nods. I don't know if she agrees with me or if she's making her own conclusions in her head.

I let out a breath. 'And maybe I don't love Isla yet. Or maybe I already do, and I'm just scared to say it out loud. But what I do know is I'm not going backwards. Not when something real might be unfolding right in front of me.'

Silence stretches between us.

Dahlia exhales, slow and steady. 'Well,' she says, rising from her chair, 'I'll be in Florence for a while. A week, maybe two. I don't expect anything, Luca. I just . . . wanted to see you. Say the things I couldn't before. And if you ever want to talk again—if there's anything left unsaid—I'm staying at the hotel by the Arno.'

I nod, quietly. 'I appreciate that,' I say. And I mean it. Even if I'm not entirely sure how I feel, or what I'm supposed to do with any of this. But I appreciate the honesty. The effort. The strange, full-circle symmetry of it all.

She lingers for a second, then picks up her bag and the now-empty coffee cup. 'Goodbye for now,' she says.

'Goodbye, Dahlia.'

I watch her step out of the cafe, the hem of her dress catching in the breeze. For a long time, I thought I'd chase that woman to the ends of the earth. I did, in a way. Even after she left, some part of me stayed waiting at the door, in case she ever came back.

And yet now, watching her walk away, I don't feel the urge to run after her. I don't feel broken. Just . . . still.

I've only known Isla for a week. Seven days. That's barely enough time to learn someone's favourite colour, let alone what their laugh sounds like at midnight. But what I feel for her—it's different. Deeper in a way I can't explain. It's not wildfire like it was with Dahlia. It's something else. Just a slow light.

Love doesn't follow a timeline. It doesn't care about logic or pacing or what promises you made to yourself in the aftermath of heartbreak. I told myself I wouldn't fall again. That I couldn't afford it. Because when I fall, I don't do it halfway. I go all in.

And that means the fall always hurts.

But maybe this time, I don't have to fall. Maybe this time, I can just . . . walk.

I step out into the street, crossing towards Isla's hotel.

This day started like any ordinary day. But I've already worn an amulet and met the ghost of my past, all before I had my morning coffee.

I guess a lot *can* happen in a day.

29

Isla

Come on, come on, come *on*.

I flip through the book like someone in a Nicholas Sparks adaptation who just realized she only has forty-eight hours to stop a wedding. Or to live. Whatever, I'm not even reading. Just skimming for a letter that starts with 'Dear Isla'. I'm pretty sure the book will spit out a new letter from Luca telling me he's gone to follow his heart or something.

Because who wouldn't follow that gorgeous bombshell to the ends of the Earth? I should've given him a luggage tag instead of that stupid cornicello. At least he could've used that for his future romantic getaways with Dahlia. But *no*, I had to be sentimental and cute. Why did I even give him that? For good luck? Protection? A passive-aggressive charm to remember me by while he falls in love with someone else?

My phone rings all of a sudden, and I jump at the sound. I answer mindlessly without checking who it is.

'What is it this time?' Harriet says, and I suddenly remember I texted her earlier while I was walking (casually, if I may add), so I did not look back at Luca and Dahlia. 'Are you even writing the book?'

'Yes I am! But that's not the issue,' I say.

'Okay . . . then what's the update with your hot pasta daddy?'

'First of all, he's not mine,' I groan, flopping dramatically onto my bed, narrowly missing the spine of the book digging into my ribcage. 'He never was. He never will be. Because now? There's a real-life Barbie in the picture.'

'Oooh. A curveball. Tell me more.'

'She's tall, she's blonde, she's effortless. She wears long summer dresses like she just stepped out of a Tuscan vineyard. She looks like someone with a second refrigerator full of spring water and antioxidants.'

She snorts. 'And how's your self-esteem?'

'Like a damp tissue.'

Harriet hums. 'So let me guess. He didn't chase after you. He stayed to talk to her.'

'Yes.'

'Did you give him the opportunity not to?'

I pause.

'Shut up.'

She cackles. 'Look. You like him. It's painfully obvious—'

'I don't! I can't. I'm not supposed to,' I say, sitting upright and removing all the strands of hair from my face. 'Who the hell can like someone in just seven days? I need more foundation for my feelings, Har.'

'Please. I've slept with guys after meeting them for seven minutes.'

'It's not the same!'

'Whatever, your constellation-based beliefs are null and void.' I hear a crunch. 'So, as I was saying before you rudely interrupted me,' she continues, 'you like him, and he likes you too.'

'What makes you say that?'

'You don't just trauma dump to strangers, sister.' I had obviously called her the moment we returned from Rome and told her all about the Gianicolo moment.

I sigh and get up from the bed to walk to the window. The Florence sky is scorching, the buildings catching the light like they've been brushed with antique paint. Down below, a kid runs in an alley with a scoop of gelato so large it looks structurally unsound. I envy that kid. He knows what he wants. Me? I'm floundering in emotional quicksand. I would give half my life savings and maybe my pinky finger to be in a room facing the cafe right now.

'Look,' Harriet says when I don't respond, 'you like each other—*don't* argue with me. So maybe . . . don't spiral yet?' she offers gently. 'This isn't the end of the book, Isla. You're, like, barely halfway through.'

'How do you know that?' I pick up my coffee from the table—the one I managed to take out of the cafe before *the* situation.

'I don't. I'm just trying to play into your magic book thing. It's so hard to be enthusiastic for you when I'm not there. Especially when there's alleged magic involved.'

I let out a frustrated sigh, fingers threading through my hair as I circle the room again. 'I know you still don't believe me.' I take a sip from the coffee, and it's disgustingly lukewarm.

'It's not that I don't believe you,' she says. 'It's just . . . Okay, it *is* that I don't believe you. But *I believe you believe it*, and that's what matters. Also, you sound like you're about to combust, so clearly something real is happening.'

I stop in my tracks.

'Because I feel like . . .' I trail off, heart thudding. 'Like I'm on the edge of something big,' I whisper. 'Like whatever happens next might change everything. I don't even know if I'm ready. But I can't look away.'

'But seriously,' Harriet adds, 'whatever happens, don't let your fear be louder than your instincts. If you want something . . . run at it.'

I smile quietly, and I think that she's right. I can do this. If it's written in the stars, then great! If not, then . . .

I don't know.

Harriet and I talk about anything and everything. I tell her about the progress of my actual novel, my craving for rice and sinigang, and everything in between. We laugh. We comfort. We distract. She crunches through her chips, and I pace the room like I'm waiting for a sign from the heavens—or at least from the magical book, which frankly has been suspiciously quiet for the last hour.

When the call ends, I stare at my reflection in the black screen of the TV, catching the slouch of my shoulders, the frizz of my hair, the anxious twist in my mouth. I try to straighten up. Tilt my chin. Practise a smile that you give to someone who might be about to gently tell you he doesn't see a future with you.

It isn't long until I hear a knock on my door. My heart does something deeply inconvenient in my chest. I speed-walk to the door, stub my toe on the leg of the bed (because of course I do), and nearly spill my now-cold cappuccino as I place it down on the table. The cup wobbles but rights itself.

When I open it, Luca's there.

Wearing the same dark shirt from earlier, hair messily perfect, eyes unreadable. And—oh my God—the cornicello amulet is still around his neck.

'I'm still in,' he says, voice low.

I blink. 'In?'

'For the book,' he clarifies. 'I'll still help you. If you still want me to.'

I step aside and gesture for him to come in, which he does.

We sit on opposite ends of the little bed, and it feels weirdly formal. Like we're about to draft a peace treaty.

'I thought you might not . . .' I start, then trail off.

'I know,' he says. 'And I thought maybe I wouldn't. But the truth is . . . I want to figure this out too. I want to know what this book is. Why it chose us. Or you. Or whoever.'

I nod. 'You believe Dahlia's theory then? That the book is a warning? That it shows us a future that we're supposed to avoid?'

Luca's jaw tightens slightly. 'I think the book shows you something. But it's not fate. It's just . . . manipulation. It's what you do after you read it that matters.'

I study him. The way he's fidgeting with the cornicello, twisting it between his fingers.

'What did you tell her?' I ask before I can stop myself.

He purses his lips. 'I told her I think she's my actual soulmate.'

'Oh,' I say. So he's just helping me decode the book as a friend? Why does it hurt? It's not supposed to hurt.

'But,' he says softly, 'I also told her that I don't believe in soulmates.'

I blink. 'Wait—what?'

He leans back, lets his head rest against the cushion, and closes his eyes briefly before answering. 'I told her that she made me fall so fast, it hurt. It was fire and wind and lightning. And that kind of love . . . it burns too quickly.'

I stare at him, the weight of his words hanging in the air between us.

'And real love?' I ask, more curious than bitter now. 'You know what real love is?'

His eyes open, meet mine. 'I think I do,' he says, quieter this time. 'I think it's something you build. Not fall into. It's a choice. Over and over.'

He twists the pendant one last time and lets it go. It rests against his chest.

'I don't know what this thing is between us,' he admits. 'I just know I didn't want it to end before it even began.'

My heart does a weird, hopeful flip. But I don't smile. Not yet.

Instead, I lean back and look out the window. 'That sounds dangerously close to romantic, Luca.'

He chuckles under his breath. 'Well . . . Princess Ann fell in love in a day. Imagine what a week would do.'

I laugh. 'Is that your new favourite movie now?'

'Close,' he says with a chuckle. And then he sighs. 'Do you want to take a break from all this?'

'All of what?'

'The book. The Dahlia encounter. *Rome.*' When he says that, I realize that the past few days were unbelievably tiring.

'What do you suggest?' I ask.

He grins. 'The Uffizi.'

30

Isla

The Uffizi Gallery is one of the most famous museums in the world. I'm not only here because of the novel I'm writing (though that *is* the main reason), but I'm genuinely fascinated by art and history. I'm not an expert, not even close. I'm pretty sure *The Birth of Venus* is the only painting I can name in here. But there was a phase in my life when I spent days googling the difference between Baroque and Rococo. So even a novice like me knows that seeing historical artworks lumped in one building can make anyone feel giddy.

'Marco's on duty today,' Luca says as we make our way through the Florence crowd. 'He's a tour guide for multiple attractions in Florence. Sometimes in the Vatican.' He chuckles when he sees my shocked face.

'Your friend slash bartender Marco?'

Well, he looked like a bartender, that's for sure.

Luca nods. 'He's also an art history graduate and a really good painter.'

My mouth opens wider.

'Yup,' he continues. 'He just finished his Master's in Fine Arts. Or History. I forget.'

'Wow,' I say, 'who would've thought?'

He just shrugs and smiles.

The moment I step into the Uffizi's courtyard, I pause. It doesn't look like a museum—at least, not the kind I'm used to. No grand dome. No ornate facade.

I'm standing between two long, imposing buildings, and the space stretches out like a narrow corridor, gently curving towards the river at the far end.

The architecture is stark and geometric, with clean lines and rhythmically spaced windows that feel more bureaucratic than artistic. The stone is grey and worn, but still elegant. Tall columns rise from the ground, giving the space an almost theatrical symmetry. Statues of artists peer out from niches like quiet sentinels, watching as tourists fumble with cameras and maps. Overhead, the sky is framed perfectly between the buildings, like a living canvas.

We reach the entrance of the museum and are immediately greeted by Marco. He's standing outside, wearing a suit.

'Welcome to the Uffizi, my friends,' he says. 'So nice of you to come here.'

'We needed a break from all the book-decoding. And I really did plan on coming here,' I say, looking around. 'Though, I have to admit, I expected it to look more artistic.'

'Fun fact: The term Uffizi translates to 'offices'. Because this building was originally built to serve as the office for the magistrates, before it opened as a public museum in 1769.'

'Okay, you're cool. And that's amazing,' I say.

'Wait till you get inside,' Marco says. He pats Luca's shoulder and says, 'I'm heading a private tour right now, but I'll catch you later,' Marco says, waving goodbye.

'Do you come here often?' I ask.

Luca smiles. 'Yes. History nerd, remember?' He leads me to the staircase with surprising ease, dodging tourists left and right.

We reach the next level of the museum, and this time, I can feel the excitement brewing. There's a long corridor that stretches further than my eyes can see. Along the corridor are doors with labels, probably a homage to the most famous artist in the room.

We walk slowly, taking it all in. There's something deeply humbling about being surrounded by so much human achievement. These paintings survived plagues, wars, heartbreak, power struggles. And now, here they are, hanging on pristine walls, with audio guides buzzing in six languages and tourists walking by in sneakers.

I pause in front of a portrait of a woman. Her expression is calm but guarded, her fingers delicately clasped together on her lap like she's hiding a secret she'll never tell.

'She looks like she's got a better poker face than those alive do,' I murmur.

'She probably does,' Luca says. 'Women in Renaissance portraits always look like they know something we don't.'

I glance at him. 'Maybe she knows how this weird book thing ends.'

He chuckles. 'Then we should've started here.'

I roll my eyes at him, but I'm smiling. And with that, we step into the first room: Sala di Giotto.

The temperature dips slightly as we pass through the threshold. The walls are lined with gold-leaf altarpieces, saints with impossibly long fingers, halos glowing like actual light sources.

'I feel like I'm being watched,' I whisper, because it's too quiet. I glance at Luca to see him, in fact, watching me. 'Apparently I am.'

He chuckles. 'You're just . . . so nice to admire. Your face speaks for you. It's incredible,' he says, walking towards me with his arms crossed.

'Thanks?' I say.

'That wasn't supposed to sound creepy, I swear.'

'It's fine,' I reply, trying not to remember the way he said I was nice to admire. 'We're in a room full of saints with penetrating gazes. You're, like, fourth on the list.'

We chuckle as we make our way out of this hall. We step into a smaller gallery with softer lighting. The walls are lined with delicate portraits, most of them featuring people with very animated expressions, as most Renaissance paintings are.

'Look at that guy,' I say, stopping in front of a portrait of a man in a knight's armour, looking uncomfortable. 'He looks like he's thinking about switching professions.'

'*I should've taken law like my brother*,' Luca replies. I snort, not expecting him to indulge me. He looks at me and says, 'How about that one?' He points to a painting of a dinner scene where one guy is clearly yelling and everyone else looks tense. 'What are they thinking?'

'Duh,' I say. 'Obviously they're thinking, *Bartholomew's sourdough is a war crime. Someone should say something.*' I put in an obnoxious accent for effect.

Luca laughs—loud enough for another tourist to look our way. I put my index finger on my lips to shush him.

We walk out and into another room, continuing our game. 'How about him?' Luca asks, pointing to a man holding a golden compass while looking confused.

I chuckle. 'He obviously went into a room and forgot why. Happens to the best of us.' I shrug.

I don't know when we started playing this game, but it's better than thinking about the other things. Like the book. Like Dahlia. Like the fact that I am in Florence with a man who is slowly becoming my undoing.

It's disarming and satisfying at the same time, seeing Luca laugh at my jokes. Surprising too, every time he butts in with one of his own. His jokes are especially funnier because he doesn't usually make them.

'What's he thinking?' I say, pointing to a man holding a lute but not playing it.

Luca narrows his eyes, then says, in the most neutral expression, 'He's thinking, *If I start playing, she'll know I only know Wonderwall.*'

That makes me snort. Loudly. Enough for another tourist to look at us with disgust.

'Wonderwall?' I hiss. 'Are you kidding me? How did you come up with that?'

He shrugs, smug. 'I contain multitudes.'

We weave through more rooms, more jokes, more paintings, and more moments of awe and wonder. I still can't believe I'm here, in Italy, making fun of Renaissance paintings with Luca.

We keep walking, and the room opens into something grander. I check the label on the door, and it says, *Da Vinci.*

'Oh, okay. I thought his paintings were in the Louvre,' I say, more to myself than Luca.

'His paintings are everywhere. Like most painters.'

'What's here?' I ask as we enter the room, with a spotlight on three paintings, one on each wall.

'This is the most famous one,' he says, leading us to the painting on the right. It's one of Mary, I think, and a winged stranger delivering a message.

'That's the moment the angel announces that the Virgin Mary will carry a baby,' Luca says.

'Jeez, imagine getting *that* information,' I say, more to myself. 'I'd probably fake a faint to buy myself some time.'

'Probably why you weren't the chosen,' Luca says with a chuckle. I snort and walk a step closer to see the information card. It reads 'The Annunciation'.

I didn't realize I said it out loud until Luca agrees and says, 'Yup. This one always fascinates me. Check it out.'

He puts both of his hands on my shoulders and leans a bit closer to me to whisper in my ear, 'Look at Mary's arm.' I shiver at the closeness. 'What do you notice?'

'Uh . . . weirdly long,' I manage to say.

'Exactly!' he says, excited like a golden retriever 'But now look here.' He guides me a few steps to the right. And suddenly, the cursed noodle arm becomes . . . totally normal. Proportional. Beautiful, even.

'What kind of witchcraft,' I breathe.

'It was originally hung in a corner of a church,' Luca explains. 'So Da Vinci painted it with the angle in mind. From this spot, it looks right.'

I blink at the painting, then at him. He's beaming like he made it. His excitement is borderline contagious. And infuriatingly adorable.

I look back at Mary. Her hand is mid-air, delicate and calm, accepting divine responsibility with a grace I absolutely would not have. I would've panicked, cried, or demanded to speak to the archangel's supervisor.

And still—there's something about her expression. That moment frozen between what she was and what she's about to become. The whole painting hums with it.

Maybe this is the universe speaking and yelling at me in Renaissance metaphors. Telling me that things make sense when you stop looking straight at them. Shift a little. Tilt your head. Rethink the weird arm.

Luca's hands finally drift off my shoulders. Slowly, like they're reluctant to go. Or maybe that's just my wishful thinking. Either way, I feel them long after they're gone. A soft, ghostly warmth that makes my stomach do a little somersault and my thoughts spiral like a broken slinky.

For a second, I pretend I'm still looking at the painting. But really, I'm trying to breathe like a normal person.

Perspective. It's not just a buzzword my therapist uses. And maybe it's not just Mary who needed it. Maybe we need it. Me and Luca. The book. This trip. Life.

31

Luca

She's still staring at Mary's arm, brows drawn together like she's trying to solve a riddle only she can hear. Meanwhile, I'm stuck wondering if I held her shoulders too long. I probably did. It wasn't intentional—I mean, it was. But it just . . . happened.

'Where to next?' she asks, finally turning to me, and I let out a breath of relief.

'*The Birth of Venus*,' I say, a little too quickly. 'It's one floor down.'

Her face lights up. 'Finally, something I know. The lady in the seashell. I've been preparing for this moment since my Tumblr era.'

I smile. 'Botticelli would be thrilled to know his work lives on through teenage mood boards.'

We walk in step, our shoes tapping softly against the polished floors. The crowd has thinned out now—just a few lingering visitors trailing behind tour guides or standing in awe. The late afternoon sun spills through the tall windows, turning everything it touches into something a little more holy, like it functions as a personalized halo for the paintings.

'Let's walk through the other rooms until we get there,' Isla says, already half a room ahead of me, her voice echoing with the kind of enthusiasm that makes it impossible not to follow.

She disappears briefly around a doorway, then pops back in to wave me forward like we're kids sneaking through an unlocked castle. Her energy is bright—like she's always mid-thought, mid-laugh, mid-falling into something.

In the next gallery, she stops abruptly in front of a dramatic painting. *Judith Beheading Holofernes*. Judith's face is determined, her arm steady as she slices through the neck of a man who looks both terrified and resigned.

'Well, that's . . . tragic,' Isla says, tilting her head and scrunching her nose. 'That's not Venus in a seashell.'

I step beside her. 'That's actually a really interesting one. One of my favourites, actually. Very underrated.'

She turns to me with a raised eyebrow. 'You like the painting of a beheading?'

I shrug, hands in my pockets. 'You would too, if you knew the story.'

'Okay, murder me with the backstory then,' she says, gesturing to the painting. 'Convince me.' She wiggles her fingers in front of her face.

I glance at her, then back at Judith. 'Holofernes, the *poor* guy,' I quote, 'was a general sent to destroy Judith's city. She seduced him, got him drunk, and then killed him in his tent. Saved everyone.'

Her mouth opens. 'Wow.' She looks back at the painting, in awe. 'Go, Judith,' she says. She takes out a little notebook—the same one she's been using to jot down notes for her books. She looks so focused, so much so that her mouth is moving as she recites whatever she's writing down, and so I give her a minute. I drift. Not far, just a quick orbit around the room, scanning the other paintings. They're all intense in their own way—scenes of sacrifice and judgment, of martyrdom and vengeance. But I keep glancing back at her.

She's still standing in front of Judith. And now that I've told her the story, she's looking at the painting like she understands something about it that she didn't before. Like maybe she sees herself in it, just a little.

When she finally closes the notebook, she sighs. Not a tired sigh. Something else.

'I think that's my favourite now,' she says, turning to me. 'And not just because she decapitated someone.'

'Oh, good. I was starting to worry.'

She smirks. 'Don't worry. I don't have a sword.'

'That we know of.'

She grins and starts walking again, back into the maze of art and time. I fall into step beside her. We walk a few minutes more, Isla still making up funny notes about the paintings.

And then we reach the doorway that leads to Botticelli's room. I spot the familiar soft pinks and seafoam greens through the arch.

'There she is,' I say. 'Your seashell girl.'

Isla lets out a theatrical gasp. 'Finally.'

I chuckle as we walk inside and towards *The Birth of Venus.* Floating on her clamshell, her hair like waves, everything soft and gold and impossibly surreal.

Isla stops in front of it, a reverent kind of silence settling over her. She doesn't pull out her notebook this time. She just stares. I watch her take it in.

I've been in this room far too many times to look at this painting in awe. So I just look at her, and watch her experience it.

After a few minutes, I step closer to her. The sound of our shoes on the museum floor barely registers now, muffled by the high ceilings. Dust floats lazily through shafts of golden light, cast from tall windows that line the gallery's upper walls.

Venus stands before us, soft and luminous, her body impossibly serene as she floats on her scallop shell across a sea so gentle, it seems to whisper. The wind gods swirl beside her in a frenzy of motion, while a nymph waits at the shore with a billowing cloth.

Isla hasn't said anything in a while—just standing there with her arms loosely crossed, as if she's afraid speaking too soon will break whatever spell she's under.

'What are you thinking?' I ask, voice low.

She doesn't look at me. Her eyes stay on Venus. 'I'm thinking she looks surprised.'

I blink. That's . . . not what I thought she'd say. 'Surprised?'

She nods, glancing briefly at me. 'Yeah. Like no one told her she was about to be born this way,' Isla goes on, her tone soft but certain. 'Like, imagine being a full-grown goddess and suddenly—bam—you're standing naked on a seashell with the wind in your face and no idea what to do next.'

She shakes her head gently. 'Everyone always talks about how beautiful she is. How she's this symbol of love and perfection and femininity. And yeah, sure, they're right. But look closer.'

I do.

'She doesn't look joyful,' she continues. 'She's not exactly sad either. But there's this look—like she's bracing for something. Like she doesn't know if she's being celebrated . . . or sacrificed.'

The light shifts across the painting as a cloud moves outside. I squint and, for the first time, I see it too. That moment of tension. Of uncertainty. The slight tightening of her mouth. The way her body turns slightly inward, like she's unsure whether to step forward or fold into herself.

'I think,' Isla says, voice quieter now, almost like she's talking to herself, 'that sometimes we're thrown into things we didn't ask for. Love. Grief. Reinventing ourselves after everything changes. Showing up on a giant clam. We just . . . wake up there. In it. And we're expected to smile and pose and be grateful. Or worse, be graceful.'

I don't say anything for a moment. I'm not sure I can. She's cracked something open, and it's so profound I'm scared a single word might collapse it. I remember what she said about her sister. About the guilt she carries. And it hits me—grief is like waking up on a seashell. Completely exposed. With people expecting you to move forward when you don't even know which way the shore is.

'That's not what I expected you to say,' I admit finally.

She finally glances at me, her expression gentler now. 'What did you expect?'

I shrug, trying to play it cool even though my chest is tight. 'I don't know. Something about seashell splinters. Or how much conditioner it would take to keep that hair under control.'

She laughs—a short, bright sound that bounces softly off the gallery walls. 'Well, yeah. That's a ridiculous amount of volume. Like, she's definitely born with it, but also—maybe it's Maybelline.'

I grin, the tension easing just a little, but her eyes still hold that reflective edge.

'And that shell?' she says, tilting her head. 'Zero lumbar support. Just a terrible ergonomic situation.'

I chuckle. 'So tragic.'

'But also,' she adds, voice softening again, 'I've just been thinking a lot about the way we look at things. Like . . . perspective really is everything, right?'

She gestures vaguely behind her, towards the doorway we just came from. 'Back there, with Mary's arm? That felt like a metaphor. It only made sense when we shifted. And now . . . maybe Venus isn't just this perfect beauty standard. Maybe she's a symbol of arrival. Of becoming. Of not knowing what the hell comes next. Of being okay anyway.'

She pauses, fingers toying absently with the corner of her sleeve.

'I think I needed that reminder,' she says. 'That sometimes you don't need to know the plan. Sometimes you just have to stand on the seashell and let the wind do what it does.'

She says it like it's no big deal. Like she didn't just give voice to something I've never found words for.

We stand in silence again, this time not heavy, but full. Like the space between two thoughts. The gallery feels quieter now, though I know it isn't. It's just us—slowed down. Softened by something we can't name.

'Hey,' she says suddenly, nudging me with her elbow. 'Thanks for bringing me here.'

I glance at her, and before I can stop myself, I say, 'You're kind of like that painting, you know.'

She raises an eyebrow. 'Meaning?'

'You say funny things, bright things, like you're always gearing up for a punchline. But underneath, there's a whole ocean of thought happening. And sometimes I get a glimpse of it. Like just now.'

She looks at me for a moment—really looks. Then smiles.

'I'm definitely not wearing enough conditioner to pull off Venus,' she says.

'Yeah,' I say, nudging her gently. 'But you've got the wind part down.'

And then she pulls out her notebook, opens to a fresh page, and writes something down.

Then she tucks it away, and we both look back at Venus, and I look at her, and I can't help but point out the similarity.

They're both just . . . there. Still standing, still bracing, still beautiful.

Still becoming.

32

Isla

Here's a fun fact they don't tell you in art history class: After you spend an afternoon walking through centuries of religious trauma, bare-chested angels, and sword-wielding heroines, your brain sort of . . . wobbles. Like it's been gently scrambled with a fork.

Also, you start seeing things differently. Not metaphorically—I mean literally. Like, everyone on the street now looks like they stepped out of a fresco. There's a guy leaning against a Vespa who could easily be a lost apostle. And that old lady feeding pigeons? Cherub energy.

The sun's just beginning to dip, turning the streets of Florence into something warm and so beautiful. It's this type of afternoon lighting that makes you want to confess things. Or write poetry. Or, I don't know . . . kiss someone you're maybe not supposed to be thinking about kissing.

'Where to next?' I ask as we step out of the Uffizi, back into the real world. If this counts as the real world. (Still unclear.)

He gestures towards the Arno. 'Want to walk by the river?'

My brain immediately jolts back to that old letter from the book of amore, where we kiss by the Arno after our day at the Uffizi. This sounds alarmingly on track with that. I should probably pivot and suggest something else, but I nod, because yes. Obviously. Walking is good. Walking means motion. Walking means I can keep my feet moving and maybe keep my heart from doing that ridiculous *thump-thump-halt-thump* thing it does when he looks at me for too long.

And he *has* been looking at me for too long. Back when we were at Da Vinci's painting, and then during my Venus breakdown. I wonder what he's thinking.

Luca leads us into a stone arch, the entrance to a small, covered stairway. There are small potted lemon trees on each step. At the end, I can just about see the narrow footpath right beside the river. It's less travelled here, almost hidden from the noise and movement of the world above. Only the occasional ripple of water and the faint hush of traffic softened by distance.

We pause near the edge of the stairway, just before we reach the footpath, where the stone wall dips low and ivy creeps over the side—leaning in to listen. Across the river, even hidden in this little stairway, I can see the Ponte Vecchio glowing with lanterns twinkling like stars. But down here, it feels like Florence is hidden just for us.

'I always forget how magical this part of the city is,' he says, his voice echoing in the secluded tunnel.

'Even after living here?'

'Especially after living here,' he replies. 'You get used to it. Then someone like you shows up and makes everything feel new again.'

Okay. That's illegal. That tone and that sentence. That sincerity disguised as a casual conversation. Someone arrest him. Call the polizia.

The wind blows and Luca's shirt ruffles, and his scent becomes richer. He smells like bergamot and an expensive perfume, and something else I can't name but still want to have in candle form.

Luca leans on the wall beside me, looking out at the water.

I, meanwhile, am trying to memorize him—the slope of his nose, the faint dimple that only shows up when he's not trying to be charming (which is rare, because he is charming, and it's *rude*, really), the way his knuckles tap the stone absentmindedly when he's deep in thought.

'You know,' he says, 'the last time I was here with someone was when I was ten years old and my parents were together.'

I look at him expectantly. 'You didn't bring anyone here after that?'

He shakes his head. 'This place has always been special. It was a reminder of the love my parents had before . . . you know,' he says.

'Then why are we here?' I ask. It's quiet, but I'm pretty sure he can hear my heartbeat from here.

He hums, thinking. Not rushing it. Letting the silence fill up with weight, not awkwardness.

Then, finally, he says, 'Because you make things better. Not by fixing them. Not by pretending they're not hard. But by . . . being there.'

He still doesn't look at me. His eyes stay trained on the water like it's easier to speak to something that won't speak back.

'You didn't try to make me forget about my dad. You let me be angry with him. You let me say the things I wasn't allowed to say before. You never told me to move on from Dahlia—you just kept showing up until one day, she appeared and it didn't hurt the same way.'

My breath catches, but he keeps going.

'And when I think about this place—about the version of me that froze it in time—I think . . . maybe you're the one person who could walk through it and not break it. Maybe even make it new.'

He finally turns to me then, eyes soft and uncertain.

'I guess I brought you here hoping you'd do what you always do. Sprinkle that impossible Isla energy and make something sad . . . a little less sad.'

And God.

God.

It's the simplest thing and the heaviest thing anyone's ever said to me.

Because I don't fix people. I know that. I make messes. I joke when I shouldn't. I deflect and overthink and talk too much when silence would do. But Luca—he sees all of that and still thinks I carry magic?

It's not fair. It's not fair how much I want to believe him.

'And I don't know if it's too much to ask,' he says, quieter now, 'but I want this place to mean something new. Not just to me. To you, too.'

I turn towards Luca fully now, leaning back slightly against the stone for balance, because I have suddenly developed arthritis and my knees are wobbly, untrustworthy.

'I'm not good at this,' I say.

'At what?'

'Moments like this. Big ones. I always want to say the right thing and end up quoting a cartoon or tripping over a leaf. I feel like I have to borrow the courage from someone else. The courage to do what I want to do,' I say.

He turns to me too, and he takes my hand. 'Then borrow it from me. Borrow it and never return it, Isla,' he says as he takes a step towards me, sandwiching me between him and the stone wall. The river Arno swooshes behind us.

'What do you really want to do?' Luca asks, with a voice so gentle I don't know if I've imagined it. 'And don't think about the signs. Don't think about anything.'

He tucks a hair strand behind my ear, and looks into my eyes. I blurt out, 'I want to kiss you.'

Then freeze, mortified. 'Oh my God—I mean—I didn't mean to say it like that, I just—'

But he's already smiling.

'You didn't mean to say it like that,' he repeats, his voice low and warm, 'but I'm really, really glad you did.'

His hand reaches up and his fingertips graze the side of my jaw. His thumb brushes just beneath my cheekbone.

And then . . . he leans in and kisses me.

Warm.

Certain.

Deliberate.

His lips are soft but firm against mine, moving with a tenderness that steals the breath right out of me. His other hand slips to the small of my back, steadying me, grounding me—and wow, I need that grounding, because everything in me is lifting. Floating.

I kiss him back gently, like I'm testing if the water's too cold to swim. My lips part as his follows, and suddenly I'm lost. I don't overthink it any more, and just . . . go with it.

The kiss deepens, his mouth moving with more confidence now. His palm curves around my waist, pulling me closer, and I rise onto my toes instinctively, my hands curling into the fabric of his shirt. I can feel the heat of him, the way he exhales through his nose like he's been wanting this more than I have. And it also makes me realize that I *have* been wanting this a lot.

His head tilts slightly, and our mouths find a rhythm. My knees tremble, and I lose myself in the warmth of him—the press of his chest, the slide of his thumb now tracing a circle behind my ear. Everything.

After our make-out session, we pull apart. But even as the kiss breaks, he lingers, his lips brushing mine once more, like a punctuation mark.

'We did exactly what the book said we'd do,' I whisper.

The words hang in the air between us, like I've just cursed something beautiful.

Luca is quiet for a beat. His fingers are still in my hair. And then he says, 'Screw the book,' his voice rougher now, almost a growl. 'It doesn't get to decide how this ends.'

And before I can answer—before I can fall deeper into the part of me that wants to believe him—he kisses me again.

This time, it's fiercer and more certain. Like he's trying to rewrite fate with the shape of his mouth.

But even as I kiss him back, even as we walk along the Arno a few minutes later, passing the same lamp posts that his family walked by, I can feel it.

In the quietest corner of my mind, where fear still whispers, I know that if the theories are right, then this is where we'll start to fall apart.

33

Luca

I know three things for sure.

One—I'm hopelessly falling for Isla. Except it doesn't feel like falling. Falling sounds chaotic, out of control. This feels like landing. Almost like I've been bracing for impact my whole life and now I'm finally on steady ground. A place to rest.

Two—the book will find a way to ruin this. It always does. That's the trick. It lets you believe for a while, lets you get comfortable. I could rip it apart, drown it, torch it—but I have no doubt it would still find a way to crawl back out. Like it did with my father.

So far, it hasn't written anything new. No fresh letters. No cryptic warnings. Just the same letter of me professing my love to Isla and asking her not to leave. But that's what scares me the most. The silence. The way it's waiting. I don't trust it. I've seen what it does—how it unravels people, rewrites the rules right when you start to hope. And maybe I could handle that. But Isla? I don't want to watch her bear that weight. Not when I want to make everything easier for her.

Three—she's still leaving in a week. She says it like it's simple logistics. But every time she mentions it, I feel something in my chest cave in.

Still, these past few days have been amazing.

She writes at the restaurant almost every day now. She sits near the back table, curls her legs under her and loses track of time. Nonna makes her extra biscotti like she's trying to bribe her into staying longer. I hope it's working.

She even comes over to my place. She laughs with Nonna and fills the quiet corners of my life with colour and motion and meaning.

And I know I should protect myself. Start pulling back before the goodbye breaks me in two. But instead, I find myself remembering her even before she leaves. She likes carbonara, and always leaves a stain either on the table or on her shirt. She always hums while she works. She always ties her hair up and puts a pen behind her ear. Her coffee always goes cold because she talks too much and writes too hard and forgets to drink it.

'Stop staring at her, she will melt,' Marco says as he helps me wipe the cups. I've been staring at Isla through the window from the kitchen, and it hasn't been helping.

'I only have a few days left.'

'Who says you do?' he challenges.

'She's leaving in a week,' I say, deadpan. I take the cup I'm drying and set it on the towel beside me.

'So go with her,' Marco says. And then he adds more quietly, 'You would have, with Dahlia.'

Her name used to trigger my darkest memories, but now, it's just a name. 'Yes, but we both know that was wrong and still would be. To uproot myself for someone who may or may not leave me again.' I didn't mean for it to sound so bitter.

I know Isla shouldn't suffer for my trauma, but we haven't even talked about it. We just established that this would end in a week. Or maybe I just assumed it. I don't know, but Isla seems like she's waiting for signs from the book or some divine intervention. Maybe she's waiting for a winged stranger to deliver some news.

'Just ask her,' Marco tells me before he sets off to wipe the tables.

As he leaves the kitchen, Enzo appears behind me. 'Capo,' he says. 'Have you thought about it?'

I know he's talking about the investor from the Philippines. I have been thinking about it. It's the perfect opportunity to follow Isla. To let her know that I'm in this, if she is.

'I've been thinking,' I say, still watching Isla through the window. 'When do you need an answer?'

'A few weeks, maybe,' he says. 'It's not urgent. But they're waiting.'

He begins untying his apron, slow and methodical. 'Kitchen's clean. Let me know.'

Before he heads for the door, I call after him, 'Why don't you take it?'

He stops, turns, and shrugs like it's obvious. 'I have a wife and son, Capo. I'm not flying them across the world for a chance.' Then he looks at Isla. 'You, though . . . you have nothing to lose.'

He smiles, just a little. 'And everything to gain.'

I sigh as he leaves the restaurant.

It's now quiet. The lights are dim, the tables are clean, and the people are out. Except for Isla. She's still here. I walk over to her and take a seat beside her.

'How's writing going?' I ask.

She looks up slowly, blinking as she returns from whatever world she was just building.

Her brows scrunch the way they always do when she's surprised by her own progress. 'I'm almost done,' she says, in a voice that's part-exhausted, part-amazed. Like she can't believe she actually did that.

'Never doubted you for a second,' I say.

She narrows her eyes at me. 'Three weeks ago, I remember you telling me I won't finish this novel if I obsess over a book.'

I laugh. 'Three weeks ago, you were a stranger who told me you were the love of my life.'

She chuckles, then softly says, 'And now?'

'Now, I think you really might be.'

Isla sucks in a breath, like she's shocked. 'Me too.'

And then I see tears forming in her eyes.

'What's wrong? Is it because you're leaving? I'd go with you.' Apparently it only took seeing her in tears for me to make this decision.

She shakes her head rapidly. 'It's the book.'

'What about it?'

'It's surely going to wreck us, no matter where we are,' she says, wiping a tear off her cheek. 'Ugh, sorry. I'm being dramatic.'

'You're not,' I say. 'Come here.' I gesture for her to come closer, and she rests her head on my shoulder. I put my arm around her. 'We'll figure it out.'

She breaks away immediately, then looks at me intently. 'Are we being rash? What if this is just some summer romance? What if we're making a mistake?'

I take a breath, press my hand over hers, and say, 'Isla.'

She doesn't look away.

'I've spent my life being careful,' I tell her. 'Planning, guarding, second-guessing everything. And you . . . you made it all collapse in the best possible way. I don't know what the book will do, or if it's already done it. I don't know what will happen next. But I know this doesn't feel like a mistake.'

A long pause.

'I've never felt more certain about anything.'

She stares at me, unmoving. Her lower lip trembles just slightly.

Then she whispers, 'You're going to ruin me.'

I smile. 'Only if you let me.'

I'm walking Isla to her hotel.

Nonna is at the nursing home tonight. She insisted. Said the card game was getting heated and she couldn't let Teresa win two nights in a row. I think she was joking. Maybe not. The nurses laugh every time I visit, already teasing me that I should reserve her a room. I wouldn't be surprised if she's filled out the forms herself. She loves that place. Says she sleeps better there. Says her dreams are funnier.

Anyway, I was planning to stay with Isla tonight. I haven't said it yet. I've run the sentence through my head a few times, but the words never quite make it to my mouth.

I'm about to try again when something catches my eye.

A street sign, glowing faintly in the dark. Not lit, exactly—just . . . illuminated.

Isla notices too.

'Is that sign—' she begins.

'Glowing?' I finish. 'Yeah. It's not just you. I see it, too.'

We stop walking. I squint, but I can't make it out from here. 'Want to go closer?'

She nods. Her eyes are wide, curious. We cross the cobblestones slowly, deliberately.

The light flickers slightly, casting strange shadows on the wall. As we get closer, Isla gasps and grabs my arm. Then I see the letters. Simple, small, painted in white.

And there it is.

Via Lullina.

34

Isla

Okay, the weird little street that doesn't exist . . . has sprung up again after Luca and I professed our feelings for each other. Wonderful. This is totally normal and totally not ominous at all.

'This isn't where I saw it last time,' I say. I don't remember exactly where I saw it, but I know there was a giant statue somewhere around.

'It's a magic street that doesn't exist. I *think* it can pop up anytime and anywhere,' he replies with a chuckle.

When I don't laugh or respond, he looks at me. He takes my hand and presses his lips to my knuckles. 'I know what you're thinking,' he says, leading me inside. 'It's not a sign, Isla. Maybe it just wanted to reveal itself to me for a change.'

I slow down, just slightly, letting my fingers trail against the old stone walls as we walk. The space here is narrow, and I scoot a little closer to Luca in an attempt to feel safe.

I only vaguely remember what it previously looked like. I do remember, however, the whole street being quieter and less lively. Like a really empty aisle made for the sake of performance.

After a few steps, we see the library: Librería dell'Amore Perduto.

I quickly point to it. 'That's it!'

Luca wordlessly leads me towards the library, my hand still in his. He holds the doorknob, and slowly turns it. We hear the faint jingle of the bell as we enter.

Like before, the library looks bigger inside. Stacks of books are everywhere, and there is no blank shelf.

'Ah, *Benvenuto*, Signor,' I hear a woman say. And when I fall into view, she quickly adds, 'Welcome back, Signorina.' She winks. It's the same woman from before. Same silver-streaked hair, same glasses perched on her nose.

'You remember me?' I ask, bewildered.

She nods. 'The same way you remember me.'

My hand slips out of Luca's instinctively as I step forward, pulse pounding in my ears. 'Okay. No. No, no. What is happening? Who are you? What is this place? And what the hell does the book want?'

She doesn't flinch. Doesn't even look surprised. Instead, she says, 'Only you can tell what the book wants.'

'That's not true. The book predicted everything we've ever done. And it hasn't written any new letters in the past few days,' I say.

'Then isn't that good? That it's satisfied?' she asks, pushing her glasses up the bridge of her nose.

Luca tenses beside me. 'What does that mean?'

She doesn't answer him directly. Instead, she walks to the edge of the desk, her fingers ghosting over the cover of a different book.

'Love is a flame,' she murmurs. 'Beautiful in its warmth. Dangerous in its hunger. You came with open hearts and lit a match.'

'You're not making this easier for us,' I say.

'I'm not trying to make it easier. I'm trying to make you see.' She goes around the room, and then, she comes into full view. She is dressed like a tarot reader at a local fair—the whole gypsy aesthetic.

'Who are you anyway?' I ask, trying to get her to answer us directly.

She tilts her head at me, like I've asked the wrong question. 'Names change. Roles shift. Sometimes, I am the keeper. Sometimes, I am the guide. Sometimes, I am the one who locks the door after you leave.'

'I hate this,' I whisper to Luca. 'I hate that I don't understand.'

His response is a soft pat on my back.

The woman moves towards a low table in the corner, where an old leather-bound book—familiar and ancient—rests under the flickering light of a lantern.

She doesn't touch it. Just stands near it like it might wake.

'You said it hasn't written anything in days,' she says. 'But you haven't asked why.'

Luca's breath catches. 'Okay . . . Why?'

'Because it doesn't write the middle,' she says, quietly. 'Only the turning points.'

'What turning point?' I ask. My voice comes out too fast. Too sharp.

She looks between us. Her expression softens in a way that somehow makes it worse.

'That,' she says, 'is between the two of you.' She walks behind the counter and once again disappears from view.

Luca and I step out into Via Lullina, then out into the Florentine air.

'That was the most frustrating encounter ever.'

We glance back—but the narrow alley we just exited is gone. No soft lights, no arched entrance, not even a crooked signpost. Just the plain side of a building, as if the street never existed at all.

At this point, I'm unsurprised. I'm still disappointed, though. 'It's just . . .' I start, 'we've spent so much of our time decoding this, and every time we feel like we're moving forward, every time we see a little bit of light at the end of the tunnel, we hit a dead end.' My shoulders slump. 'This was supposed to be some major turnaround, Luca, but again, we're left with nothing but stupid metaphors and useless crumbs.' I pout so aggressively that Luca chuckles.

'Isla,' he says. 'She's just being cryptic. All she's really saying is the book makes a letter every time there's a turning point. And so far, it hasn't written any. So that means we're in the sweet middle. Maybe we're just where we're supposed to be.' I know he's saying that to comfort me, but somehow that makes it worse. Because it can't be the sweet middle forever.

He wraps his arm around me as we continue walking towards my hotel, his thumb gently rubbing my arm like he's trying to soothe both of us.

'We can check the book now, if you want,' he says, casually, like he's inviting me to watch a movie instead of opening a possibly cursed object.

I glance up at him. He doesn't say it outright, but I can tell—he wants to come up. And I want him to. I've been meaning to ask him to stay, if I'm being honest with myself.

'Okay,' I say, with a smile that feels too small for everything I'm holding in.

I try not to think about the upcoming doom that is my flight back home. I'm supposed to feel better, since I've been making progress with my novel. I'm going back home to see Harriet and maybe even visit my parents again. But somehow, all that pales in comparison to leaving Luca and everything else Florentine behind.

It also doesn't help that I'm still the same superstitious mess who feels like everything will get worse if I don't follow the signs. And it especially doesn't help that I'm afraid the book's silence is just the calm before the heartbreak.

When we reach my hotel room, it's quiet. I unlock the door and step inside, the dim light spilling in behind us. The book sits on the bedside table, already giving me an eerie feeling.

When I walk towards it, Luca catches my wrist. I whirl around to look at him.

'Before we open this, I just want to say,' he tells me. 'Nothing this book says will change anything for me. Not the way I feel about you. About this.'

My fingers loosen. The fear in my chest shifts—still there, but softer now. Held by him.

I nod. 'Okay.'

And together, we walk towards the book.

I run my fingers over the cover, half-expecting it to be warm, or to jolt me like a defibrillator. But it's just a book.

'Ready?' I whisper.

Luca steps closer. 'With you? Always.'

I sigh as I open it to its last pages, and as expected, there's a new one. Dated a week from now. The room is so quiet, my heartbeat is the only thing I can hear as I read the words.

Dear Luca,

I've sworn off love for as long as I remember. After too many heartbreaks, I closed myself off to it. And losing my sister only added to that hatred towards love. It reinforced my belief that love was the root of every loss.

It also doesn't help that my horoscopes somehow always tell me to avoid it.

But you changed all that. You made me believe again. Not just in love, but in softness. In slowness.

And I love you. So much. But I can't do this to you.

You can't uproot your life for me. You can't leave your world behind—not for someone who still doesn't know where she belongs. You deserve someone who doesn't need a sign to stay. Someone who isn't always looking for the exit sign.

And I know I've said before that we don't get to decide for the people we're leaving behind . . . And yet here I am. Doing the thing I swore I'd never do. Writing the goodbye before we've even had the fight.

But maybe this isn't self-protection. Maybe this is love, finally learning to loosen its grip. To want the best for someone even if it means stepping aside. May this be my apology to the version of me that thought staying was always the braver choice.

I hope one day, when this doesn't hurt as much, you'll believe that I meant every second. That you weren't a chapter, you were the story. The kind I'll reread every time I want to believe in love again.

Always,

Isla

The room is so quiet, I can hear everything—the buzz of the minibar, the hum of the hallway light, the sound of Luca's breath stalling in his throat.

I don't know how long I stare at the letter. It's dated a week from now. I haven't written it, not yet. And still, somehow, it feels like I already have.

Luca moves behind me. I can feel him reading over my shoulder, his breath brushing against my hair. He doesn't speak right away.

Then, softly, 'You don't really believe this . . . do you?'

I swallow hard, the taste of guilt bitter on my tongue. 'I don't know what I believe any more.'

'I didn't fall in love with you so you could make decisions for me,' he says, voice thick with worry. 'If I want to be with you, that's my choice. Not the book's. Not the stars'. Not some version of you from the future.'

It's not lost on me that it's the first time he's said that officially, and even in the heaviness of it all, I have to point it out. 'You fell in love with me?' I ask, softly.

He leads me to the edge of the bed and sits beside me. 'I wouldn't call it falling, it's more like . . .' he trails off.

'Like landing?' I finish for him, and he nods. 'I feel the same way.' Tears sting at the corners of my eyes. 'But what if I hurt you? Or you hurt me? What if this really ends the way all the other letters did?'

'Then it ends,' he says simply. 'But I'm not going to take a book's word for it.' He shifts, so he's now kneeling in front of me. 'I'd rather love you knowing it might hurt, than never loving you at all.'

For a moment, I believe him. I reach forward and cradle his face, leaning in until our foreheads brush. 'I knew you were a romantic Italian all along,' I murmur.

He laughs against my mouth. 'Don't tell anyone.' And then he proceeds to kiss me. Softly, warmly, beautifully.

35

Luca

The first thing I hear is a groggy voice muttering, 'If this is heaven, it's a little drafty and someone's elbow is digging into my spleen.'

Isla.

I open my eyes and find her lying half on top of me, one leg tangled with mine, hair everywhere.

'Your spleen's in no danger,' I murmur. 'That's your hip. And that's my knee.'

She groans and flops onto her back dramatically, arm flinging over her face like a fallen Victorian woman. Doesn't bother to open her eyes.

The light through the curtains is pale, and everything about this room feels unreal. Like we've slipped into a pocket of time that's untouched by reality. Untouched by flights. Or books. Or goodbye.

But the ache is still there. I brush it off. I turn onto my side and brush her hair away from her face. 'Did you sleep okay?'

Last night was incredible. It's like we sealed whatever unresolved feelings we had, and we just celebrated love.

'I had a dream I was in a library that ate people,' she says. 'But then you showed up with a sword . . . but now that I think about it, it was more like a kitchen knife.'

'Is that your way of saying you want breakfast?'

She nods. 'Florentine pancakes. Dusty with powdered sugar. Served by a shirtless man who looks suspiciously like you.'

'Suspiciously?' I lean over and kiss her shoulder. 'That hurts.'

She peeks from one eye. 'Fine. He is you.' She rolls over, so she's on my chest. She traces my face softly with her fingertips. 'I love you,' she says.

And I freeze. Not because I haven't felt it—I have. For days. Weeks, even. But because hearing it from her, in the morning light with no distractions and no theatrics, feels like someone just handed me the rarest thing in the world and trusted me not to drop it.

'I love you too,' I say, pressing a kiss to her hair, my voice steady even as my heart trips over itself.

She lets out a long content sigh and nuzzles into my chest. 'I wish we could stay like this.'

'So stay,' I say. It slips out before I can stop it. Before I remember that reality is just outside this room, crouched and waiting to pounce.

She doesn't respond right away. And for a moment, I wonder if I've broken the spell. But then she whispers, 'Let's not think about that yet. Let's just stay here, in this little morning bubble.'

And so we do.

Isla's still at the hotel, and I've finally mustered enough self-control to leave her there—for now. She said she needed to make a few last-minute edits to her novel, and I pretended not to take that personally, even though every part of me wanted to stay tangled up in her presence for as long as she would allow.

Still, responsibilities don't disappear just because you're in love.

I walk down the street towards the restaurant, inhaling the scent of rising dough and roasted tomatoes wafting from the neighbouring cafe. The sun is already high.

Enzo and Marco are in when I arrive, prepping for the lunch crowd. I force myself to walk through the doors like I'm still the steady version of myself. The one who knew his rhythm. The one who wasn't completely undone by a girl with a pen behind her ear and magic in her laugh.

I nod in the general direction of the kitchen. 'Give me ten minutes, and I'll go over everything with you.'

'Take your time, Capo,' Enzo says, already elbow-deep in dough.

Before I start the meeting, I step into the quiet corner to call Nonna. It's been a day since we last spoke.

She answers on the second ring. 'Ciao,' she says.

'Hello, Nonna. Remember me? Your charming, reliable, devastatingly handsome grandson?' I tease, smiling as I sink into a chair.

But her voice comes slower this time. Duller. 'Luca . . .'

I sit upright. 'Nonna?'

'I feel ill,' she says softly.

That's all she says. And it's all I need.

I don't remember hanging up. I don't remember calling out to Enzo. But suddenly I'm outside again, the air hitting my face like cold water as I sprint through the streets.

I arrive at the nursing home minutes later. She insists on spending more and more time in here these days.

The hallway smells like a weird combination of lavender cleaner and onion soup. I take the stairs two at a time, ignoring the sting in my calves, the ache in my lungs. A nurse sees me and immediately gestures down the right wing.

'She's resting, Signor,' she says softly. 'Room eleven.'

I push open the door quietly, already bracing myself.

And there she is.

Nonna lies in bed, propped up against pillows. She's wearing her usual floral nightdress, her white hair pinned neatly away from her face. She looks pale, but still normal.

'Nonna,' I breathe.

Her head turns, and a smile tugs at her lips. 'Ah, *il mio ragazzo bello*. You didn't have to run here like the building was on fire.'

'You said you felt ill.'

'I am ill,' she says, like I'm being dramatic. 'I have a fever, not the plague.'

I sit on the edge of her bed, careful not to jostle her. 'You scared me.'

She reaches for my hand and pats it. Her skin is paper-thin, warm. 'You scare easily when it comes to people you love. That's a good thing.'

A doctor walks in, clipboard in hand, and gives us both a polite nod. 'She'll be okay,' he says. 'Just a virus. But she should stay here a few more days for rest and monitoring.'

'Can't she rest at home?' I ask.

'She won't,' the doctor says, already smiling like he knows her. 'Too many friends. Too much chiacchiere.'

'I heard that,' Nonna says.

He chuckles and heads out, closing the door behind him. I glance back at her, relief flooding my chest—but also something else. A dread I can't name.

'I can bring you home,' I offer. 'Once you're stronger.'

Nonna squeezes my hand. 'Why? So I can sit alone and wait for you to come home from the restaurant?'

'I'll be there more often—'

'Luca,' she interrupts gently. 'My life has already been lived. Yours is still stretching ahead of you. Let me spend my days here with my friends, gossiping about television and yelling at the soup. I want to be surrounded by people who are as old and cranky as I am.'

I laugh, though it's watery. 'You're not cranky.'

'Yet,' she says with a wink. 'But give me a week on hospital food and I'll be unbearable.'

Silence falls for a beat. She strokes my knuckles with her thumb.

'I know you're scared,' she continues. 'You lost your parents too soon. In different ways, but still. You've been holding your heart so tightly ever since—afraid to lose anything else. And that Dahlia woman made you feel like you could open again. And then she left.'

I sigh, pushing a hand through my hair. 'I really hope there's a "but" coming, otherwise this is just a very eloquent recap of my tragic history.'

She chuckles, her eyes glinting. 'But, *tesoro mio*, life is not meant to be held in a tight fist.' She positions her hand in a soft fist. 'It's not a thing to control. It's meant to be lived.

Fully. Honestly. Let it break your heart. Let it hurt. That's how it makes room to heal.'

'I've been thinking,' I tell her. 'I don't think I would've gone with Dahlia after all. Or maybe I would've, but I would've returned immediately . . . but now, I think you're right. Life is . . . meant to be lived. It's . . .' I trail off.

She studies me for a moment. 'Is this about the girl?' she asks, because of course she knows. 'The one who leaves soon?'

I nod. 'I want her to stay. With her, I'm sure somehow. I don't know why, but it doesn't feel scary. And so I really want her to stay.'

'But?'

'I don't want to ask her to. I don't want her to feel trapped. And if she leaves, I don't know how to be okay.'

Nonna's exhale is soft and full of something that might be heartbreak or wisdom—or both. She leans her head back against the pillow.

'Then you love her,' she says simply. 'And that, Luca, is the best and worst thing in the world.'

I offer her a small smile, one that barely holds together.

'You think she'll stay?'

Nonna closes her eyes for a moment, then opens them slowly, calmly. 'I think,' she says, 'that's not the right question.'

'What is, then?'

She turns her head to me again, her eyes sharp now, crystal-clear despite the fever. 'The question is: If she doesn't stay . . . will you still love her anyway?'

I freeze. The question slices clean through the part of me that thought I was protecting myself.

'You've convinced yourself, reasonably so,' she says softly, 'that love only counts if it stays. If it roots itself into your routine, fits neatly into the hours you've already measured out. But love isn't a tenant, Luca. It doesn't show up with a lease and promise to stay tidy. It doesn't owe you permanence just because it appeared at all.'

She pauses, her voice soft like a whisper from a dream. 'Love isn't meant to stay in one place to prove it existed. It's meant to move you. Shape you. No matter if it stays or it goes, it will change you . . . and then you just adapt.'

Well, that sticks.

She's right. I've spent so much time believing that love only matters if it doesn't leave. Because my father did. My mother passed too early. And Dahlia . . . She made me believe that love meant giving everything up. And when she walked away, it felt like proof that I wasn't enough.

I think about Isla. About the way she laughs with her whole body. About how she writes like she's chasing something important. About how her being near makes everything brighter. Her joy, her chaos, her warmth. She's filled places in my life I didn't even know were empty.

I think of the book. Of the letters. Of every sign she's tried to follow, just to make sense of something as wild and uncontainable as us.

I take Nonna's hand again and rest my forehead against her knuckles.

'Thank you,' I whisper. 'Not just for the words. But for knowing what I needed before I did.'

She's nearly asleep now, but she gives my hand a tired squeeze.

'Go live,' she says. 'Whatever that means for you.'

I guess I will.

36

Isla

'Love? Isla, are you out of your mind?' Harriet's face takes up my entire phone screen like she's about to crawl through it and shake me. She's got chip crumbs on her hoodie and a look of complete betrayal on her face.

I'm currently in the bathroom of my hotel room, halfway through doing my eyeliner, which is now crooked because of this ambush. 'Har, I know how it sounds—'

'Delusional is how it sounds,' she interrupts, crunching down on another chip. 'And I say that as someone who has listened—patiently, might I add—to you ramble about a book that writes your fate. You made me promise not to date someone just because Mercury was in retrograde, and now you're telling me you're in love with a man you've known for—what, three weeks?'

'Three and a half,' I mutter, wiping away the smudge of eyeliner with the back of my hand.

She throws her head back and raises her hands in mock surrender. 'Oh, sorry. My bad. That extra half really cements it.'

I exhale and sit on the closed toilet lid, make-up brush dangling in one hand. 'I don't know how to explain it. Normally, I wouldn't have let this happen. Maybe before Ivy died. Maybe then I would've jumped into something like this, no questions asked. Summer fling? Sure. Why not? But not post Ivy. Not after I started believing that signs meant everything. I mean, you know me—I break up with people if a fortune cookie tells me to.'

'That guy from Cebu never recovered,' Harriet says.

'Exactly. But with Luca . . .' I pause, trying to find the right words. 'It's like—I forgot how to be afraid. Like, when I'm with him, I don't need a sign. I don't need a plan.'

Har doesn't interrupt. She just munches softer, her brows now pulled together, listening. She looks at me like she's trying to decide whether to hug me or slap me. 'You sound like someone in love.'

'I am someone in love.'

A soft sigh from her end. 'Okay. Listen to me, and listen closely, because I'm only going to say this once before I go back to mocking your poor life decisions.'

I smile faintly.

'If you love him, Isla . . . If you love him like you say you do, then maybe you should reassess.'

'Reassess?'

'Maybe your life led you there for a reason. Maybe you should, I don't know, stay.' She immediately follows up with, 'I mean return. You still have to come back here for me, so I can have a final hug before you drive off into the Italian sunset in your princess carriage.'

I blink, stunned by the simplicity of her suggestion. I never considered that. I only thought about the impending doom of this ending. And I thought about him following me, which was probably the reason why I 'wrote' in the book that he shouldn't uproot his life for me. But I never considered leaping for him. I close my eyes, taking it all in.

'Your silence is creeping me out.'

I open my eyes again. 'I thought you said I was delusional.'

'Oh, you are,' she says, pointing at me with a chip. 'But you're also in love. And those two things? They tend to overlap.'

I laugh—relieved, shaky, a little breathless. 'What would I do without you?'

'Probably get hit by a symbolic bicycle,' she says. 'Now go. Be brave.'

I chuckle as she ends the call with a chip in her mouth.

I arrive at the restaurant expecting it to be bustling, but instead it's closed. I come closer to check if I'm mistaken. Maybe it's just 'No Lights Night' or 'Candlelit Carbonara Day' or some other Florentine gimmick I haven't heard of. But no. There, on the door, is the 'Chiuso' sign. I frown and I squint, check the time, then double-check the date. Did I get it wrong? Did he cancel? Did I dream this entire dinner thing?

But just as I'm about to text him, I see it. Through the glass, past the empty tables and chairs stacked like forgotten thoughts, there's one table glowing under the warm flicker of a candle. A single setting. A small bouquet of flowers.

Okay. I'm either about to get murdered . . . or romanced.

I enter the restaurant and get a clearer view of the scene. The table is set up like a scene from a movie: flickering candle in the middle, fresh wildflowers in a mason jar, and two glasses of wine already waiting. There's soft music playing—something jazzy, something old.

And then he appears.

Luca.

He steps out of the kitchen like a main character from every Italian drama ever made. Seriously. I blink twice just to make sure I'm not hallucinating because what in the actual James Bond madness is happening here?

He's wearing a navy, checkered suit that looks tailored, like it was sewn directly onto him by an ancient Italian tailor who only works under moonlight. His hair is pushed back, and the candlelight hits his face just right—accentuating his stupidly perfect jawline, those stupidly kind eyes, that slight smile that already has me weak in the knees.

'Ciao, *bella*,' he says in a soft voice.

Oh, come on. 'Hey,' I say with the bright, chirpy voice of someone pretending not to be wildly flustered. 'So . . . um . . . what's with all this?' I make a vague jazz hands motion at the set-up, as if the romance is some theatrical set I'm still trying to process.

'I made you a feast. Then freshened up.'

I chuckle. 'Multitalented. Incredible.' I step closer, suddenly aware that my black dress, which I thought was cute, now makes me feel borderline underdressed in the presence of his glow-up. 'You look . . . really, really good.'

He smiles—soft, a little shy, like he's still not used to compliments. 'You look beautiful.'

He wraps his arms around my waist and pulls me a little closer, gently swaying us in place. He leans down to speak near my ear, his voice velvet and danger. 'I wanted to give you a special evening. To say thank you. For being here. For being with me.'

My heart performs a little backflip. I pull back slightly to look at him. 'Thank you, too. For this . . . and for being you.'

He looks at me for a beat, and then—

'Can I come with you?' he asks, almost too casual.

My brows furrow. 'What?'

He laughs, but there's a tremor in it. 'To the Philippines. I've been talking to the investor Enzo introduced me to. I want to help open the restaurant there. I've already told Marco and Enzo—they'll take over the place here. It's time.'

My stomach drops and flies at the same time.

'You're serious?'

He nods. 'I am. I want to be where you are.'

I blink at him, heart stammering like it's forgotten how to function.

What if this is another test? What if this is the book manipulating him?

'I know it's a lot to take in. Maybe we can have dinner first.' He pulls out the chair and I sit. I try to give him a smile that says I'm not spiralling. But I know I'm failing.

'That's a lot, Luca . . .' I say.

I feel like I'm watching the opening scene of a perfect love story—the candlelight, the suit, the man who would literally cross oceans—but I've already read the final chapter. I've seen how it ends. Quiet. Cracked. Me alone in my condo, wrapped in a blanket, eating cold noodles and pulling tarot cards until one finally lies to me in the right way.

'I know.'

'You're leaving your home. Your nonna. Your business—'

'I'm not leaving them,' he says gently. 'I'm growing from them. And I'm not doing this blindly, Isla. I've thought about it. I've really thought about it. And I still want to come with you.'

I swallow. My fingers tremble a little as I reach for his. 'I don't want to be someone you give everything up for.'

His hand wraps around mine, warm and certain. 'You're not,' he says, voice low but sure. 'To give something up means to lose it. To sacrifice it. But being with you . . . It doesn't feel like losing anything.'

'And that book, it's not gonna stop. I know it will affect us. Me. I—'

I trail off, because the words are starting to taste like fear now. Bitter and familiar.

Luca doesn't flinch. He just squeezes my hand, steady and patient. 'I'm not afraid of the book,' he says. 'I'm only afraid of letting go of something this . . . right.'

I smile and nod, because what else can I say to that?

We continue dinner. The food is warm and rich, and I enjoy it. Because, apparently I am someone who can spiral *and* enjoy a decent meal. We talk more—about childhood stories, favourite songs, irrational fears. He tells me about the time he got locked in the freezer during a delivery mishap, and I confess that I once broke my wrist trying to rollerblade down a hill because I was 'manifesting balance'. We laugh more than I expected.

I know everything should be perfect. I know that I should stop thinking too much. That the book is just a book and I can ignore it. But I can't shake off the feeling that it's already influenced us more than we thought.

I've admittedly been listening to that book more than I've been listening to myself. As a matter of fact, I don't know where the line is any more. Which part of my heart is mine and which part is just following instructions.

I glance at Luca. His eyes are warm. Devoted. So sure.

Or maybe he's not. Maybe he's also being influenced by the book? What if his courage to love me is actually a rebellion against it? What if this isn't free will, but a reaction? What if the book wanted him to stay behind and he said no just to prove he could?

I clink my wine glass against his and smile again. This time, it's more convincing. I try to spend the rest of the evening as present as I can.

But in the back of my mind, I swear I can hear a page turning.

37

Luca

Manila is hot. And I'm used to the heat. Summer in Italy can be hot, too, but it's not humid like this. My shirt, linen and supposedly 'breathable', has surrendered all its dignity.

Beside me, Isla is laughing. She's wearing denim shorts and a sleeveless cotton top. Absorbent. Efficient. Practical.

'Don't look at me like that,' I say as we step out of the airport.

'I warned you,' she says, still beaming. 'I believe the phrase I used was *prepare to sweat through your soul.* You accused me of being too dramatic.'

'I thought you *were* being dramatic.'

She gasps, mock-offended, then nudges me as we push the luggage trolley forward.

'Welcome to the tropics, Signor.' She winks.

Before I can respond, a voice cuts through the air. 'GIRL!'

I whirl around and see a redheaded woman running towards us. Isla squeals beside me and runs towards the woman, and they crash into each other in a whirlwind hug, the kind that knocks the air out of your lungs. Arms flailing. Shrieking. The works.

'Before anything else, put your bags in,' the redhead says as she pulls away, already moving towards a nearby SUV parked a little too confidently by the curb. 'I can't stay parked here long. The guards here *do not* play.'

'Right, yes,' Isla says breathlessly, turning back to me. 'Luca, this is Harriet. Harriet, Luca.'

'Loverboy!' Harriet grins at me like we've already been friends for years. 'Pleasure. Bags first, pleasantries later.'

I grab the suitcases and follow the chaos. Harriet flings open the back of the SUV and Isla helps me toss the bags in. Once everything's packed, we pile into the car (she insists we both stay in the back, because her front seat is cluttered), and Harriet peels out of the curb recklessly.

'Sorry about that,' she says as she flicks the signal light and then completely ignores it. She's adjusting her hair in the rearview mirror with one hand and steering with the other. I'm not totally convinced she's using either efficiently. 'The guards here get snappy.'

'No worries,' I say, glancing around the SUV. It smells faintly of coconut. 'You're Isla's best friend?'

'Unfortunately,' Harriet says, giving Isla a quick eyebrow raise in the mirror. 'I've known her since before she had eyebrows.'

'I had eyebrows! They were just . . .' Isla lifts a finger, swirling it vaguely in the air. 'Expressive.'

'Non-existent,' Harriet deadpans.

I glance out the window as the city begins to unfold. The streets are busy, loud, bursting with colour and motion. Jeepneys pass us—gleaming metal painted in neon oranges and purples, slogans scrawled across their sides. Vendors line the sidewalks under patchy tarps, selling everything from sliced mangoes to smart phones. The traffic sounds are less like horns and more like constant punctuation.

'It's loud,' I murmur.

'It's alive,' Isla corrects.

She leans back against the seat, one arm looped casually with mine, like she's never belonged anywhere more. There's sweat gathering at the base of her neck, but she doesn't seem to care.

Harriet swerves to avoid a pothole the size of a small bathtub, then immediately turns to me like she's not actively operating a motor vehicle.

'So, Luca,' she says, dragging out the 'u' like she's evaluating the name itself. 'Italian. Tall. Can cook. What's your deal?'

'Har!' Isla screeches, slapping her arm.

'What? I'm trying to understand!'

I cough, eyes wide. 'I, uh—'

'Ignore her,' Isla says, putting a hand over mine. 'She's part-dragon and can get a bit cranky because she can't have dairy.'

'Excuse me, I'm evolving,' Harriet says, flipping her hair with one hand while turning into another narrow road with the other. 'I've started eating real cheese again. Life's too short to pretend cashew tastes like camembert.'

I blink. 'You're . . . very brave.'

'So whatcha doing here?'

'I . . . like your country,' I say, immediately regretting how diplomatic and vague that sounds.

She cackles. 'So do backpackers with commitment issues.'

Isla sighs loudly. 'He's not a backpacker. He's opening a restaurant here.'

Harriet once again looks behind her like her car self-drives. (It doesn't.) 'Oh, so it really is serious. You're moving here?'

'That's the plan,' I say.

Then Harriet slaps the steering wheel. '*Damn*, Italy Boy. That's bold.'

I relax slightly. 'Thank you, I think?'

'I mean, I'd personally never relocate across oceans for a woman who leaves her coffee half-finished, but to each their own.'

'I do finish it sometimes,' Isla mutters under her breath.

I chuckle as I try to process this entire dynamic while sweat drips down my back.

We pull up to a gated condo building and she swings the car into a parking slot with the precision of someone who's been here a lot.

Harriet unbuckles, twists around, and levels her full attention on me. 'Alright. I don't hate you.'

'High praise,' I murmur.

'But,' she adds, raising a finger, 'if you hurt her, I will re-open the Colosseum to get your ass eaten by a bunch of lions.'

I nod solemnly. 'Understood.'

Then she smiles. 'Great. Welcome to Manila, Loverboy.'

Isla snorts and grabs my hand. 'Let's get inside. You coming, Har?' she asks.

Harriet sighs dramatically, like we've asked her to give up her social life. 'As much as I would love to see Luca's reaction to your curated throw pillows, I have work. You sent me that manuscript last night, remember? The one I had to download on data at 1 a.m. while stuck in traffic? I need to start the edits. I'll see you two disgusting lovebirds tomorrow.'

'Don't be jealous,' Isla sings as she pulls me towards the building. 'You'll find love. Or a dog. Or maybe both.'

'Don't put that kind of pressure on a girl!' Harriet calls, pulling the door shut behind her with flair.

As we walk into the building, luggage in hand, my shirt is clinging to me like regret and my brain is still processing everything that has happened. I can't help but feel it again—the surrealness. The total disorientation. I'm thousands of miles away from home. The humidity is trying to eat me alive. I've been verbally wrestled by a woman I met ten minutes ago.

And yet Isla's hand is in mine.

And all is well.

The elevator dings, and we step out into a hallway that smells faintly of floor polish. Her condo door clicks open with the usual jangle of keys, and we step inside.

Immediately, my eyes go to the sofa.

As Harriet mentioned, the throw pillows are . . . something. There's a pink one that says 'manifesting', a yellow one shaped like a fried egg, and a rectangular pillow that simply reads 'NO'.

Isla laughs, tossing her keys into a bowl (a bright orange one with white polka dots) by the door. 'Be glad I changed it before I left. There used to be one that said "Don't talk to me until I've hexed my ex".'

I chuckle as she walks to the kitchen. I follow her into the space—small, lived-in, hers. There are stacks of books on nearly every surface. A string of fairy lights hangs half-heartedly above the TV. A candle labelled 'Emotional Stability' sits completely unused on her bookshelf.

As I look around, I realize this is her world. Her rhythm. Her life.

And I'm in it.

And even though I'm far from everything I've ever known—my restaurant, my nonna, my neighbourhood back in Florence—this cluttered, cozy space feels like an open door. A beginning.

I take a step closer to her, where she's pouring water into a glass. She looks up at me and smiles.

'What are you thinking?' I ask.

'I'm thinking,' she says, 'that I really want you here.'

'Good,' I reply. 'I'll be where you want me to be.'

I press a soft kiss on the top of her head. 'I know you're worried about the book,' I say.

She looks down at the glass in her hand, not drinking it, just holding it like it might anchor her. 'It's just hard not to,' she says after a while. 'Every time I think we've outrun it, it finds a way to sneak back in.'

I nod. 'I know. But I don't care what the book says. Or doesn't say. I care about you. And I care about right now.'

She smiles softly, and places the glass of water back on her small counter. She faces me and wraps her arms around me in a tight hug. 'Thanks,' she says, her voice muffled as she sinks into my arms.

'Anytime,' I reply.

'Do you wanna eat something?' she asks, pulling away just enough for me to see her face. I push a strand out of her face.

'What do you have?'

'I can cook something. I miss eating food from home,' she says, already looking around the kitchen, scrambling for ingredients as if she has any left.

I chuckle as she decides on cooking adobo, and she points a wooden spoon at me like a weapon. 'Out, shoo. My turn in the kitchen.'

'Yes, Chef,' I say with a mock salute, stepping into the living room.

Her condo is small—just a single-bedroom unit, with barely enough room to stretch. But it's hers. And somehow, every inch of it feels like her. The throw pillows are mismatched but charming, her bookshelf is overflowing with both poetry and paperback romances, and there's a framed photo of her and Harriet mid-laughter by the TV.

I walk slowly to the shelves, taking in snapshots of the life she's built, one tiny memory at a time. There's one of her with her parents. One with Ivy, I assume. I recognize the short hair and the sharp features from photos she's shown me before. My gaze lingers there for a moment longer.

Behind me, I hear her humming softly, the scent of soy and garlic beginning to bloom in the air, smelling like . . . home.

38

Isla

For days, it's bliss. Luca and I move through my condo like we've lived there for years. We share a toothbrush cup. Fold laundry together. Dance to music from my tinny speakers like it's the most romantic ballroom in Europe. From the way we scoot up next to each other on the couch, I could be in a shoebox studio and still feel like we had space.

His meeting with the investor went well. Really well. They're planning to open the restaurant somewhere in Manila City—a place he insists has 'the best traffic to test your patience and the best food to reward it'.

We fall into a rhythm that makes it easy to forget that we were once just strangers in Florence, unravelling mysteries and folding in confounding feelings.

'Your novel was amazing, by the way,' Harriet says as we stroll down a quiet street near my condo, the sky dipped in lavender. We each have ice cream cones in hand—mine's rocky road, hers is coconut pandan—and we're walking like we've got nowhere to be. 'Made me cry buckets. And I don't even cry teaspoons, so that's saying something.'

I laugh. 'Har, you literally sobbed when that one food truck show ended.'

'That was grief. Actual grief. They had the best grilled cheese sandwich in Southeast Asia and then they shut down to 'pursue other interests'. Whatever that means.'

I grin, licking a smear of chocolate off my knuckle. 'Thanks for editing it. It wouldn't exist without you.'

'Correction: It would exist. But it would be riddled with typos. How can you not know how Botticelli is spelled?' She bumps her hip against mine. 'But seriously, you did good. It's beautiful, and honest, and just painful enough in the right places.'

'Thank you,' I hug her jokingly.

When we reach my condo, she says, 'Okay, I have to go.' She takes her bag off her shoulders to get the keys to her car that she parked in front of my building entrance.

'I have a date with that George guy,' she says.

'Who is this George guy?' I ask. 'Why do I not know about him?'

Harriet rolls her eyes. 'Because I met him this morning. It's not a big deal. We're just grabbing coffee. No alcohol on the first date, no giving addresses—don't worry, I still remember our cardinal rules, Sister Safety.'

I raise my eyebrows as I climb the stairs. 'Uh-huh. Is he at least cute?'

She grins wickedly. 'Does it matter? He's six-foot-five.'

I cackle. 'So that's the bar now? Just tall enough to change the lightbulbs?'

'Exactly,' she says, already walking backwards towards her car. 'If I'm gonna date a stranger, he might as well reach the top shelf.'

I shake my head as I fumble for my keys, a smile lingering on my face. I take the elevator and enter the condo.

The space is still warm from the life we've been filling it with—Luca's jacket tossed over a chair, our half-finished puzzle on the table, a faint trace of garlic from this morning's tapsilog.

And then I see it.

The book. Sitting where I know we didn't leave it. I know, because we left it in Florence. Wrapped in cloth. Tucked behind a false panel in the back of a library. Luca even said goodbye to it. We *both* did.

But here it is now, sitting casually on my console like it's always been there.

I don't scream. I don't throw it across the room. I just stare, numb, as I walk closer to it.

The Book of Amore. It's the same book. The same cover. The same spine.

I breathe heavily as I open it, taking my time until I reach the final pages. Now, here's one thing I probably should have mentioned: The book usually has empty pages after our letters. Even if the letters change, there are always empty pages.

But now, there's a final page. No empty pages. Just one last letter, in Luca's handwriting.

My Dearest Isla,

I waited.

I don't say that to guilt you. I say it because it's the truth. I waited the way people wait for spring in the middle of a long, cruel winter—with anticipation, with hope.

When I left your condo, I told myself it was just space. Just time. That you'd call and I'd hear your voice again, and it would sound like home. But the days stretched into weeks, then into months, and the silence started to sound like an answer.

So I came back to Florence. Back to the restaurant, to Marco and Enzo, to Nonna and her relentless critiques of my hair. Life feels familiar again. A little quieter. A little lonelier.

But here's the part you might not expect: I'm not angry. I was, maybe, for a day or two. Not at you, at myself, for thinking I could rewrite someone else's story.

So here's what I want to say: I love you.

I loved you when you were unsure. I loved you when you were afraid. I loved you when you laughed with your whole body and when you couldn't meet my eyes. I loved you when you read the signs and I chose to challenge them.

And I probably still will. But I'm learning to live without waiting. Without expecting your return. But I will still love you, because if we only love someone when it guarantees presence, or permanence, then that isn't love.

If you ever find your way back here, not to Florence, but to me, I'll know. And I'll smile. And I'll take you back, no questions asked.

But I won't hold my breath.

Con amore,
Luca

I stare at it and read it again. Then again. And ten more times, thinking that if I read it enough, I'll find some kind of loophole or a hidden symbol. Or a message. But there's nothing left to decipher.

I take a seat on my couch, and wipe the tears I didn't even know were there.

When Luca returns, the sun is already low. He looks tired, his sleeves rolled up, collar slightly loose, like he's walked through the whole of Manila trying to chase something down. But his eyes light up when he sees me, just for a second, like instinct.

Then he sees my face.

'What happened?' he asks, his voice dipping into concern as he steps inside and drops his keys on the counter. His gaze follows mine, and when he sees it—the book—his expression shifts. It's subtle, but I catch the flicker of something beneath his eyes. Confusion, maybe. Or dread. He blinks, just once, slow and uncertain, then schools his features into something gentler.

'It came back,' I say finally. 'The book. It just—showed up.'

Luca doesn't move. He blinks for a few seconds, but then he regains composure. He sits down beside me on my small sofa, and takes my egg-shaped throw pillow to put on his lap. He takes my hand in his, and says, 'What did it say?'

I look up at him. He's doing that thing where he tries to hide how tense he is. His jaw is tight, his eyebrows just slightly furrowed—but when he sees me watching, he smooths them out. Like he wants me to feel safe. Like he wants to give me room, even if he's unravelling on the inside.

His thumb brushes slowly across my knuckles, grounding me.

'It's a letter,' I say. 'From you. Well . . . not you, but the version of you a year from now. One who's already back in Florence.'

He nods, silent. Still steady. Still listening.

'It says you waited for me. That I didn't reach out. That you finally decided to move on.'

My voice catches, but I press through it. 'Do you want to read it? Maybe you'll make more sense of it than I can.'

He shakes his head almost instantly. 'No, amore,' he says, voice low but firm. 'I don't need to read it.'

I stare at him. 'Why not?'

'Because whatever version of me is in that letter . . . it's not me. Not the me sitting here. Not the one who loves you now.'

I exhale shakily. 'But what if it *is* you? What if that's what's coming? The book's been right about everything so far. We subconsciously did what it told us we would do. And now, what if I'm just dragging you towards something that's doomed, and you're trying so hard to hold on while I'm—' I cut myself off, too aware of how much I'm spiralling. I hate that I do this. That I can't seem to not do this.

Luca squeezes my hand, not to stop me, but to remind me he's still here. 'Isla,' he says, and my name sounds like a promise in his mouth. 'Amore mio, I'm not afraid of what might happen. I'm not afraid of heartbreak. I've been through it before, and I survived. But I'm more afraid of never giving us a real chance just because you're scared of what a book says.'

'I know,' I whisper. 'But I don't trust myself. Not fully. I thought I was better, but I saw that letter and I just . . . broke.'

His eyes soften even more. 'Do you need time?'

'No,' I immediately respond, but I trail off a little, and look at him, tears pooling again. 'I don't know.'

He doesn't say anything right away. Just sits there for a moment, like he's making peace with something he knew might come.

Then, finally, he speaks. 'Okay,' he says. 'I'll give you space. But I'm not disappearing. I'm not going far.' He stands slowly and walks to the counter, scribbling something on a piece of paper—an address. 'I'll check into this hotel. Just for now. I'll be there if you want me . . . When you want me.'

He doesn't wait for me to respond, and goes straight to the room to collect his stuff.

I don't follow him, I don't talk, I don't even stop him. But when he's done with filling his luggage, he approaches me.

He gives me a hug and presses a kiss on the top of my head. 'I love you,' he says.

'Me too,' I say, unable to look at his eyes.

When he walks out the door, I'm left alone. I stand in the middle of the room for a while, unsure of what to do with my hands or my heart. I've lived here alone my entire adult life, but it's never felt emptier than it is now. The scent of his cologne is still in the air, and I'm scared of the day I won't smell it again.

I sit on the couch with the consequences of my decisions.

I don't know why I think like this. I don't know why I'm letting this book influence me, or why I see it the way I see all the signs around me. Like little instructions for me to follow or else something else will go wrong. Someone will leave. Or die. Why does my brain twist something good until it becomes something dangerous?

I know it doesn't make sense. On paper, I sound ridiculous. But fear can't be explained all the time, and I know for sure that my attachment to my signs is fear speaking.

I try not to think of Ivy. Of how she's gone and how I can't see her again because I ignored the signs. I try not to think about how the opposite is happening now. How I'm losing Luca because the signs are all I see.

But no matter how I try, it's all I think about.

39

Isla

My parents live in the more provincial part of Manila, in a small village where there are sari-sari stores and neighbourhood barbecues, *not* in a twenty-storey condominium.

I don't remember the last time I was here. I know for sure that it was after Ivy's death. The memory is so vivid, because it was a time when everything was new. When we were adjusting to a new life without her. We'd tiptoe around each other, smile in places where we used to laugh, and set dinner like the empty chair didn't exist.

At that time, I stayed for a week, trying to help my parents 'adjust', whatever that meant. I washed dishes. Cooked meals. Tried to make conversation about anything other than her. But grief, I've learned, is sticky. It clings to the walls. To your voice when you try to speak. It sticks to everything it vaguely touches.

I remember the night my mother looked at me—not with anger, but something worse. Disappointment. Disgust, even. It was subtle, but unmistakable. A flicker across her face when I told her I wished I could go back, do something differently.

When I finally said out loud that I felt responsible. And she didn't argue.

'If you hadn't been so wild, Isla,' she said, 'if you weren't always dragging her along, maybe she wouldn't have felt the need to prove she could keep up.'

She didn't say it to hurt me, I think. But she didn't try to take it back either. And once those words were out there, they stuck. They became part of the foundation I built my newer self on—the version of me that second-guesses everything, that waits for signs, that overcorrects and overthinks.

Now, standing in front of the house, I wonder if that version of me is the only one they remember.

The white walls are a little more faded now. The garden is patchy, overgrown in some places and bare in others. The wind chimes still hang on the porch, but one of the pipes is cracked. The gate still squeaks. And in the distance, I hear the familiar buzzing chorus of cicadas under the mid-afternoon sun. Somewhere nearby, someone is selling taho. My childhood, all at once.

I don't even know why I'm here. Is it closure I want? Forgiveness? Or maybe I just want to prove something to myself. That I can walk into this house without breaking apart. That I can sit across from my mother and not shrink under the weight of her gaze.

Maybe I want her to say it—that it wasn't my fault. Or maybe I just want to stop needing her to.

I take a deep breath, my hand hovering over the gate, the rusted metal warm beneath my fingers. I don't know what I'm going to say. I don't even know if I'll make it past the threshold.

'Ma?' I call out, stepping past the gate and into the garden. The vines are thicker now, heavy with bougainvillea blooms, and a rogue papaya tree leans into the path.

I push the door open. It's still painted the same pale blue, chipped on the edges. Still unlocked. When I enter, I call out again, 'Ma? Pa?' I shouldn't feel like a guest in my old home, but somehow, I do.

Ivy and I moved out for good around seven years ago, to stay in the city for our jobs. We still went home monthly, but it stopped after the incident.

As I hover by the door, I can't deny that the house smells like . . . home. Frying oil. Food. Eucalyptus. A little bit of old wood and detergent.

My mom peeks out from behind the wall, spatula in hand. Her eyes widen. 'Isla?' she says, like I've materialized from smoke. Her apron is stained with oil and flour, and her hair is pulled back in the same lazy bun she's worn for decades. She looks exactly like she did in all the memories I've tried to avoid.

She doesn't wait for an answer. 'Anak, look at you!' she says, voice breaking into a laugh as she wraps me in a tight hug. 'You didn't even text you were coming.'

'I wasn't sure I would,' I say honestly, but I hug her back.

'Well,' she huffs, stepping aside and ushering me in, 'you're here now. That's what matters. Come in, I'm making pancit.'

I follow her to the kitchen, and take a seat as she breezes through the room, pulling a plate from the cabinets, scooping a heaping amount of pancit, and setting it in front of me. She hands me a fork and a glass of soda.

After a few spoonfuls, she sits beside me, and just observes. 'How are you?' she asks. When I don't answer immediately, she adds, 'Still writing?'

'Yeah. Just finished something. Harriet's editing it,' I say. She's always been fond of Harriet. She used to say that I needed a friend like that to keep up with me. Little did she know, I'm the one trailing behind now.

She nods and smiles, and I can't help but notice how it still feels like we're dodging the giant elephant in the room. She talks about the neighbours, about her garden that keeps getting eaten by ants, about how my cousin got married but didn't invite the family because it was 'intimate'. I nod, I smile, I laugh in some parts. And then—without a shift in tone—she says, 'I cleaned Ivy's old room last month.'

My fingers still. My fork hovers mid-bite.

'I still put flowers in there sometimes,' she says, casually, like it's something as ordinary as sweeping the floor. 'Sunflowers. They last longer.'

I can't find the words, so I just look at my glass, at the condensation beading on the surface. There's so many things I want to ask, but I don't even know where to start. Instead I say, 'I know I stayed away. After.'

I push around the food on my plate with my fork. She wipes her hands on her apron and looks at me. Her eyes are softer now, older than I remember. 'We all stayed away in our own ways, Isla.'

'You were angry at me,' I say in a whisper.

She shakes her head. 'No, we weren't.' She takes my hand and rubs it gently with her thumb. 'It's just that . . . when we grieve, we find things to hold onto. And sometimes we hold the wrong ones.'

I see in her face that she's trying to think of more things to say to make me feel better, but I don't think I'm ready for a big emotional talk yet. This is a good place to be, and it's enough to me for now. 'Thank you,' I say.

Then I hear the shuffle of slippers from the hallway. My father steps into the kitchen, wearing his favourite old T-shirt with a faded basketball logo and holding a newspaper he probably didn't read.

He looks surprised to see me. 'Anak,' he says. His voice is quieter than my mom's, but it always has been.

'Hi, Pa,' I say.

He comes closer and gives me a gentle pat on the shoulder, like he's still unsure if he's allowed to hug me. But he does—awkwardly, a little stiff—and I lean into it.

'Your mom's been talking about you. Every week she says, "Maybe Isla will visit today."'

My mom rolls her eyes at him but doesn't deny it.

'I missed you both,' I say.

'You can visit more often, yeah?' he says. And I nod.

We continue to eat our *merienda*, talking about Ivy, not in the heavy, calculated way we used to try to, but more openly. We talk about how she used to burn everything she cooked because she did so many things all at once. We even laugh when we recall how she would judge every soap opera ever made, but still sit in front of the TV to watch them every night.

They don't take away my guilt completely—not in a single conversation, not in one afternoon. But they chip at it. They remind me that love and loss are tangled, and no one comes out of it clean.

'Any boyfriends we should know of?' my mom casually asks when we're cleaning up the dishes.

I hesitate for a while, but I tell her about Luca. About how I met him in Florence. I don't mention the book—it feels like too much, like trying to explain a dream you haven't fully woken up from. But I tell her how he made me laugh. How he cooked for me. How he listened. How he said he loved me before I even knew what I wanted from him. How I pulled away—not because I didn't feel the same, but because I was scared. Because all the signs I've built my life around told me to.

'Anak,' my mom says slowly, drying her hands with a towel and looking at me, 'sometimes, the signs we follow aren't signs at all. They're fears. And fears are not facts.'

I blink at her, amazed at what she has said and how unbelievably simple it sounds. I can't believe I didn't think of it that way.

I've been building my life around signs, like little breadcrumbs scattered by the universe. A car honk at the wrong time. A chill down my spine. A sudden gust of wind. I interpreted everything like it had meaning. Because I needed it to. Because after Ivy died, the world stopped making sense—and it felt safer to pretend that something, anything, was guiding me.

I nod, but it's more to myself than to her. My chest aches, but in a good way—like something's finally breaking open after being sealed for too long.

Later, as I say goodbye and step outside into the soft orange haze of the Manila afternoon, I feel lighter. I'm not healed. Not fixed. But . . . fine. The street looks the same as it always did. A tricycle sputters by. There's a group of kids chasing each other around a basketball hoop that's half nailed to a mango tree. Someone is sweeping leaves into a corner.

I remember this one time—I must have been sixteen, which means Ivy was eighteen—we were at the beach with our parents. The same beach where we'd go every summer, armed with packed lunches and gallons of SPF 80. I had spent the whole afternoon running into the waves, daring them to knock me over.

Ivy, on the other hand, never let her feet leave the shore. She sat on a towel with a book propped on her knees and a hat so big it made her look like she was in disguise. She was always like that—watching before joining, thinking before doing.

That day, I remember grabbing her hand and yelling, 'Come on! Just once!'

She hesitated, of course. She looked back at our parents, like she was asking permission. Then she looked at me. 'What if I get hurt?'

'You won't,' I said with full, reckless confidence. 'You'll float.'

She let me drag her into the water. Just to her knees. But it felt like a win. She squealed when the cold water touched her legs and tried to pull away, but I held her there, laughing. 'You're fine! See? Told you!'

And for a few seconds, she smiled. I mean, really smiled. Her nose crinkled and her eyes turned to crescents. It was rare, and I remember it vividly.

After she died, I kept thinking of that day with a stomach full of guilt. I felt like I planted the seed of recklessness in her. Like that smile was the start of something dangerous.

But now . . . I wonder if that moment wasn't about me at all. Maybe it was Ivy choosing something for herself. Choosing wonder, even if it scared her. Maybe the things I thought I gave her—wildness, spontaneity, risk—weren't mine to give. Maybe she had them all along and was just learning how to reach for them.

I'm pretty sure grief doesn't go away. Guilt probably doesn't, either. But I guess, like the paintings in the Uffizi, all I needed was a different perspective.

40

Luca

Manila hums differently without her.

Of course, I've only been here for about two weeks. And only four days without her. But I can already compare the feel of it to when she was with me. Already, I miss her voice breaking into my thoughts, her laughter tumbling over the noise of traffic. I miss the way she made the city feel more alive than it is.

Today, I'm walking the side streets of Makati. The sun is low, caught in the glass of high-rise buildings. Pedestrians sweep past in office clothes and worn slippers alike. I duck into a quiet coffee shop nestled between a pharmacy and a printing shop.

Inside, it's cool and dim. The air smells like cinnamon and coffee. A student taps away at her laptop in the corner while an elderly man reads the newspaper by the window. I order an Americano and sit near the back, the buzz of the city muffled by the soft jazz playing overhead.

'Ciao,' I say as my phone rings.

'How's the restaurant?' Marco says on the other line.

'Well, we're planning to set it up in Intramuros,' I say, adjusting the cuff of my sleeve. 'It's a beautiful district. Old stone walls, horse-drawn carriages, churches from centuries ago. Patrick, the investor, wants a sort of Filipino–Italian fusion. I'm working on recipe prototypes.'

'You can do that better than anyone,' he says. 'And Isla?'

'Um . . . she's good.' I'm not in the mood to talk about everything that happened, so I deflect. 'How are things there?'

'Good, actually. I mean, we miss you, but we're thriving.' Marco chuckles, the sound warm and distant through the phone. 'Enzo's reinstated happy hour, and the influx of people at night is incredible. It's like the old days—wine flowing, tables full, everyone shouting over each other just to be heard. You'd hate it.'

I smile faintly. 'I probably would.'

He continues, 'I also visit your nonna every once in a while. She keeps telling me to leave her alone, but then asks for a serving of carbonara the next day because, and I quote, the nursing home's food "tastes like ash".'

I smile. Nonna's like that. 'Grazie, Marco, truly.'

'Don't mention it. I'm enjoying this,' he says.

We catch up for a while, then end the call. After we hang up, I sit for a while, letting the warmth of the coffee seep into my hands. The cafe is half-full now. The student in the corner has packed up, but the old man is still reading, his thumb resting on a creased page.

Florence is quieter this time of year. Marco said the piazza's still lively at night, but I can imagine how the cold might be creeping in, how the wind tunnels between the old buildings. I imagine my apartment there, the uneven floors, the too-narrow kitchen. My cookbooks. My mother's framed recipe for ragù I've kept hanging by the spice rack since I was eighteen.

I think about Nonna, and how she always told me to live my life, but also to text her as soon as the sun came down because only fools stay up late in the streets of Florence.

I miss it. So I fire a quick call to her.

She answers immediately. 'I hope you're not already thinking of coming back,' she says. I can hear the faint chatter of her friends.

I chuckle. 'I'm not . . . Just a little homesick, I guess.'

I can hear her shuffle, until I can't hear chatter in the background any more. 'Where's Isla?'

'She, uh, she's not here,' I say quietly. Nonna doesn't say anything. I know she can hear the hesitation in my voice.

'Well, she's not a plant, mio dio,' she says. 'She can go where she wants. Just don't forget to water your own damn self while you wait.'

I laugh at her absurd metaphor. And then she tells me that it's her turn in Scopa, a famous card game, and we end the call.

As I sip my coffee, my thoughts drift to Isla.

I wonder, for a moment, if all this—crossing oceans, opening myself up again, loving someone so thoroughly—was foolish. If I'm simply setting myself up to be left again. To sit in a different city, in a different cafe, mourning another almost. But I remember when Nonna told me that if I only love someone because they're here, that isn't love.

My mother used to tell me the same thing, but I was too young to know or pay attention. When I was thirteen, she used to take me on walks in the late afternoons. She always wore her red scarf—no matter the season—and she'd loop it around her wrist while I asked her about everything: the art in the Uffizi, how she managed to do everything by herself, whether she believed in fate.

She would say no. That she believed in choices. 'Love, Luca,' she told me once, her arms looped around mine because I was already taller than her, 'even if it doesn't bloom the way you imagined, it's not wasted. Nothing real ever is.'

She never got to meet the version of me that stayed in relationships long enough to see them fall apart. Never got to see me take a risk that wasn't safe or certain. And yet, I think she'd be proud of this. Of me. Sitting in a strange city, waiting. Hoping. Choosing.

I look out the window. A child chases bubbles that catch the sunlight. A street musician is setting up his guitar case with a hopeful grin. In a country halfway across the world from mine, life continues with the same unshakable rhythm it always has.

There's no promise of what happens next. No divine certainty. No cosmic instruction manual. But that doesn't mean it isn't okay to hope.

If there's anything I learned from Isla, it's that there are things beyond my control. And how she feels about me is one of those things. But what I can control is what I feel about her.

And no matter which way I look at it, I still love her.

So maybe I'll stay here, waiting and hoping for as long as I can.

I step out of the cafe, and walk around until I reach a bookshop. On a whim, I step inside. I wander for a moment before making my way to the counter.

'Hi,' I say. 'Do you happen to have any books by Isla Mendoza?'

The woman behind the counter—maybe in her fifties, with salt-and-pepper hair tucked into a clip—looks up from her receipt log. 'Isla Mendoza?' she echoes, thoughtful. 'Ah . . . yes, I think we have a few copies of her latest work. One moment.'

She disappears into a back aisle, and I trail behind her until we reach a dusty corner. She gestures to the bottom row of a shelf. 'Here. Didn't sell much when it came out, but I personally liked it.' She shrugs.

There are ten copies of the slim book with a matte cover that's faded with time. The title is simple: *The Distance Between Stars.*

I thought she always wrote romance books. I guess not. I kneel down and pick one up, brushing off the dust on the corner with my thumb. I flip to the first chapter and read a few lines. Then a few more.

It's fiction, technically, but I see her in every paragraph I read. She writes something about losing someone who has anchored you, and then being afraid to float. I don't need to ask who it's about. This is about Ivy. And the writing is all of Isla. And I don't think she ever thought anyone would notice.

I stand up and walk back to the counter, holding all ten copies.

The woman raises an eyebrow. 'You sure you want all of them?' I nod as she smiles faintly and begins to ring them up.

'Graz—' I stop. '*Salamat.*' I smile at the woman, and leave the bookstore.

For the rest of the day, I read the book in pieces–on the park bench, in another cafe, in the silence of my hotel room. And it's her. All of it. The story is fiction, technically—but only just. It's Isla bleeding between the lines, trying to soften her grief by shaping it into plot.

The book is short, but I appreciate how Isla has tried to give her character a moment of redemption that she hasn't yet given herself. That takes a different kind of strength.

I run my fingers over the spine and think about what to do with the books. I consider mailing them to Florence. Leaving them in cafes, one at a time, where someone might pick one up by accident.

Or maybe . . .

At the new restaurant we're opening in Intramuros (and maybe every restaurant I'll have after that), I'll build a small wooden shelf. A tiny book nook, tucked near the entrance where people can browse while waiting. A place for the overlooked stories. The ones that didn't hit bestseller lists or win awards—but mattered anyway.

And hers will be the first.

Not as a grand romantic gesture. Not even to win her back. Just . . . because stories like hers deserve to be read. And as I sit there in the quiet, the irony isn't lost on me.

The Book of Amore.

I used to laugh at it. A ridiculous thing. A book that rewrote itself, that claimed to know who belonged with whom. I told her it was nonsense, that love doesn't follow scripts.

But now here I am, holding a stack of books written by the girl I love. Creating a shelf so that strangers might stumble across something that changes them.

Exactly like the thing I never believed in.

So maybe that magic book wasn't some prophecy.

Maybe it was just a reminder that sometimes the stories choose you.

41

Isla

There's a butterfly on my balcony railing.

Normally, I'd say something weird to it. Like 'Hey, Ivy, nice wings today' or 'Flap your wings twice if I'm making the right decision'. You know—normal sister-from-beyond-the-veil kind of stuff.

But today, my brain isn't doing that thing where it assigns a hidden message to every mundane thing. Weird.

It's just me and a pretty butterfly. And a very lukewarm mug of three-hour-old coffee.

I go back inside my condo, wearing the shirt Luca left behind. It's still not making sense to me what I should do with the whole thing. I know he won't wait for me forever, and it wouldn't be fair of me to expect him to. But I feel like I have more to uncover with myself before I worry about that part of my life. And I won't let someone orbit around my unfinished self.

I sigh, as I take the quickest shower and leave my home. For some reason, I put the book in my tote. Maybe muscle memory. I've been doing it in Florence. Make-up bag, wallet, keys, Magic Book That Ruined Me. Maybe I just subconsciously want to keep it handy in case it changes over the course of today.

Anyway, I ride the bus on the way to the office where I'll get the printed manuscript with Harriet's comments. It's nearly empty, probably because it's almost noon. I sit by the window because I've always been dramatic like that. I take the giant book out of my tote and check the last page. It's still the same. The same final letter from 'Luca'.

I read it again, my eyes skimming through the familiar words.

But today I fixate on that one line: *If we only love someone when it guarantees presence, or permanence, then that isn't love.*

I stare at it for a while, really trying to think about what it could mean. From Luca's perspective, it's easy to deduce. He's been left by his father, his mother, Dahlia. And he learned that loving someone for real doesn't just mean loving them when they're here. Well, that's what the book says. I don't know if Real Luca actually thinks like this now.

As I read it over and over, I realize something.

That's what I've been doing all along, isn't it?

Loving Ivy like she was still here. Loving her by punishing myself for outliving her. Loving her only as long as it felt like I was keeping her close through guilt. Almost as if the moment I become happy again, she disappears. And if she disappeared, it would mean that I didn't love her.

Jeez.

And maybe I've been doing the same with Luca. Pulling away the second love looked uncertain. Convinced myself that I was doing it for him. Even when I hated people for leaving.

Presence. Permanence. I was worshipping both. So much that I didn't see that love isn't something you can measure like that.

I press my hand against the closed book's cover. For the first time, I don't feel the need to open it again. And when I reach the bus stop, I don't go down. I stay. Because there's somewhere else I'd rather go.

The cemetery looks the same as it did the last time I was here: The day we buried Ivy six feet underground. I didn't visit her after that. I couldn't bring myself to. Instead, I looked for her in everything else around me. I looked for her in signs. In constellations. In random flying insects (sorry, Ivy).

But now, I'm here. I stand in front of my sister's headstone, awkwardly clutching a paper bag with two sunflower stems I bought from a sidewalk vendor.

I take a seat on the patch of grass, and run my hand over the stone with her name engraved on it. I still feel a heaviness in my chest. Like I still can't believe that she's there, and I'm left here. But I power through.

As I set the sunflowers down, I say, 'Hey . . . so, I haven't been great at this. Talking to you. Visiting you.' I fumble with the sunflower stems as I talk to Ivy.

'I think I convinced myself that if I didn't come here, then you weren't really gone. That you were still out there, being a butterfly or something.' I chuckle to myself, because I know she'd roll her eyes at me.

I smile faintly, tracing a petal with my thumb. 'But you're not. You're here. And I've been carrying that, Ivy. All of it.

The guilt. The what ifs. The idea that if I had just been better, more responsible, less . . . *me*—then you'd still be alive.'

A breeze lifts the edge of the paper bag. I press it down gently. 'I feel like,' I continue, 'if I punished myself for being the one left behind, I'd earn back some piece of you. Some piece of meaning.' My voice catches.

I look up at the sky. It's bright blue and sunny. The only thing stopping me from being fried is the giant tree behind me.

I tell her, 'Anyway, I thought loving you meant clinging to the ache. But maybe real love isn't like that. It's less mourning, and more . . . remembering. Choosing to carry you forward, not hold myself back.'

I laugh through my nose. 'Ew, that sounded poetic. I've clearly been reading too many of my own books.' I shift in the grass and let myself go quiet for a moment.

And just like I used to when we were kids—when she was mad at me, or teasing me, or just being her all-knowing older self—I imagine Ivy sitting beside me. Her arms crossed. That tiny frown she always had when I did something she didn't approve of. I picture her shaking her head, rolling her eyes, saying, *I miss the old you. The version who wasn't scared of everything.*

'I miss her, too,' I whisper back.

'You know, you'd like Luca,' I say suddenly, as if she's still there and we're just picking up a conversation from the night before. 'He's responsible. A good cook. Annoying. Mildly judgmental. He told me he loved me, and what did I do? I panicked. I ran. Because apparently, that's my main personality trait now.'

Ivy always told me I never took anything seriously. And I always argued with her, but for that I know she's right. For some reason, no matter how much I joke about everything else, I can't help but be so serious about all this. About my feelings. About my love for Luca. My love for Ivy. And maybe even the love I have for myself.

I place my hand over my heart for a second. Then I whisper, 'I miss you, Ivs. But I think I'm ready to miss you in a different way now.'

And then something shifts. A soft breeze passes through, lifting the hem of my shirt and rustling the sunflower petals. It's not dramatic. The clouds don't part. No butterflies descend from the heavens.

But a weight has been lifted off me, I can feel it. Maybe not totally, but there's something.

After all, healing isn't a light switch. It's not a flashing neon sign that says *Congratulations, you are emotionally well.* It's not one big cry over a Pinterest quote or a song bridge. Healing is slow. It's not linear. It's very awkward. It's like growing out a bad haircut. You dread it and hate it until one day you look at the mirror and realize that it isn't so bad any more. It's a bunch of invisible moments, like a laugh that doesn't feel forced. Or a memory that doesn't make you want to disappear and cry into a void. Tiny shifts that you don't even realize are happening until they pile up and you feel . . . fine.

I spend a few more minutes with Ivy, just remembering her, and missing her, and giving her all the details about my life.

Then I stand, brush off my pants, and make my way back to the city. I still have to drop by the office to get

Harriet's printed edits on my manuscript. Which feels like a very grounded, practical thing to do for someone who just emotionally reconciled with her dead sister.

On the bus ride, my phone buzzes.

It's a notification from my daily horoscope app. I still read it. Of course I do. Maybe some habits die hard. It says that I should trust the turn I wasn't meant to take.

Maybe that means something. Maybe it doesn't. But right now, I don't let it dictate my choices. Once I take my manuscript from the office, I stuff it in my overloaded tote bag. At this point, I'm convinced my tote bag is enchanted. It holds my wallet, keys, make-up, a full manuscript, and a magic book. And probably snacks. Always snacks.

When I step back outside, I realize I don't want to go home yet.

Instead, I decide to stroll around Manila for a bit. Let the city hold me for a while. I tell myself it's because I want fresh air, but maybe I'm hoping to catch a glimpse of Luca's restaurant. I know it's still being built, still in its early stages, but maybe he'll be there. Maybe I'll see him laughing with someone, tasting food, I don't know. Or maybe, if my courage doesn't bail on me at the last minute, I'll talk to him.

Or I won't. I'll just confirm that he's still real. Still here. Still within reach.

I take a cab this time, because I'm too emotionally delicate for another three-hour bus ride. Of course, it's rush hour. Manila traffic welcomes me with open, unmoving arms. Students are walking out of schools, workers are getting off work, and I'm here. Stuck. A few blocks before my stop, I glance outside and my eyes widen.

A few blocks before my supposed stop, the cab makes an unexpected turn—some kind of shortcut through Intramuros. I don't know what makes me look out the window just then. But I do. And when I do, I freeze.

There, just past the blur of jeepneys and an overgrown bush trying to be a tree, is a small alley. Narrow.

I shake my head, but I tell the taxi driver to stop. '*Kuya, para po*,' I say. Then I get out, walk towards the street sign, and squint, just enough to make out the words.

Kalye Laluma.

42

Isla

I almost laugh at the absurdity of it. Of course even the street transcends geography. Of course it found a way to reappear here, in the middle of Manila, hidden between two buildings that don't quite seem to match. I don't know why I'm surprised. Maybe I thought the magic was exclusive to Florence. Or Italy.

I take a breath and step into the alley.

The moment I cross the invisible threshold from Manila Proper to Whatever-This-Is, the air feels different. Like the first time in Florence, the sounds from the outside are suddenly muffled. Like someone put a pillow over that world.

I walk forward, down the cobblestones and deeper into the alley. Maybe the alley only appears in cobblestoned streets. It reminds me of Old Intramuros, but it's less crowded and less polluted. Wrought-iron balconies cling to the upper floors of the buildings, some with trailing vines, others with hanging laundry swaying lazily in the breeze. Bougainvillea peek from crumbling windowsills in colours that feel a little too bright.

Everything smells faintly of old books. And sampaguita.

The lamps lining the street look like they were stolen from a period film—glass globes with a warm amber glow even in daylight. There's a small fountain in the middle.

I glance around.

A bookstore sits at the far end of the lane, and my pulse quickens as I approach it.

I open the doors, and it's exactly the same interior. Exactly the same stack of books. The same floors, tables. The same counter, and the same woman behind it.

She doesn't look up. Just says, softly, without fanfare, 'You're right on time.'

'Okay,' I say, stepping in front of the counter. 'I've thought multiple times about what you could be. A spunky little demigod who's in charge of love and heartbreak, or a time-travelling librarian who's messing with people's hearts. I've even considered that you were just a figment of my overactive imagination.'

She chuckles. 'That's fair . . . but I'm no one special.'

I shift the tote bag on my shoulder, switching it to the other side. 'See, that's what magical people always say.'

Her eyes crinkle at the corners. 'I'm just someone who makes sure the right stories find their way to the people who need them.'

'That's it?'

She shrugs, but there's a knowing glint in her eyes. 'Stories have a life of their own. They know where to go. When to arrive. Whom to nudge. I only help them along.' She wiggles her fingers.

I take the book from the tote and set it on a counter with a resounding thud. 'So, this book,' I say. 'Why me? Why him?'

She leans forward on the counter, folding her hands. 'Because you were both stuck. And it wanted to help you get unstuck.'

I blink. 'Books can want things?'

'All things with meaning do,' she says. 'You're a writer. Don't pretend you haven't felt it.'

She has a point. I've argued with characters in the shower, begged stubborn plot lines to cooperate, even cried over dialogue that refused to sound human. I've dreamed about scenes I hadn't written yet, and had story ideas show up uninvited at 2 a.m. So, yeah, I've felt it. But this is an entirely different kind of thing.

I nod slowly, my fingers brushing over the worn cover, and say, 'I'm returning it now.'

She doesn't reach for it. Doesn't move. Just smiles like she's been expecting that answer for a long time.

'You're the only one who's returned it,' she says, her voice soft, almost amused. 'Everyone else tries to bury it. One woman threw it into the ocean. A man in Amsterdam tried to set it on fire, but the pages wouldn't catch. No one's ever just walked in and . . . placed it gently on the counter.' She chuckles.

'I don't hate this book,' I say, flipping through its pages for a final time. 'And I'm not afraid of it any more.'

She watches me carefully, like she's trying to understand if I mean what I say, or if I'm just saying it to get rid of the book. 'That's rare. People usually think they have to destroy the hard things in order to move on from them.'

I glance down at the cover. 'I think I did, at first. I thought this book ruined me. But it didn't. It just . . . held up a mirror.'

'And you looked.'

'I looked,' I echo. 'And then I kept reading.'

For a moment, it's silent, and we just smile at each other in understanding. I take a deep breath. 'Does it . . . go to someone else now?'

She shrugs with a secret smile. 'If it wants to.'

'Do you even work here?' I ask, narrowing my eyes at her playfully. 'Or are you just the metaphysical embodiment of healing?'

She laughs, and for the first time, it sounds real—like a laugh that belongs to someone who's known grief, and joy, and all the weird, squishy bits in between. 'Well, we often forget that healing is part of loving. And that we should heal on our own before we attempt to help others with theirs. Because if we don't learn to care for our own wounds, we'll end up bleeding on people who didn't cut us.'

I smile, stepping back from the counter. 'I think I'm finally learning that,' I whisper.

She smiles softly, and this time, she does take the book. Just lightly, like she's cradling something sacred. 'Then you're ready to let it go.'

And so I do.

I know now that the book is not cursed. It's not unstoppable. It doesn't carry the power to dictate our futures or doom us to heartbreak. It isn't magic in the way people warned me.

It isn't like what Giodani said, that it's this beautiful, tragic thing that shows us who we're destined to be with—some romantic, cosmic roadmap. And it isn't like what Philip Rossi believed either, that it's a cursed object, designed to reveal what we're most afraid to want. That it punishes us for wanting too much. It's not what Dahlia thinks. That it's a warning.

The truth is quite simpler than all that. The book never spoke for fate. It only spoke for us. Our desires, our wounds, our what-ifs and what-could-bes.

It took pieces of me I tried to hide and turned them into ink. It mirrored back the parts I was too scared to say out loud. The longings I tucked between laughter. The guilt I buried under superstition. The grief I never gave myself permission to name.

It changed, not because it was enchanted—but because I was. Changing. Growing. Hurting. Hoping. Every time I turned a page, I wasn't discovering some divine plan. I was confronting the version of myself I was too afraid to meet.

And now, I think I finally understand. The book only gave what I brought into it. It never wrote the story—I did.

And that means I can choose how it ends.

43

Isla

Intramuros at twilight is beautiful. Not in a cinematic, postcard-worthy kind of way. Just warm light pooling on cobblestones, the scent of grilled barbecue from a nearby stall, and the faint hum of someone's radio playing an old love song like the background's been pre-picked for me.

It reminds me of Florence—sort of. Not the way it looks, but the way it feels. Like the air is softening for the day to end. Like the past is close enough to touch.

I'm walking a little too fast, like if I slow down, I'll change my mind.

I don't know what I'm expecting. Maybe that he won't be there. Maybe that he will and won't want to see me.

I'm wearing the same clothes I've been wearing since this morning. My hair's doing that thing where it can't decide if it wants to frizz or flatten so it somehow does both, and my heart is definitely trying to jump out of my body.

But I keep going.

The restaurant Luca's working on isn't open yet, but I know where it is. When I reach the street, I slow down. The lights are already on inside. The front door is slightly ajar. There's soft jazz playing—of course. A woman in a long skirt is holding a few curtain swatches against the window, and I can see his silhouette. (Yes, I know it's him. I'm obsessive, remember?)

I take a deep breath and summon the courage to step in.

The bell above the door chimes quietly. I'm half-hoping the floor won't creak, that I can back out and pretend I just wanted to check the menu. But of course it creaks. Loudly.

He turns around.

His eyes land on me, and for a second—just one second—his whole face goes still. I wonder if he's going to smile. I wonder if he's going to frown. I wonder if he'll just nod and pretend everything's fine.

Instead, he just says, 'Isla.' Nothing else, just my name.

'Hi,' I say. I suddenly feel very aware of my arms. Where do people usually put them in these situations?

The woman holding the curtain swatches gives us a look and slips out the door like she's seen enough movies to know this scene isn't for her.

He's wearing a white shirt, sleeves rolled, with a smear of something that looks like chocolate on his collar. His hair's a little messier. His face is a bit scruffier. He looks . . . stupidly handsome.

'You came,' he says, stepping forward.

I nod. 'I know. It's so off-brand of me. I usually run.'

He smiles—relieved, tired, happy—and gestures towards a table by the window. 'Sit with me?'

We do. There's a pot of something simmering in the back, and someone clattering around the kitchen. But for now, it feels like we're the only two people in the world.

We talk about everything and nothing. About my 'reconciliation' with Ivy. About my parents. About the magic book (which he *totally* believes in now, but he pretends otherwise). About how he's making an Italian–Filipino fusion menu. About how he misses his nonna.

And to that, I say, 'Do you want to go back?'

He doesn't answer right away. After a beat, he says, 'A part of me does . . .' he trails off. Then he takes my hand and looks at me. 'But a bigger part loves you and doesn't want to build a life without you.'

I stare at him. 'That's a really good line,' I say, chuckling.

'It's not a line.' He smiles.

I look at our hands—his thumb tracing lazy circles on my skin—and think about what it would mean. It's not like I have so much to leave behind. It's not like I'm uprooting myself. I mean, I can still visit. I can write anywhere, anyway, and—

'But I'm not going to ask you to come with me and leave the life you know,' he says, cutting through my thoughts like he can read them.

'Then what?' I ask, confused.

He shrugs. 'I haven't really thought about it, but maybe we can spend half the time there, and half here.'

'So,' I say, cautious, 'like . . . what? Six months here, six months there?'

He nods. 'If that works for you.'

'And if it doesn't?'

Luca shrugs with a soft smile. 'Then we change the plan.'

I blink at him. 'Just like that?'

'Just like that.'

There's no threat in his voice, or hesitation. It's just . . . calmness. And it's a foreign concept to me to just change plans like that. To be so free, so sure, that you can just change whatever the universe gives you. But maybe life is about writing things in pencil, and editing it along the way. It's just one big draft.

'Okay,' I whisper. 'Let's try.'

He smiles and gets up from his seat, inviting me to join him outside. I take his hand and let him drag me out.

The sky outside has gone from lilac to indigo. People are lighting candles in their windows. I lean against him and close my eyes for a moment.

'I love you, Isla,' he says, planting a soft kiss on the top of my head. '*Ti amo. Mahal kita.*' He chuckles as he says the last one, with the thickest, clumsiest accent. 'I'm working on it,' he says.

I laugh and say, '*Mahal din kita.*'

And then we just . . . stay in the moment. He looks at me, eyes still crinkling from laughing at his bad Filipino accent. And then he leans in, slowly, as if giving me a chance to pull away.

But I don't. Instead, I kiss him first. I kiss him first, and it feels right. Real.

So maybe . . . some people believe in signs.

I still do. I still read my horoscope. I'll probably still look at things like they're signs from the universe. But the difference is now I won't let them dictate my life.

Because now, I believe in choice too.

And I'm choosing this. Choosing him. Choosing me.

Whatever happens next . . . I guess we'll just choose again.

Epilogue (One Year Later)

Isla

I have learned that no matter the cuisine, garlic is a central ingredient. It's the first thing I smell when I enter the restaurant.

'Where have you been, Amore?' Luca asks me. He's wearing his apron and his chef's hat as he peeks out the kitchen door.

'On the phone,' I say with a sigh, waving my phone like it betrayed me. 'With Harriet. Her flight's delayed. And she insists I pick her up at the airport.'

He raises an eyebrow. 'But the guests start arriving in—'

'Exactly. Two hours.' I toss my tote bag onto one of the empty chairs and start tying my hair into a messy bun. 'I can't leave. There's still signage to fix. And the playlist. And one of the table numbers is missing. I think table six is table twice now.'

'Can't she take the train?' Marco emerges from the bar. 'Rome is very accessible. Much more than Florence.'

'Can she? Yes. Will she? Absolutely not.' I point a finger at him as if that seals the deal. 'My best friend has a long-standing belief that she is a very important person. Like, possibly royalty.'

Marco chuckles—a low, amused sound. 'I got it, Isla. I'll go. I'll pick up your Very Important Best Friend. Might even roll out a red carpet at the terminal.'

'You're a hero,' I say dramatically, already halfway through reorganizing the dessert station. 'And possibly her next crush.'

He gives me a look. 'Then I'll comb my hair.'

Luca laughs from the kitchen, and immediately makes me feel better. I glance towards him and our eyes meet. For a moment, I don't care about anything else. I just want to get lost in those eyes, in our home, far from this restaurant.

Okay, our home is technically on top of this restaurant, so that's not very far, but the point stands.

Today is the opening day of Tahanan, a restaurant Luca and I are opening in Rome. A fusion of both our homes, tucked between centuries-old buildings.

We moved here four months ago, after I signed a global deal with my publisher. I still split my time between Manila and Rome—we both do. But lately, Rome's been feeling more and more like home. Not because it's perfect, or easy, or Instagrammable (though it is all of those things). But because we chose it. We keep choosing it. And each other.

The name of the restaurant means 'home' in Filipino. And Luca agrees that the name best captures that feeling, especially for those whose homes are not in Italy.

And maybe that's the most romantic thing I've ever written: a place where people come together over food that tastes like memory.

Exactly two hours later, guests begin to arrive. The first one through the doors is Nonna, walking arm-in-arm with two friends from the nursing home. She never did move back in with us—she claims she has 'too much drama to observe' at the home—but she shows up dressed to the nines, pearls and all, and asks loudly for a glass of wine before appetizers even land.

The music plays and candles flicker on every table. Guests settle in with glasses of prosecco, the scent of adobo and truffle pasta wafting through the space. I glide from table to table, laughing too hard at half the jokes and probably oversharing whenever some curious diners ask how Luca and I met. We don't tell them about the book. We just stick with the other story. That we met, and fell in love immediately. It's easier to explain that way.

Luca finally emerges from the kitchen once the first two courses are served—his sleeves rolled up, his hair a little messy from the heat, and a grin that still does things to my spine, my stomach, my heart, my liver (kidding, but you get the point). He loops an arm around my waist and kisses my temple.

'Your table six was definitely duplicated,' he teases.

'I know,' I mutter. 'They're bonding over it.'

And just as I'm about to check in on Nonna's request for more wine—her second glass, for 'digestive purposes'—the front door swings open with dramatic flair.

'*Ciao!*' a voice sings out. 'Is this where the world-famous author and the super hot chef live? I've arrived!'

'Har!' I scream, nearly running into a tray of appetizers as I launch into her.

Harriet is in a floral-print dress that dips dramatically at the neckline and flutters at the hem. Her sunglasses are still on indoors, and her red curls are pulled into a messy bun. 'I love this city,' she declares as she lowers her shades. 'No one has side-eyed my cleavage since I landed. I might never leave.'

Marco appears behind her, holding her luggage.

'Even Marco here didn't look.' She removes her sunglasses and winks at Marco.

As Luca walks up to us, Marco smirks. 'Signorina Harriet, I don't look in lobbies. I reserve that for the bedroom.' He stands in front of her, waiting for her response.

For the first time, Harriet looks amused. 'What a gentleman,' she says. 'Dangerous and polite, just the way I like it.'

'Harriet!' I swat her arm.

Marco ignores me and winks at her instead. 'I'll leave your luggage in the corner, Your Highness,' he says.

'You didn't tell me the restaurant came with entertainment,' Harriet says as Marco sets her luggage properly.

I just roll my eyes as Luca laughs. 'Who knew two people could be so alike?' he says to me.

'Do I at least get a glass of wine for surviving international air travel and a panic attack caused by Italian customs?' Harriet walks inside and takes a seat at one of the tables.

Marco doesn't miss a beat. 'Red or white?'

'Surprise me,' she says with a wink, and he grins like he already knows what he's getting.

I watch the two of them trade another lingering look, and I know—I just know—I'm going to regret introducing them. Or maybe not. Maybe I'll end up writing about them someday.

The restaurant begins to hum louder as more guests trickle in. Candles flicker. Laughter bounces off the old stone walls. Plates are passed. Forks clink gently against porcelain. Luca disappears into the kitchen with a wink, and I get back to work—checking the seating plan one last time, refilling water glasses, hugging old friends as they walk in. But there's a joy humming under my skin I can't shake. Maybe it's the adrenaline. Or maybe it's something better.

By the time the final course is served, the playlist hits the perfect acoustic version of our song. Nonna raises her glass. Luca slips beside me, flour still on his sleeves and that boyish grin that makes me fall in love all over again.

'Well?' he says softly, brushing a lock of hair behind my ear. 'Did we do it?'

I glance around the room—at our friends, our food, our beautiful chaos—and smile. 'Yeah. We did it.'

Dear Reader,

First of all, thank you. For picking up this book. For flipping past all the pages. For letting these characters into your world, even for just a little while.

I don't know if you believe in fate. Or love. Or if you're just here for tropes. (Respect—because I do that too.) But here's what I do hope: I hope you know love and life are weird. Beautiful, ridiculous, and weird. Sometimes, life hands you exactly what you wished for. Other times, it gives you the unexpected, like a magic book and an Italian man.

Either way, I hope you know that you get to choose: from who to love to when to give up, let go, and start again (and yes, it is okay to choose that). I don't know your story. But I hope you write it. In bold choices. In late-night honesty. In bravery. Even in fear.

And if you're waiting for a sign, be it to leave, to book that trip, to start that messy, possibly doomed but hopefully magical thing? Don't. You don't need the universe to give you permission. And you don't need to have things figured out. None of us do. Even the ones who say they do really don't. The secret is to just keep showing up.

So thank you for showing up for me. For reading, for dreaming, for wondering if love letters still matter. (They do.) And if all else fails, know that someone, somewhere, is rooting for you. Including me.

Just remember: If you ever find yourself on a street that doesn't exist on any map, stuck with a book that shows you what you're scared of, do not panic.

You got this.

Yours,
The Book

Acknowledgements

This book is my child. And it certainly behaved like one: It kept me up at night, it never listened to me, and it ran all over the place while I chased it around screaming. And since it takes a village to raise something like that, I want to take this moment to thank the community that carried me through it.

To the Penguin SEA team that I worked with (Nora, Sakshi, Divya, Amberdawn): Thank you for being the calm adults in the room while I was obviously not. Thank you for your patience, your clarity, and your support. I'm sorry for not knowing UK English and for my crimes against the comma. You are superheroes.

To my friend Kayla: for designing the most beautiful cover in the world. I am forever in awe of your art.

To the early readers of this book—advance readers, industry partners, friends who got copies against their will—thank you. Your comments live in my head, and this book is a million times better because of you.

To my friends and family: my parents, my sister, and my best friend Stephanie, who became unwilling witnesses to the entire process. Thank you for the pep talks, the distractions, and the gentle interventions. Your patience deserves to be rewarded with something fancier than this acknowledgment, but here we are.

To my actual human child Uno: Thank you for existing. Just looking at you takes the stress away.

To my husband Patrick: Thank you for taking me to Italy, where this book found its setting and its stubborn sense of place. Thank you for indulging my need to wander, observe, and romanticize everything, and for taking the photos that accompanied this book. I couldn't have written this book without Italy—but I wouldn't have found Italy without you. I love you.

And to you, reader: Thank you for choosing this book. Thank you for trusting me with your time, your feelings, and your attention. I hope Isla and Luca's story keeps you company for a while—on a train, in a coffee shop, or in bed at 1 a.m. when you promised yourself that you would stop at the next chapter.

Thank you for giving my little book-baby a home far beyond anything I could have imagined.

Now it's yours. Be gentle with it. Or throw it across the room. Whatever, it never listened to me anyway.